# REVENGE RITUAL

## C J Browne

To Aileen

I hope you enjoy the read

Lots of love

C J (or Chris)

First published 2015 by Endeavour Press Ltd.

'Black widow' has become a universal term for a deadly female, largely due to the spiders' mating habits. Female black widows sometimes kill and eat their male counterparts after mating in a macabre ritual that gives the insect its name. Her vibrant markings are a visible warning to potential predators that she is toxic. The markings, however, do not appear to frighten off prey.

*The Oxford Guide to Arachnids*

# Prologue

*Western Evening Gazette, September 18th, 1987*
*MENTAL NURSE KILLED IN CLIFF TOP TRAGEDY - PATIENT STILL MISSING*

*Elliot Wagner, 34, a nurse at Pastures Mental Hospital was killed last night when his Norton motorcycle plunged off the cliffs near Orcombe Point, Exmouth. A patient from the hospital's secure unit was believed to be with Mr Wagner at the time. Rescue Services confirmed that although a woman's possessions were recovered from the scene her body is still missing, believed to have been swept out to sea.*

*

Twenty Eight Years Later

Looking at him now it's hard to believe I ever found this pathetic streak of manhood attractive. So as I bend down to remove his shoes I try to sound sympathetic.

'Put your feet up, Terence. You look exhausted.'

He's still wearing the old fashioned Oxfords. He always fussed about his shoes: just one of the many things I hated about him. Last thing at night, he'd sit at the end of the bed polishing away and looking everywhere but at my naked body. It was always an effort to get him interested and that hasn't changed.

I touch the only part of him that's sweating. His socks feel unpleasantly moist as I lift his feet up on to the chaise longue. His sweat clings to my hands and I wipe them against the cool silk of my dress. The clingy fabric's too hot for this weather but I'm wearing it to please him – for one last time. And he did look pleased watching me unfasten the top two buttons to remind him of what I can do for him. That was before I'd devoured the exotic meal he'd lovingly prepared - he always was a good cook – and he'd downed the 1998 Grand Cru, Cote de Nuits without noticing the Restoril I'd dropped in.

He looks pathetic. His eyes have glazed over and his silver speckled hair is sticking to his forehead. Now sweat stains are spreading from under his armpits across his crisp Italian-style shirt. He's run out of conversation.

'Well, say something,' I encourage - but of course he can't. The drugs are starting to work. He can still move his mouth but the words come out like half formed bubbles.

'Tha ... thanks.'

Always polite but then manners are so important, aren't they Terence?

He struggles to sit up, 'Wassup ... with?'

'What's up with me? Absolutely nothing.' He feebly wags his head from side to side and I watch in disgust as more spittle runs down the side of his chin. 'Oh, you mean what's up with you? Well, that would be telling.'

Sunbeams stream in through the half drawn shutters and cast a strip of brightness across his face illuminating dust motes hanging in the air above his drooping head. I enjoy the bemusement clouding those puppy dog eyes. He's trying to make sense of what's happening - how an evening of pleasure could go so horribly wrong. Don't worry Terence. There's worse to come.

I kneel next to his shaking body, lean in close to his face so he can feel my breath and whisper, 'I know I promised there'd be no sex in your precious home – but when I want you ... well, you can't resist.'

He grunts something as I undo his trousers and pull them away from his scrawny backside and down his legs. I can't tell if he's calling out in protest or pleasure but his eyes look more focused as I grab his hair and jerk his head back.

'That's right. That's why I'm here. Did you think I just came round for dinner?' I let his head drop back again. 'You'd do anything to stop that daughter of yours finding out the truth, wouldn't you? It's pathetic. You're such a fraud.'

I remove the rest of his clothing and search his pockets before folding each item neatly and laying them on a chair. His pockets are full of dirty handkerchiefs and I reach for my antiseptic body wipes. There's a worn leather wallet with two twenty pound notes and a photograph. I hold the photograph in front of his face, 'Do you love her more than me? 'He groans. 'You'd better not or this little bitch will get hurt.'

He tries to spit at me but obviously has no saliva. 'You ... you're the bitch.' The effort of speech makes him slide back against the cushions -

blue silk with an oriental peacock design. I could lift one up, place it over his head, press down hard ... but that would be too easy.

I stand back and scan his naked body. It's lightly tanned and his firm thighs and flat stomach could belong to a man half his age. I enjoy the feel of his skin and the tightening of his muscles under the wetness of the body wipes as I stroke them around his body. Even in his half stupor he's responding to my caress - until I reach his groin and twist his testicles.

In my bag I've bought scarves to suit the occasion. Golden brown, the colour of his eyes, although they've darkened now to the colour of dirty coal. Cobalt blue like the ocean he's so fond of, faded vermillion, the colour of the tasteless brocade draped all round this house - and scarlet to remind him of his betrayal.

I reposition his body checking he is still alive. Then carefully tie each wrist to the chair backs and each ankle to the ends of the chaise longue. It takes less than three minutes.

The smell of scorched feathers fills the room. The crackle of flames from the back of the house grows louder. No time for any more fun.

I kiss his forehead one last time and say, 'She's going to suffer but you're going to die.'

# 1

Two Days Earlier

'And the award for Young Criminologist of the Year goes to ... Dr Kate Trevelyan for her cutting edge work on keeping sex workers safe.'

Kate couldn't believe it, even thought she was wearing her lucky tiger skin underwear and had thrown salt over her shoulder three times during the celebratory dinner. But she did deserve it - if only to reward her for searching out the sexiest evening dress in Oxford Street then travelling across London in record time to the Stakis St Ermine Hotel. She'd changed and refreshed her make up in the hotel toilet and joined the other guests just as they were sitting down for the meal.

'Young Criminologist of the Year,' she repeated under her breath. It had a real ring to it. Breath it in, get used to it. It might not make her fortune but it was certainly going to advance her career. Her hard work was paying off at last and it felt great to be acknowledged. All those hours spent sitting at the computer analysing statistics. Days of hanging around piss smelling back streets avoiding packs of Rottweilers. Difficult interviews with traumatised victims, she didn't think she'd ever get used to those, and being nice to the influential academics doing the peer reviews for her articles while they look down her cleavage. She'd done it. She was a high flyer now and Jake might even make her a Director.

He was standing on his feet next to her and raising his glass with a look that said he wasn't just admiring her research skills. She'd admired his work since uni - Professor Jake Williamson, distinguished author of 'Crime in Social, Biological and Moral Settings', and creator of the 'Williamson Scale of risk factors', used by governments the world over to identify the character traits of likely terrorists.

She'd felt special ever since he'd recruited her to The Centre for Criminal Research. She could still remember the warmth of his handshake and the excitement in her stomach the day she'd joined Europe's most prestigious criminal policy think tank two years ago. She'd found Jake attractive from the start, taking hours with her appearance before setting off to work - but she'd carried on disagreeing with him about his attitude to women. He'd started paying her more attention, taking her for meals to celebrate successful contracts or inviting her to parties to mingle with influential people. She'd always kept their relationship professional until now. But when she heard about her secondment to The Centre of Criminal Research's Devon office, she felt she could risk taking it further. She would be working in Sidmouth and living with her father and Jake would be in London. She'd felt even more certain of their mutual attraction when he turned up at her flat on her last night in London and the sex had been amazing.

As Kate raised her glass back to him she thought of her father and how strange she was finding it living back at home after ten years away. She'd only been there for three nights and already was finding it awkward. They'd got on better when her grandmother was still living with them. Still, her father had always supported her education and career wherever she was in the world.

'Here's to you, Dad. Thanks for believing in me; especially when I mess up.'

Jake, who couldn't hear what she was saying above the applause, gave her a knowing look and shouted, 'Up you go, Kate. This is your moment.'

He pushed her out into the aisle between the tables. Photographers' flashlights, reflected in the chandeliers and wine glasses, were capturing her big moment. It was a straight line to the steps leading to the podium. All her fellow consultants from The Centre for Criminal Research were on their feet, their congratulations ringing in her ears. As she reached the stage lined by mirrors she caught glimpses of a sleek young woman in an emerald silk dress. It had cost her two months bonus but from the way it made her feel it was worth double.

At the podium, still trying to look elegant in her too high heels, she looked down at the room of admiring faces. Next to her, the Chair of the British Society of Criminology held up her hand to quieten the applause.

'Criminology wouldn't be the science it is today without the contribution of the people we study. To present the award to Dr Trevelyan is someone who encouraged her fellow workers to participate fully and disregarded her own safety for what some saw as potentially dangerous research.'

Kate thought the introduction could have been worded better, but shared the audience's anticipation as a slight figure wearing a floppy white hat and brilliant orange jumpsuit made her way up to the stage. As she came up the steps she threw her hat in the air with a loud whoop, then rushed to Kate and enveloped her in a bear hug. That was Sophie Wippelston. It couldn't be anyone else.

They had met when Kate had started her research into sex workers' safety. Assaults on street prostitutes around King Cross had trebled in less than a year but no-one outside The Centre for Criminal Research thought the work was worth doing. Jake had his doubts but had agreed to fund the research for a trial three month period. At first, none of the sex workers would participate until Sophie intervened. An undergraduate at Westminster University, her only way of paying her rent was working the streets. Unlike the other sex workers, she'd sought Kate out and was only too willing to talk about it.

'It's just like any old screw except you get paid for it. What's wrong with that?' she'd challenged. Then grinned, 'Don't worry, I know what I'm doing,' and gone on to explain all her precautions in detail, including the mace spray and vaginal foam from Hong Kong that was supposed to kill all STD germs dead.

Kate liked Sophie. If she'd come from a family that struggled to pay the rent every week instead of her own middle class-everything-provided-for background she might have turned to sex work too. Although if Kate had needed to pay her way through uni, she'd have preferred to offer a telephone sex service from a hotel bedroom rather than walk up and down the dark and threatening backstreets of London.

Sophie handed Kate a certificate and cheque for five hundred pounds and the audience started a further round of applause, which drowned out Sophie's greeting to Kate and comment that her earnings had gone through the roof as a result of Kate's research.

When the presentation was over, Kate invited Sophie to join her at her table where she kept all the CCR staff amused with risqué jokes about her male clients. Seeing how all the researchers were being entertained, Jake asked Kate if she wanted to go up to his hotel room. She hesitated. She was enjoying herself and didn't want to leave Sophie so soon.

But the young sex worker had overheard and winked at Kate, 'I've got a work appointment too,' she said as she gathered up all the left over petit fours and scooped them into her handbag. Then, after blowing kisses to everyone and telling Jake to be good, she left.

In Jake's bedroom, Kate's skin tingled with champagne and anticipation as he slammed the door shut and started to remove her expensive silk dress. He'd remembered she liked making love under the shower and had removed most of her clothes by the time they made it to the bathroom.

Afterwards they slept, stretched out on the bed together. Kate woke up to the sound of traffic and cuddled up against Jake as he traced his fingers across her bare stomach.

'What's it like to be good at everything you do?'

She rolled over and kissed him, 'Am I?'

'You're amazing. I knew it from the moment you were rude to me at your interview. You're popular with everyone, you never miss a deadline and however difficult a research contract seems you always get a result ...' She closed her eyes to enjoy his caress as he carried on, 'and you've got a beautiful body.'

But whatever he was going to say next was interrupted by someone knocking on the door. Jake ignored it and started to massage her feet.

The knocking continued, 'Sir, we need to come in to make up the room.'

Jake reached for his iPhone, 'Shit, is that the time?'

They grabbed their clothes, which were strewn all over the bedroom after last night's antics, and started to dress, but Kate was having a hard time keeping her balance to pull her hold ups on for laughing.

*

Kate slept for most of the drive down to Devon. When they stopped at Stonehenge for a coffee Jake asked her how she was settling in at the Sidmouth office.

'Great,' she told him although it wasn't really. She felt like an outsider and the rest of the research team seemed suspicious of her London connections.

Jake didn't seem to notice her lack of enthusiasm. 'Not only will you be acting team leader and be paid more, but you will be able to spend more time with your father. There's very little crime on the Jurassic Coast so you can spend your afternoons enjoying Devon cream teas together.'

That would be nice occasionally, but so far she was finding it a bit of a strain after nearly ten years of continual absence and she missed the buzz of working in London. On the way back to Jake's Porsche she caught a glimpse of her reflection in his wing mirror. Her hair was sticking up at strange angles and, even worse, her mascara had run. The bastard hadn't even told her.

'Can you drop me at my father's?' Now she'd seen how she looked, she was desperate for a shower. There was no way she was going into the office looking like that. What she really needed was a hug from someone sympathetic and some home cooking.

'No,' Jake snapped back.

She glanced across and saw he wasn't smiling. 'Look, I know we're late already but ...' Then she noticed he was laughing at her.

'I'm not dropping you at your father's because there's some correspondence waiting for you back at the office. You've been invited to speak at the American Society of Criminology, and then stay on at the University of Chicago to work on their gang prevention programme. It's an all expenses trip to the USA and I was thinking of joining you as your bag carrier.'

'In your dreams,' she replied but was secretly pleased. 'Come on then tell me more. When is it?'

'They want you to start straight away. Attend the conference then spend some time in the housing projects. You'll be away for a year. But don't worry, there'll be time for you to enjoy a few more days in Devon first, although I got the impression you weren't really enjoying the Sidmouth office.'

But Kate was hardly listening. She was already working out what to include in her speech. Chicago, the windy city, one of the most exciting places in the world. Home of the founding fathers of urban criminology - somewhere she had wanted to work for ages.

'What kind of research?' she said, keeping her voice non-committal. She'd be damned if she'd show him how excited she really was.

Jake turned and gave her one of his infuriating grins that showed she was back in his good books. 'Come back to the office and find out. But I'd sneak in the back door if I were you.'

# 2

The shower could wait. All Kate wanted to do now was share her news. Dad's old Mercedes was parked in the drive of Brathcol, her old home. The old house looked magnificent in the sunlight with its timbered front and art deco windows, even if it could do with a coat of paint. Beyond her father's car she was disappointed to see a gleaming yellow Ferrari parked. She'd been hoping he'd be alone so she could tell him all about her trip to the States. Apart from Jake, there had been no one left at the office to share her excitement.

From the information waiting for her at the Sidmouth office, it looked like she'd be away for at least a year. She knew her father would be disappointed. Each of the three mornings since she'd arrived he told her how much he was enjoying having her to stay as if he expected her to suddenly leave - and now she was going to. She wanted to break the news to him gradually: it wasn't the sort of conversation she wanted to have in front of a stranger. In fact, she didn't want to meet a stranger at all when she felt such a mess from her steamy night with Jake - especially one who owned a Ferrari.

She found her father sitting outside in the garden on the swing seat next to an elegant woman with a designer top, white jeans and bright red lipstick. From her laughter, it sounded like they'd been sharing a joke and Dad looked rather startled at Kate's appearance. The red lipped woman on the other hand appeared totally unphased and immediately jumped to her feet and held out a perfectly manicured hand.

'Hello, you must be Kate. I've been dying to meet you. I've heard all about your prize for working with prostitutes from your father. He's so proud of you.'

Kate's ebullient mood dipped. Dad didn't go in for small talk. Who was this woman who seemed to have persuaded her father to share some details of her life she'd prefer to remain private? She looked familiar but Kate couldn't quite place her.

She remained where she was with her arm held rigidly by her side and said, 'You seem to have an advantage over me then.'

The woman was still smiling, 'Of course, what am I thinking. You don't know who I am. Why should you? I'm Elaine Pierce. Your father has been helping with Kidpower, one of my charities. I called round to tell him about one of his mentees, a boy called Micki. He's doing so well with your father's help that the Youth Offending Team is shortening his attendance order.'

Kate gave her father a quizzical look. Dad looked flustered, uneasy at the praise. 'Well, it's not down to me really. Everyone at Kidpower does their best and young Micki is a grand kid. It's not his fault he's been uprooted from his family and friends in Poland. If he was still living at home I doubt he would ever have started stealing.'

It was the first Kate had heard of Kidpower, or knew of what appeared to be a developing friendship between her father and this woman, judging by the way he looked at her. He held Elaine Pierce's gaze long enough to be rewarded with an engaging smile, then turned to his daughter, 'I'm sorry Kate, I should have introduced you. Elaine is the CEO of Pierce Enterprises, the development company behind the Ladram Heights New Town.' Her father stopped talking as if he'd noticed Kate's less than enthusiastic response. 'You must remember Ladram Heights. It's where I teach. I took you out there when the community school was being built, the last time you were home.'

That was when it was mainly fields, scaffolding and piles of mud but Kate had heard a lot about it since. The local papers were full of the scandal of building in an Area of Outstanding Natural Beauty and that the promised quota of affordable housing was far too low. Some of the team in the Sidmouth office had suggested Pierce Enterprises had bribed local officials to get away with it.

'Elaine is making an amazing difference to people's lives all along the coast. The charity helps young people in trouble with the law to go straight. It's one of her company's ways of compensating locals for any disruption during the development.' Kate didn't like the way he looked at Elaine for approval before continuing. 'You could get involved with Kidpower too, while you're staying here. Working with young offenders, you'll be ideal.'

'I'm sure I could Dad,' Kate was in no mood for volunteering, 'but I won't be here after next week - I'm going to America.' Her words wiped the smile off his face. She hadn't intended to spring her news on him like that.

She started to explain about her research job in Chicago. What a wonderful opportunity it was: how she'd be working with some of the world's best criminologists.

But he just stared back at her.

'Oh, and there was I, hoping you'd stick around a bit longer this time. You've only been here three days and now you're off again. You treat this place like a hotel.'

They sat in an awkward silence broken only by the mewing of a buzzard circling overhead until Dad got up and said he was getting them a drink.

After he'd gone Elaine pulled her chair closer to Kate, 'That sounds like an amazing opportunity. I can understand that you have to go. I'd do the same in your shoes. Don't worry about your father, he'll understand. He's just disappointed.' Kate was thinking she might have misjudged her when Elaine added, 'I don't think he sees very much of you normally so it shouldn't make any difference. Of course, your timing's not great. He's under a lot of strain at school at the moment. Who'd want to be a headmaster these days? He won't thank me for telling you but I know he depends on you for support.' Elaine flicked a fly off the sleeve of her shirt with a red finger nail. 'Of course you could consider putting off your trip for a while. But I gather you usually put your career before anything else.'

Kate glared back. The woman had a nerve. She was talking as if she and Dad had some special relationship. She should stick to property development and keep her opinions to herself. When Kate arrived at Brathcol, she had everything planned out. She was going to spend some time finding out what her dad had been doing since the weekend then mention the subject of working abroad gradually, in a way that would involve him in her decision to go. Of course he supported her career, hadn't Elaine Pierce said as much when she arrived. This was supposed to be a special moment between the two of them and this woman was ruining it.

She was about to tell her so when her mobile rang. Kate's spirits lifted as soon as she saw who was phoning. It was her grandmother. Kate missed her a lot. Nan had practically brought her up after her mother died and she had never understood the reason why her grandmother had left her son and granddaughter to live in Bermuda. Although she loved her father, it hadn't been the same when there was just the two of them. Maybe that was why she hadn't been home to visit him as often as he wanted.

She strode away from Elaine Pierce to have her conversation in private. Nan would tell Elaine to mind her own business. She would understand why Kate wanted to go to Chicago. She saw her dad walk back across the lawn with a tray of homemade lemonade and lemon drizzle cake and rushed over to share the phone call with him. He mouthed 'who's that?' as he placed the tray down on the wrought iron table next to Elaine.

'It's Nan. She's at the airport - yes, Heathrow. She's back in England for some sort of art convention in London and she's coming to stay with us. Arrives the day after tomorrow. Isn't that brilliant?'

Her father stumbled and spilt the lemonade. Kate was so busy arranging to meet Nan at Exeter station that she hardly noticed until she saw him wipe down his trousers. As she finished the phone call she saw her father was staring back at her and Elaine hadn't touched her drink.

'You didn't think to ask me then?'

Kate hadn't. 'I'm sorry Dad.'

'Well, I hope you're going to be around to look after your grandmother, because I'm needed at the Kidpower fundraising weekend. I've already promised Elaine and . . .'

Elaine was already on her feet with her hand on Kate's father's arm, 'Oh, that doesn't matter.'

But Kate could tell it did. Elaine smiled back at them both as she reached in her bag for her car keys, 'Look, I've taken up enough of your time. You two obviously have things to discuss.'

This time Kate shook the hand that was offered as Elaine said, 'It's been a pleasure to meet you. Good luck with your plans in the USA,' then strode away without looking back leaving Kate feeling that somehow she was in the wrong. Maybe she had been rude to Elaine. Sometimes she forgot about other people's feelings.

She went over and put her arm round her father. 'I'm sorry if I was inconsiderate. You go to your Kidpower weekend and I'll look after Nan. I'll take a sabbatical from work before I go to the States. I'll have plenty of time to be with both of you.' But he shrugged her off and strode back into the house.

# 3

Micki Hamereski hadn't forgiven his pa for making him leave Poland for England and attend Ladram Heights Community School. Four months in and it still hadn't got any better. They made him join the stupid English kids that needed extra lessons. He'd tried to tell them he was good at English but no one listened. The other kids ignored him. The older ones waited around corners and forced him to do shameful things. Last time they made him lick the floor where someone had left dog shit while they took photos on their mobile phones. He didn't want to think who'd viewed them by now.

He made it to school as the last of his class were sidling into the class room. As usual the only seat was right at the front. The first lesson should have been English with Mr Trevelyan so Micki was disappointed to see Miss Blundell standing at the front of the room. She wasn't as bad as some of the other teachers but he didn't like the way she fussed around him. She was busy arranging books on her table but looked up as she heard the usual commotion that greeted his entry. Micki was forced to take the only empty seat at the front and tried to sink down into it, but it was no good. Miss Blundell had noticed and was heading in his direction.

'Glad you could join us, Micki.'

As she drew closer he could smell her chalky perfume and hear some giggling behind him. Better to talk to her and hope she would go away.

'Thank you, Miss.'

She asked if he'd managed to do his homework and if he needed any extra help with his essay. There was more giggling. Ms Blundell coughed and shuffled from one foot to the other. 'As you're all so keen to be heard this morning, we'd better get started.'

She went back to her table and started handing out books. 'We're going to read 'Shadow' by Michael Morpurgo. It's a story about a refugee boy from Afghanistan and his friendship with a dog called Shadow. As you read, think about the boy, Aman, and what he is going through as a refugee in this country. Think about children being locked up in places like Yarl's Wood Detention Centre and if you think that's right.'

Micki looked up; maybe for once English might be interesting. He took the book from Miss Blundell with more enthusiasm than he usually felt for school books, but prayed she wouldn't ask him to read it aloud. She seemed to interpret the look he gave her correctly. Maybe she'd heard someone behind him muttering that he should be sent to Yarl's Wood.

'We'll start with the back row. Simone, will you read the first chapter.'

He risked a quick look round and saw Simone take the gum out of her mouth and flick it away. 'Do I have to, Miss?'

Miss Blundell stood over her 'Yes, Simone, you do have to.'

After a drawn out pause, Simone started to read from the book.

He could have done a better job at reading out loud, but the story was interesting and he could follow it easily from the book. He didn't even notice when Miss Blundell asked someone else to read, he was so absorbed. There were lots of things in it that he liked. He liked the boy called Matt who was Aman's best friend and wished he had a best friend in England like him. Matt wanted to get Aman out of the prison he was being kept in before he was sent back to Afghanistan. Micki thought if he had a friend like Matt he might not want to go home so much and Ladram Heights Community School might be bearable. Matt had taken Aman to see the night sky in Devon because the stars were so much brighter than in Manchester and Micki remembered Mr Trevelyan saying that he would take him to the Observatory in Sidmouth, something he had been looking forward to.

He was sorry when the lesson came to an end.

As he was leaving Miss Blundell came over to him, 'Did you enjoy the story, Micki?'

'Yes, thank you, Miss Blundell,' he answered without thinking.

'Yes, thank you, Miss Blundell,' was echoed behind him, followed by more giggling.

Micki walked away, leaving her standing alone in the classroom. He could feel his cheeks getting hotter and hoped that no one would notice. But the giggling was right behind him. He speeded up and walked straight into a purple t-shirt being worn by someone big and solid. As he recovered his balance, he saw the wearer was Connor O'Brian's friend from Kidpower - and that wasn't good.

Micki was trying his best not to cry. They had pinned him down on the floor and were forcing the contents of the nearest waste bin into his mouth. He'd tried wriggling and resisting but the movement made him choke. Gasping for breath and feeling hot tears run down his face, he knew it was going to get worse.

One of the gang shouted, 'Eat that you mother fucker,' while he poured something vile down his throat forcing him to swallow it.

The other kids from his class stood round cheering and mocking or shouting 'Yes, Miss Blundell.'

'I love you Miss Blundell.'

'Can I fuck you Miss Blundell?'

'Oh, you're so tasty teacher.'

Just when Micki thought he was going to pass out everything went very quiet. He opened his eyes and saw the youth with the purple hair and t-shirt being hauled away from him.

He was relieved to hear a familiar and authoritative voice ring out somewhere above his head, 'Everyone, stay where you are.' But the echo of feet running away down the corridor suggested most of the onlookers had disobeyed.

Mr Trevelyan bent down to lift Micki's head off the ground and started scooping the shit out of his mouth. Then whispered, 'Don't worry, I know who they are. They won't be doing that again.'

Micki knew he meant well but wasn't convinced. Mr T was doing his best to put a stop to the gangs at school but even he looked defeated when he'd called all the students together and told them, violence wouldn't be tolerated and there would be penalties for bullies, as if he knew it wouldn't make any difference.

As Mr T helped him to his feet, Micki spat out the last smelly mouthful and allowed Mr T to guide him onto a chair. He handed Micki a handkerchief that smelt of washing powder to wipe his face, then offered him some water from the drinks machine.

'Feeling better now?' Mr T asked.

Apart from some bruises, a sore mouth and the deep humiliation, Micki felt alright.

He tried to say this but went into a spasm of coughing.

'So it's still happening?'

Micki just nodded, and Mr T said he would take him home. He tried to say no, he'd be fine, but Mr T insisted he needed to tell his father what had happened. Micki knew his pa would be out working on the building site but he didn't argue. He lay curled up in the back of Mr T's car as they drove out of the school car park, his eyes tightly closed.

As they arrived at the builders' hostel in Salterton Avenue where Micki lived, Mr T looked round, 'Those boys who attacked you. They go to Kidpower, don't they?'

Micki didn't say anything. He was in enough trouble just being himself without being thought a grass.

He hated his weekly visits to Kidpower more than going to school. It was a place full of gang scum. It was where he'd been sent for some 'therapy' with Mr T, which was supposed to stop him thieving. Mr T was trying to help but he didn't get it. He had to steal. Connor and his cronies would have made his life more miserable if he turned up at Kidpower empty handed. A part of him hoped he would get caught again. Then his pa would have to send him home to Poland. But it wasn't so bad now Mr T was his mentor as well as his teacher. He liked Mr T, who tried to stop the kids at school getting at him, and these days Pa was so hard to talk to that it was good to have someone else who would listen.

He opened the car door, hoping to make a quick dash into the hostel so that Mr T wouldn't come inside, but he hurt all over from the kicking. Mr T supported him to the door and rang the bell. No response, Micki knew the place was empty. He got out his key muttering, 'I'm fine. You go now Mr T,' and noticed how sad his teacher looked.

'I should really wait until your father comes back from work.'

'No need Mr T. I'm good.' Then as an afterthought, 'I'll see you tonight.' Micki had no intention of turning up at Kidpower but only said it to encourage his teacher to leave.

Mr T gave a weary smile, 'No Micki. You don't need to come tonight. In fact I don't want you to come to Kidpower any more.' He reached into his pocket for a pen and notebook and wrote something out, 'Here's my home address. I live in a house called Brathcol in Otterford, it's between Ladram Heights and Sidmouth. I think our mentoring sessions should be held there in future.'

Micki watched Mr T head back to his car, curious to know what his house would be like and grateful that his visits to Kidpower were at an end.

# 4

When Kate had been asked to manage The Centre for Criminal Research's West Country office she was delighted, she felt ready for some downtime. She spent the last couple of years working in the country's poorest communities investigating the causes of crime. It was exciting work and dangerous at times and had provided the material for her thesis and then her postdoctoral research post at Oxford, but she needed a break. She'd always loved Sidmouth, the jewel of the East Devon Jurassic coast. The building stood out from its neighbours in the middle of a Georgian terrace overlooking the cricket ground: the only house in the row that hadn't been given the pastel Portobello paint job. Beyond the glossy green door, the severe black striped carpet and tubular metal office furniture contrasted sharply with the gentle opulence of the building's exterior.

The pace of the working day here was tortoise like compared to London, but she loved her new office overlooking the sea with its high ceiling and original cornices. Here the other researchers left her alone to get on with her work unlike the incessant interruptions of The CCR's London office. Kate like to escape the communal kitchen downstairs and bring her coffee back to her office where she would sit at the window and imagine Jane Austen's Elizabeth Bennet looking out at the bathing machines on the beach, eager to go in for a swim.

Returning to work in Devon had triggered lots of memories of Kate's childhood. How Nan would be waiting for her after school on Fridays when the two of them browsed the Sidmouth gift shops and boutiques, finishing off at the Mocca Cafe for cakes and ice cream. The Mocca had survived but many of the old family businesses like the cafe had closed, although the place still retained its Victorian elegance and charm. Especially at this time of year, before the rush of the holiday season started.

Kate's eagerness to see her grandmother again was heightened by her father's moodiness at breakfast. He still hadn't forgiven her for being rude to Elaine Pierce, but as usual, he'd avoid saying it. He'd hardly spoken to her since Elaine Pierce had left last night. Of course, it could be the prospect of Nan's visit. They hadn't got on that well when Kate was a child. She'd often fled to her bedroom to avoid the raised voices between her father and grandmother when Nan lived with them. Still, she hated hurting her father and had tried to kiss him goodbye as he left for community school, but he pulled away from her. She'd shouted sorry after him but he hadn't replied. To make up for parting on a sour note she had taken a detour to Ladram Heights, intending to call in and see him at the community school, but his secretary said he was in an important meeting and couldn't be disturbed. Now she was late for Jake's regional briefing.

As she made her way towards the meeting room her thoughts about her father were interrupted by the sound of shouting on a soundtrack being played at maximum volume. She wondered which of the Sidmouth researchers was risking Jake's disapproval. But Jake was the one holding the remote control in his hand, even turning up the volume.

He acknowledged her arrival with a brief nod and paused the recording long enough to say, 'So you are going to join us this morning? I thought you'd better things to do now you've become an international criminologist.'

Kate ignored the sarcasm and sat down next to him. 'Sorry, just a bit of a spat with my father. Nothing for you to worry about.' Then looking round at the rest of the team gathered round the video screen she shrugged, 'Sorry everyone, I didn't realise you'd started the team briefing.'

Ginny, the administrator, raised her eyebrows behind Jake's back while most of the other researchers smiled back at her. All except Denise, who hadn't forgiven Kate for taking her place as Head of the South West office, and who gave her a disapproving look, 'We were just checking out the local news coverage of the demonstrations.'

Jake started the video again and said, 'The Home Office is concerned that the demos are escalating and becoming more violent. Of course it might be an everyday happening in London, but here in sunny Sidmouth it's the last thing you'd expect.'

Some of the team glanced at Kate, identifying her with the London comment. Kate was about to say that a visit from Father Christmas in May was the last thing she'd expect. But the sight of the Sidmouth

Esplanade packed with demonstrators, some charging at the few police officers, was surprising. 'When did all this happen?'

'Yesterday, when you were enjoying yourself in the Stakis St Ermine Hotel.' Jake replied. 'Three police hurt and a two year old crushed in the crowd had to be taken to hospital. Local officers didn't recognise many of the demonstrators. Think they've been bussed in to cause trouble, but if you listen to some of the interviews, there is plenty of local antagonism to immigrant labour. It started with taxi drivers. Now most of the anger is directed against the migrant labourers bought in to build Ladram Heights New Town.'

Jake increased the volume and the sounds of protest filled the office again.

'Local jobs for local people.'

'Gangs must go.'

'Give us back our countryside.'

'Surely it's just a one off?' Kate said, moving closer for a better view. The demonstrators were mainly young women with children holding balloons with slogans. If it was happening in Balham High Street nobody would take any notice.

'Look at those women.' Denise interrupted, 'What an earth are they thinking taking children on demonstrations?'

'That's what we're going to find out,' Jake replied, turning the video off, 'and no, Kate, it's not a one off. There are daily demonstrations all across the West Country, anywhere with a high migrant population. But the worst area is Ladram Heights.' Jake was on a roll now, 'However, the good news for us is that the demonstrators are bringing some new business our way. The Government are desperate to stop this kind of thing. If it spreads it's going to cripple the tourist industry. The Home Office want to know who or what is behind the disorder. They want us to look into what's causing it and find a way of stopping it before it goes viral.' He paused to look hard at Kate, who was thinking about what Jake had said about Ladram Heights and wondering if Elaine Pierce employed any migrant labour. 'CCR have been given the contract because one of us has done some outstanding work in the area of community relations. The Government is insisting that we do the research and that Kate leads it.'

Everyone looked at Kate as Jake said, 'You grew up round here didn't you Kate? You know the area.'

'Well, I haven't lived here since 2005. I don't mind helping to gather some information but don't forget I'm off to the States in a couple of weeks.'

Jake was passing her one of the familiar red box files that CCR used for new research contracts. 'You'll do more than that, Kate. You'll be leading the contract, scoping the problem, identifying research subjects, dealing with PR - not to mention managing the team, allocating workloads, monitoring progress and attending weekly meetings at the Home Office.'

She scanned his face to check if he was being serious. Yesterday he'd been nearly as excited about her work in the States as she was. She was supposed to start in a couple of weeks. She'd already bought her air ticket. There was no way she could do all he wanted before she left for Chicago.

She was about to protest but he'd already anticipated her reaction, 'It means you'll have to cancel your work in the States, of course. But it will give you more time to spend with your dad.'

'What! You know I'm expected in Chicago, it's all arranged ...'

Jake ran his fingers through his hair looking smug, 'No, you're not. I've already cancelled the trip. Researching the demonstrations will benefit our whole organisation. If we pull this off, I've been promised a string of Government research contracts will follow. Chicago would only enhance *your* reputation. This project will be a great opportunity for all of us. So I'm putting Chicago on ice – and you're job now is to find out what's behind these demonstrations.'

# 5

She couldn't believe Jake expected her to drop the USA work just to stick around in Devon monitoring demonstrators. Chicago was too good an opportunity to miss; he'd told her that only last night – Denise or one of the others in the South West team could lead the Government contract. But when she'd tried to have a quiet word with Jake after the team briefing had ended, he'd brushed her off saying it was all agreed and if she wanted to remain working for CCR she'd better accept her USA work was on hold for the foreseeable future.

Failing to conceal her disappointment, Kate could sense the tense atmosphere in the office. She was only too aware of the looks that followed her departure. She'd ignored the questions thrown at her by the rest of the team as she'd walked past them and out of the office. She needed to cool off but knew she was unlikely to get much support after her very public show of pique. They were already resentful of her London connections.

Outside, it was a beautiful morning. The artist's favourite sort of blue sky was reflected in the intense blue of the shimmering sea. But Kate couldn't fail to notice the flash of yellow or hear the squeal of tyres as Elaine Pierce drew up level with her in her open topped Ferrari. Her sleek red hair was tied back from her face with an animal print scarf and she was wearing huge sunglasses; the look reminded Kate of Audrey Hepburn.

Elaine was already opening the passenger door, ignoring the irate motorist behind her waiting to overtake. 'Hi there, Kate. I'm on my way to The Sidoli for some lunch. Want to come?' She sounded like Kate's best friend.

Kate hesitated. She should really get back to the office to make it up with her colleagues and try to persuade Jake to change his mind. But she'd hardly eaten any breakfast and her tummy was rumbling. And then again, maybe Elaine could help her bridge the rift with her dad.

Elaine was smiling up at her expectantly, 'It's my treat. Consider it a kind of thank you to your father. He's put so much time in with the youngsters at Kidpower and never expects anything back. Beside I'd like to get to know you.'

The invitation was hard to refuse. Sidoli's was one of the best restaurants in Devon.

As Elaine accelerated away and Kate lurched back in the passenger seat the wind rushed through her hair sweeping away some of her anger. The Ferrari attracted admiring glances, Jake and the rest of the office could wait. Elaine might even be able to persuade him to change his mind about her going to Chicago.

*

Kate hadn't been to the Sidoli Hotel for years, but it hadn't changed much since the nineties when Nan used to bring her here for Sunday afternoon tea. Back then she'd thought it was the height of Georgian elegance. The place still looked stylish. The restaurant was under a new glass roof with a panoramic view out across the Jurassic Coast. Waiters in blue striped waistcoats stood around waiting for customers and as Kate entered with Elaine, The Maître d' stepped forward to guide them to a table in the corner with a sea view.

The decor of the Sidoli dining room was Arctic - reflective glass tables, whale-shaped table mats and sledge shaped vases containing white lilies. Elaine complemented the decor in her blood red dress, crimson lipstick and long ruby earrings. Kate scanned the elegant room, breathing in the aroma of good food, glad that she'd accepted the invitation, even though she felt dowdy beside Elaine.

Elaine ordered a bottle of Chenin Blanc and beckoned to the waiter to fill their two glasses. Kate usually liked to select her own wine but took up her glass and smiled back her appreciation deciding to keep any critical thoughts to herself.

'Here's to your success in the States,' Elaine said as she lifted her glass. Then as Kate responded to the toast, added, 'I hope I wasn't intruding yesterday. You were obviously so excited about the job offer, I felt I was in the way.'

Kate could see the diners around them straining to hear what Elaine was saying and waiters watching attentively in case she wanted something. There was no doubt Elaine was a woman of influence and someone who would make a good ally.

The succulent smell of duck in orange sauce wafted over from the next table as Elaine discarded her menu. 'I have a meeting to go to in an hour, so we'd better order. But first I want to find out if there's anything I can do to help with your work. I have a lot of business contacts in the States.'

Kate sipped her wine which was a good choice. She was about to ask Elaine if she'd found much opposition to her company's development of Ladram Heights and her controversial employment of migrant workers. But Elaine was waving her menu at a waiter who rushed to her side. 'We'll have the Dover sole followed by crepe suzette.'

Kate liked to take her time over ordering food, especially food that smelt so good. She also preferred to choose her own meals. She caught the waiter's arm as he walked past, 'I'll have the duckling in orange sauce followed by the blueberry sorbet.' She glanced at Elaine and was gratified to see her smile had slipped a little.

When their food arrived it tasted just as good as it smelled and between mouthfuls, she told Elaine about her research and how privileged she felt working at The Centre for Criminal Research with Jake who, for all his faults, was a brilliant boss. Elaine was an excellent listener and after two more glasses of wine, Kate was telling her all about Jake's unreasonable behaviour, not just his insistence that she ditch the Chicago contract but other occasions when he'd let her down, including the times he'd asked her out and failed to turn up and his propensity for affairs with junior researchers. When she'd finished she realised she had given more away about her feelings for her boss than she'd intended.

Elaine listened encouragingly and smiled when Kate finally paused for breath.

'It sounds as though Jake is a typical alpha male. He's hurt you probably without realising it and you have feelings for him that are more than professional. Would you like me to talk to him? Help him to appreciate how valuable you are to CCR. Philanthropy is big business in the United States and crime is a much bigger problem there than it is here. I know investors who are looking for criminal researchers and would pay well over the odds for someone like you.'

She glanced at her watch, took a business card from her clutch bag and passed it to Kate. 'Sounds like you need a bit of pampering. Serena used to work for me and I set her up in business when I moved to Devon.

She's a brilliant masseur. Please ring her and book in. I'll let her know it will be my treat.'

As Kate took the card wondering if she was doing the right thing, her smart phone rang. She apologised and answered it as Elaine settled the bill.

It was a London number. A voice she didn't recognise, 'Is that Kate Trevelyan?'

'Yes.' Kate's thumb was poised to cut off the call.

'I'm Macey Griffiths, a friend of your Nan's. She was staying with me in London.'

Kate felt her stomach lurch, 'Is everything all right?'

'She was knocked over by a car. She's in the Royal Free hospital. I couldn't get hold of your father.'

'Is she badly hurt?' Even through her shock, Kate was aware that Elaine was listening in with a concerned expression.

'Hard to tell, she's fractured her hip and was unconscious for a while.'

'I'll come straight over.' She took down details of the ward, thanked Macey Griffiths and put away her phone.

Elaine was still waiting by her side, 'Bad news?'

'It's my grandmother, she's had an accident. I need to get up to London.' She scrambled through her purse looking for cash to pay for her meal.

'Please, it's my treat.'

Kate stuffed the money in her pocket and grabbed her bag. 'Can you give me a lift to my car?'

Elaine shook her head, 'You can't drive, Kate. You've had too much to drink. Here let me ring your father.'

'When I tried to see him earlier his secretary said he would be out at meetings all day.'

'Well, he must have his mobile with him.' Kate watched in disbelief as Elaine started to try his number. It was obvious from the conversation that she wasn't having any luck getting hold of her father either.

'Look, don't bother. I want to go.'

Elaine tossed her phone back into her bag. 'I think you should wait and ring your father. He would want to know. He talks about his mother a lot, always wants to please her'.

Kate didn't appreciate the advice. 'If you don't want to give me a lift …' She made for the door leaving Elaine to signal to the Maitre d' and run after her.

'Wouldn't you be better waiting? Let your father drive to London. You need to stay here and fight your corner with Jake, insist he allows you to go to Chicago.'

Eventually Elaine insisted on driving her back to The Centre for Criminal Research to collect her car. On the way, Kate tried unsuccessfully to contact her father so Elaine promised to tell him what had happened. She also offered to pay for Kate's train ticket to London. Kate shrugged this suggestion off, knowing the journey would be quicker by car.

She was soon heading up the M5 to London hoping she wouldn't be stopped and breathalysed. To stop herself worrying about Nan, she thought about the relationship between Elaine and her father. Maybe he did deserve a bit of fun and he'd certainly get that from his friendship with Elaine Pierce.

# 6

I look around at the rubbish gathering in Ladram Heights's new affordable housing zone and wonder why I've bothered to come. The environmentally friendly street furniture has already been trashed, the latest LED illuminations destroyed and houses covered with graffiti, despite their paint resistant surfaces. I may have been persuaded to create this place but it doesn't mean I want to visit it and witness the unholy mess it has become in less than a year. Give me the aesthetically pleasing and expensive side of the Ladram Heights development any day. Now that's style. Homes more like mine with high ceilings, cornices with elegant reception rooms, Poggenpohl kitchens and private walled gardens; not some construction built in a hurry and done on the cheap. Still, it's turned out to be just what those councillors wanted: one tenth of the four thousand dwellings that make up Ladram Heights New Town are really only fit for rats.

It's humid for May and I'm sweating. I need a nicotine fix. I'm well on the way to giving up but Old Woman Trevelyan has seriously affected my plan and it's bringing out withdrawal symptoms. I crave cigarettes.

The new Ladram Heights shopping arcade across the road already looks squalid with bin bags and cardboard boxes spewing debris all over the pavement. As I go inside the newsagents and see who's serving, I'm not surprised about the rubbish.

The Asian shop assistant chats to his friend ignoring his queue of customers. The rows of cigarettes stacked on the shelf behind him seem to mock me. I'm not used to waiting. Neither it seems are the people out on the street. As their shouting grows louder everyone goes to the doorway to look out. The shopkeeper slams the door shut but it doesn't keep out the chanting.

'Immos out, immos out.'

'British jobs for British workers.'

The demonstrators get closer and the other customers crowd back behind the counter. The shouting is accompanied by banging on the window just before the brick comes through it. The woman ahead of me jumps. Her toddler shrieks in alarm and she bends down to inspect his hair for broken glass. The woman's attractive, despite her cheap clothes and unstylish haircut. The other two men waiting to be served don't bother to wait but dash out and run in the opposite direction to the demonstrators. The shopkeeper reaches for a brush behind the counter to sweep up the glass as the demonstrators' chanting drifts away through the broken window.

The kid's mother snatches at the shopkeeper's arm, 'I'll have the money by the end of the week, I know I will, but I need the eggs and milk today,' then points to her child, 'He's hungry, he's had no breakfast today . . .'

'It's too bad Mel, but I can't deal with that now.' He gestures towards the shattered glass, 'Those bloody demonstrators. That's the fourth replacement window this month. The insurance won't pay any more. I bring my family here for a better life and all I get is trouble.'

The other remaining customers and I watch the demonstrators retreating down the street. Their shouts of, 'Out. Out. Out,' grow fainter as they move away.

'They'll be back,' warns the shopkeeper.

The woman is still trying to speak to him, 'You know I always pay up, Mr Singh.'

'You do Mel, but that boy of yours doesn't. He's been in here stealing my beer again. You need to control him better.'

She shakes her head, 'Are you sure it was Finn?'

'Yes, definitely your Finn; he hangs around with the wrong lads. I don't tell the police in case they threaten me again, but I will have to next time.' The newsagent's turning away; he knows a lost cause when he sees it.

'I'm so sorry, Mr Singh. There won't be a next time. I'll make sure of it ... I will,' but she doesn't sound convincing. She grabs the child's hand pulling him towards the door. 'Forget about the milk.'

As she passes me the child collides with a haphazard display of sweets and drinks by the door sending a carton of orange juice splashing down my white designer jeans. His mother starts to stammer an apology. Something about her pale hopeless face make me feel protective, reminds me of my roots. Or maybe it's the way the shop assistant's got hold of her arm and is shoving her out of the door.

I push him out of the way, 'I'll buy you the milk,' I tell her.

Brushing aside her protests I grab two bottles of milk and some eggs from the shelves.

'You'll be doing me a favour; I don't like having loads of change.' Then pointing to the shelf above the shopkeeper's head I ask for the cigarettes that I've come in to buy. The woman looks stunned as I force the milk and eggs into her hands. As I leave the shop I'm surprised by my generosity.

Further along Salterton Avenue, uniformed officers are shoving some of the demonstrators into a blue police van and herding the onlookers back down the street. The demonstration seems over for now. I notice fresh graffiti has been splashed around. I prefer the original images the demonstrators have tried to cover up. Some are highly artistic with splashes of colour representing a reasonable likeness to Picasso's Guernica along with letters spelling out '*Miecza*', the Polish for dagger. The outline of an otter having its throat cut is a nice touch.

Strolling down the street to the bus shelter I check my watch. Something should be happening soon. There's no one around now except some stray dogs and two women arguing outside their front doors. This whole place feels like a time bomb. Hopeless babies dropped from between their mother's legs at such a rate they are hardly noticed. If they're lucky enough to have a dad he'll either be banged up or doing the rounds of his harem. It's not surprising their offspring find their way to Kidpower.

A page of yesterday's newspaper blows across my legs and I watch it dance up the empty street, following its progress until it's squashed by the wheels of a white transit van churning up grit as it squeals to a halt. The rear doors are flung open and six leather clad youths jump out. The last one out throws cans of lager at the others, who catch them deftly, hold them up like trophies, down the contents in two or three swallows, then fling the empties at each other.

A second white van, its sides all bashed in, pulls alongside and more leather-coated youths scramble out and start kicking the empty cans around, occasionally shifting their aim to hit parked cars or the windows of the nearby houses. The huddle of children playing nearby snatch up their micro scooters and dash away. Only a young girl hangs back and starts to cry. One of the youths shouts at her in Polish or Romanian and aims a can in her direction. It ricochets off her back as she flees through her front door.

The youths form a line-up like soldiers on parade then turn up their collars and take knives out of their pockets. They shout more foreign words then head down the street on either side of the road, scratching all the car doors as they pass. A couple pick up bricks lying in the road and start to smash car windows.

They stop outside the Asian newsagent's where they take dark green bottles filled with old cloths from their pockets. As they light the fabric they hold them up to the CCTV cameras above their heads. Then smash the blazing bottles into the windows of the row of shops.

It's time for me to leave.

*

All that hostile street action makes me feel horny. I drive back to Hawke Towers, my mansion up in the hills above Lyme Regis and text Connor. It's not on the coast but high enough up to have the kind of sea view people still pay a packet for. I'm taking the scenic route and driving slowly enough to enjoying the gentle throbbing between my thighs as I picture his naked body.

But when I get home, I'm still too early and Connor hasn't arrived back yet. So I take the setters for a walk, prolonging the anticipation. When I return his Norton motorbike is parked in the drive and as I reach the open front door I can hear the television blasting out from the drawing room. There's a pleasant warmth spreading through my body as I imagine what's about to happen. Connor is sitting on the sofa naked except for the damp towel half-draped around his hips, his iPad balanced on his knee.

'Everything go to plan?' I ask.

He ignores me at first, too engrossed in the images on the screen.

I stroll over to him and run my fingernail down his back. I'm expecting a reaction but he doesn't move. He's busy staring at the pictures of the blazing shops alight in The Parade. The local TV news team had filmed the aftermath of the fire. I listen as a brassy female reporter steps over piles of debris to describe the scene. Behind her back fire engines are still parked and smoke is rising all round her. A couple of young boys jump up and down in the background making V signs at the camera.

35

'Chaos hit the streets of East Devon again today when a demonstration by the protest group 'Jobs for Locals' was followed by a firebombing incident in Ladram Heights New Town. The emergency services were already on stand-by and were able to take shop keeper, Satinder Singh to hospital, where he is recovering from minor burns. Mr Singh's shop has been destroyed and the neighbouring shops are badly damaged.'

The camera pans away to show a group of teenagers clustering round the police tape. Connor pushes to the front of the group as the woman reporter approaches them. 'Locals believe the fire was started by a gang of Polish migrant workers taking reprisals against the demonstrators.'

Connor leans over the tape and talks into the microphone she's holding out to him, 'Yeah, that's right. It's them immigrants, they don't like the demos. They're taking their revenge.'

Stupid boy. Doesn't he realise what he's doing. Publicity like that is the last thing we need.

I push in front of him and turn off the television. 'Does it make you feel good, being a television icon?'

He grins back, then navigates back to his 'My Space' page and clicks on 'Connor's Highs Today.' 'See, it's not just the telly. It's gone viral.' He scrolls through images of leather coated figures and selects one of them. It's a shot of his artificially bronzed face under a black wig grinning and waving a petrol bomb, then another of him kicking a dog as the other gang members make V signs to the cameras and throw fire-bombs at the shop windows. 'Don't you think I make a good immo?'

His stupidity is becoming a liability, but he has a young firm body and he can make love all night long. I start to unwrap his towel, caressing him in all the right places to get a response. 'Do you feel good now?' I asked again.

Connor seems oblivious to the question and the caress: he's still distracted by the images on his phone. I dig my nails in harder leaving a thin red line on either side of his spine. I need him to respond: not just for my pleasure but to keep him obedient. But he pushed me away and switched on the TV again.

The reporter is still prattling on. 'The police want to hear from any witnesses to this appalling street violence,' she says as a phone number flashes up on the screen.

He looks at me at last, 'Hey, man. You could ring them.'

I hate this misuse of the word man. 'You saw me then?'

'Even in the heat of the moment I saw you. I know you like to watch me at work. Turns you on and all.'

He turns back to the television screen while I walk across to the drinks cabinet and pour out a vodka cocktail. My current toy boy is becoming too obsessed with building up his ego. My sexual anticipation drains away replaced by an incubating anger – but I need him around for a bit longer.

# 7

Mr T lived a few miles out of Ladram Heights in Otterford, a village Micki liked immediately, with its old church, water mill and village green. A stream ran through the centre of the village separating the cottages from the main road. The bus stopped outside the post office and he went in to ask for directions to Brathcol. The man behind the counter was chatting to a mother whose baby was asleep in a pushchair. He seemed in no hurry to serve him. Micki glanced at the local paper while he waited. The front page had a big red, white and blue Union Jack across it and the headline: 'Send the Scroungers Home'. They still hated people like him and his pa, even out here. Resisting an urge to rip all the newspapers off the shelves and stamp on them, he stayed to get his directions.

Further out from the centre of the village the thatched cottages were replaced by big houses with private drives and metal security gates. According to Micki's directions, Mr T's house was just round the corner behind the church. It looked newer than the neighbouring houses with a high white wall and no gate. From the road, the house looked like it was made from giant liquorice allsorts: black and white cubes stuck together and joined by two white towers. He liked the mix of round and square windows. If it was his home he'd chose the room with the large round windows at the top of the tower. He was surprised Mr T lived somewhere so interesting.

As he stood in the centre of the wide drive deciding whether to go in, a motorbike cut in front of him. He had to throw himself down onto the gravel to avoid being hit. The motorbike swung round to face him. The two riders removed their helmets, revealing the purple cropped hair worn by the Budleigh Boyz gang. Micki swallowed hard. He knew the smaller one. He was close enough to see the scar on Connor's face and catch the intensity of the glare from those piercing blue eyes. On the few occasions he made it to Kidpower he made sure Micki's life was hell.

Micki looked around for somewhere to hide as the other one passed a large container from the back of the bike to Connor, who slammed it down on the road. Micki didn't wait to find out their intentions. He scrambled onto his feet as Connor strode towards him and fled back to the road towards the centre of the village. The sound of a revving motorbike made him run faster, weaving between parked cars and jumping across the narrow stream whenever he encountered pedestrians.

Rounding the corner, he expected the motorbike to hit him in the back at any moment. He could hardly breathe but didn't dare look round. The engine was getting louder, the bike was almost on top of him. Then he felt the draft in his face as it drew level. Micki felt sick with relief as the bike sped past him and he saw it was driven by a blonde woman with no crash helmet who waved at him as she went by.

He slowed from a run to a walk. His breath was coming more naturally now and he tagged along at the back of a family group squabbling over where to eat. As they moved into single file to make way for a tractor he saw his bus pulling up opposite the village green. He swerved past the family and ran towards it, horrified to hear the engine wind into life as he approached. There was no-one left at the bus stop and the driver was closing the doors. Micki waved his arms and ran the last few yards in the middle of the road. The bus would either stop or run him over.

The bus stopped directly in front of him and the driver opened the doors. 'Have the aliens landed then?' he scoffed as Micki felt round his pocket for some change. Micki paid, said, 'Thank you,' and sat down at the back of the bus, grateful to be moving away from Otterford.

He was still gasping for breath as the bus passed Mr T's house and he saw the smoke rising from beyond the high wall. His eyes started to smart as the acrid smell of burning wafted in through the bus window.

# 8

It was well after ten by the time Kate arrived back in Otterford and she was worn out. She should have stayed in Devon and driven back in the morning. Nan was a lot better than she'd expected and she'd waited in the ward with her until she'd came round from the anaesthetic. The medics had finally hustled her away together with Macey Griffiths and the collection of Nan's friends waiting to see her.

She still hadn't been able to get hold of her father. Elaine Pierce must have told him about Nan's accident and Kate was upset that when he saw she was calling he hadn't rung her back. She'd done a lot of thinking about family on the drive back to Devon. There'd been some kind of falling out between her grandmother and her father before Nan had moved out of the house. But she'd never found out what the argument had been about. Her father never accompanied Kate on her visits to Bermuda even though they were in the school holidays. After Nan left, he'd taken to spending more time in his study - probably to avoid her sulks and her obnoxious friends. Now she was older she could understand how hard bringing up a teenage daughter on his own must have been for him.

It was a dark night and she didn't notice the smoke at first, only the acrid smell. But just before she reached Brathcol she had to swerve over the kerb to avoid colliding with the 'Road closed' sign. Then she saw all the emergency vehicles. Fire engines were blocking the road and parked police cars had their lights flashing.

Her heart was pounding as she ducked under the blue and white tape and ran into a police officer in a high visibility jacket who grabbed her, forcing her to swerve to a halt. The toxic air was making her cough and her eyes run. She rubbed them hard to get a better view, praying Brathcol was not the house on fire. In the split second it took her to pull away from the officer, she realised the smoke was coming from its windows, and froze. All she could think about was her dad's hurt expression as he left for school, after their argument. Then she was scrabbling through her bag, trying to find her phone. She prayed he wasn't still inside.

Flames were dancing up the inside of the house, visible through the blown-out windows. The police officer was shouting at her. Or at least his mouth was moving but she couldn't hear any words. Everything seemed to be happening in slow motion, in a vacuum. Then the silence was broken by a loud explosion and she was blown free. A cacophony of roaring flames, men shouting and water hoses pumping filled the air instead.

At first Kate didn't recognise the usually ultra-sophisticated Mrs Reece, Dad's neighbour, standing in front of her in dressing gown and hair rollers.

She shouted at the police officer, 'My dad? Is he inside?'

He didn't reply but reached for her arm and Mrs Reece held the other one. She burst free from them and was diving under the tape before they could stop her and sprinting towards the house. The next minute she was flat on her back with something pinning her down, a hissing hunchbacked monster. It took some time for her to recognise a firefighter in helmet and face mask, wearing breathing apparatus.

She screamed at him, 'Where's my dad?'

*

One of the police officers told her that Dad had been taken to the Royal Devon and Exeter Hospital. He couldn't give her many details about her father's condition, only that he was alive. He'd survived the fire. Brathcol was a ruin but she prayed Dad was going to be all right.

She drove into Exeter, breaking all the speed limits. Her earlier fatigue had disappeared; in fact she felt hyper. She was buzzing, hotwired. On the way, feeling so alert, she reviewed her life and choices. It took big moments in life, she thought, to help clarify your priorities - and hers had been all wrong. She had put her career and love life before the people she really cared about. From now on she would stay and work in Devon and be around to help Dad. She would contribute to Nan's recovery. Her cancelled trip to the United States and Jake were no longer important.

It was nearly midnight when she arrived at the hospital. The main reception was empty and she had to wait for someone to direct her to the intensive care ward. Their instructions contradicted the direction notices scattered liberally around the corridors and it took her another ten minutes to find it. When a male nurse finally let her in, she was told to wait while they found out what had happened to her father. As she looked around the ward, at the unconscious patients and rhythmic thud of machinery, the cloying odour of disinfectant made her feel sick. She jumped as a porter came up behind her, pushing a patient on a trolley. Kate checked to make sure he wasn't her dad.

Then the nurse returned and panic rose up from Kate's stomach at the expression on his face as she was gently guided towards a side room.

# 9

Kate hadn't expected a police officer to be waiting for her outside the ward, especially one of African Caribbean descent working in the West Country. But when DS Jacqui Sunday introduced herself, she found she had plenty of questions.

'How did Dad die?'

'Was there a spate of arson attacks in the area?'

'What the hell were the police doing letting it happen? Why hadn't someone got him out sooner?'

The nurse asked if she wanted some tea and hurried away when she shook her head. Stupid to offer it, all the canteens were closed. From the look of concern on her face, DS Sunday expected her to cry. She even had a handkerchief in her hand ready to pass over. But if there were any tears waiting to fall, Kate thought they would have frozen. She just felt very cold and detached from what was going on, suspended in some kind of vacuum.

Someone asked, 'Was the fire started deliberately?' and the policewoman was looking at her as if Kate had spoken. She must have voiced her thoughts.

The policewoman didn't respond at first. Kate could see her weighing up what category of bereaved relative she fitted. Angry and demanding, or so overwhelmed with grief that she couldn't speak. She didn't feel anything. All her emotions had drained away when the nurse had shaken his head and told her nothing could have been done to save her father. But then, she realised, she owed it to her dad to find out what had happened so she tried again.

'You think it was arson?'

DS Sunday gave a quick professional smile. 'We're still waiting for the Fire Inspector's report. We don't have many deliberate murders in Devon, thank goodness.' The policewoman touched her hand and said, 'I knew your father, you know. I used to visit Ladram Heights Community School. He invited us in to give talks about personal safety, internet bullying, that kind of thing. He really cared about his pupils. He also did everything he could to make us feel welcome which isn't always the case. Some schools organise their staff training day when they know we are coming in, to stop us talking to the kids.'

Kate tried to smile back. It couldn't be easy dealing with relatives of the recently dead. Jacqui Sunday was only trying to make her feel better. It must be a pig of a job.

'Your father was a great one for ...' Just then, Jacqui Sunday's mobile rang. Answering it, her face took on a serious look. She held the phone away from her ear, and spoke to Kate in a hushed voice. 'The pathologist says you can see your father now. But only if that's OK by you. It would be helpful if you could identify his body. But only if you want to ... if you're sure...'

Kate wasn't sure at all: something as formal as identifying his body jolted her back to reality - a world where her father would never go back to community school, a world where she'd never hear his voice again. Her stomach churned as she thought of the ordeal ahead of her. She tried to remember how he'd looked at breakfast. The crumbs on his shabby sports jacket. The thinning circle of hair at the back of his head as he'd gone out.

She took a deep breath and nodded her consent.

'This way then,' Jacqui Sunday said.

They walked side by side and Kate felt a bit less alone as they made their way to the back of the hospital. She wondered how DS Sunday was finding it, being a black policewoman working in Devon. Her own work often involved working with the police and she'd heard stories about black officers being sidelined; how women had to be better than men to get promotion.

Jacqui stopped outside a metal door. They'd arrived at the mortuary.

It didn't smell of formalin and wasn't full of the kind of cold meat cabinets she was used to seeing on television programmes such as CSI. Instead she was shown into an ordinary room, empty except for a metal hospital bed and a table.

The body lay on the bed covered with a sheet which Jacqui Sunday pulled down to uncover the face. Kate closed her eyes. The mortuary clock was ticking away the seconds. She braced herself to open her eyes and stared straight at her dad's face. His skin was grey, as if the dust from the burnt-out house had bonded with it, but she couldn't see any signs of burning. He didn't look the charred and mangled person she had expected to see.

Jacqui Sunday said, 'Is this your father?'

Kate swallowed back her sobs. At last she managed to say, 'Yes, that's him.' She rounded on Jacqui. Her words came out harder than she intended. 'What killed him?'

A man in green scrubs she hadn't noticed before answered. 'We think your father died of smoke inhalation. As you can see, he wasn't badly burnt.'

'Did he suffer? Would he have known what was happening?'

'Probably not.' Kate noted his hesitation before he added, 'We will know more after the post-mortem.'

'There's going to be a post-mortem?' She shuddered and tried not to think of this man slicing into her father.

'There has to be one after an unexpected death.' He was already covering up Dad's body.

'Will it be soon?'

'Probably tomorrow. Depends on the Coroner.'

Her head was buzzing with more questions, but suddenly queasiness kicked in. The pathologist held the mortuary door open as she pushed past, her hand pressed across her mouth.

Jacqui caught up with her in the car park just as she'd finished being sick and offered her some tissues.

Kate was thinking clearly again. 'This wasn't an accident you know. Dad was much too careful for that. He checked everything. Had smoke alarms everywhere. Always checked the doors were locked before going to bed. There's no way he'd let Brathcol burn while he was inside.'

'We'll see.' Jacqui gave her a much-practised sad smile. 'You shouldn't be on your own, you know. Is there anyone who can stay with you?'

She couldn't think of anyone and was about to say so when someone called out her name. Jake was at her side, holding her tight. She snuggled into his chest, aware of her mascara staining his tie.

'How did you know I was here?'

He held her closer and whispered in her ear, 'I was worried about you when you didn't come back to the office so I drove round to your dad's to see if you were OK. Your neighbour said you'd gone to the hospital. I thought you might need ...' He'd run out of words. Jake didn't do emotional, but Kate didn't care. It felt so good to be held.

The squealing of car tyres pulling up alongside made them both look up. The yellow Ferrari had narrowly missed hitting Jacqui, and now Elaine Pierce was getting out of it.

'Kate, this is awful. I've just come from the ward where your father died. They said you'd been there. You poor dear.'

Jake had released his hold on her and she knew he was staring at Elaine over the top of her head. She started to introduce them, then suddenly felt exhausted. Elaine caught her as she slumped forward. Her grip felt surprisingly strong.

'I'm taking you home with me.'

Jacqui started to interrupt, 'Are you a relation? Can you leave me your address and phone number, we'll need to talk to Kate again.' Elaine ignored her.

Jake was standing back, arms folded. Kate turned towards him hoping he'd insist she went home with him. 'I'll ring you in the morning, Kate.'

Kate watched him turn and walk away. She wished she was going with him instead of Elaine, but Elaine was already leading her towards the Ferrari. Kate allowed herself to be helped into the passenger seat, feeling limp and pathetic and suddenly vulnerable.

# 10

She was standing outside her father's study. He was calling out to her but she couldn't reach him. Every time she tried to open the door the flames forced her back. Sweat was running down her back and the smoke in her lungs was making her sick. She had to try harder. Open the door and find Dad, whatever it took. But she couldn't and she knew she was letting him down yet again.

'Wake up, Kate! Wake up! It's all right. You're just dreaming.'

The voice had changed. It was a woman calling her and even with her eyes closed Kate knew she was no longer in the dark. She stretched out her fingers and toes under the duvet. She was all right. But her father wasn't.

The memories of last night came tumbling back. She was in Elaine Pierce's mansion and when she opened her eyes she wasn't surprised to see Elaine standing over her.

Embarrassed at showing emotion in front of a stranger, Kate tried to laugh it off. 'Sorry, bad dream. Didn't mean to disturb you.'

Sitting on the edge of the bed, Elaine stroked away a strand of Kate's hair sticking to her cheek. 'You didn't. I've bought your breakfast up and I heard you calling out.'

Kate sat up and looked around the unfamiliar bedroom. Elaine must have opened the shutters and sunlight was streaming through the open window. On a table in front of the window a tray was laid for breakfast. Kate realised she was hungry as the aroma of warm croissants and fresh coffee wafted over.

Elaine was holding out a robe, looking concerned. 'I was going to join you for breakfast but maybe you'd prefer to be alone?'

She was tempted to say she didn't want any company and wasn't hungry. But that would be rude. She forced a smile, slipped out of bed and sat down at the table.

The view from the window was worth getting out of bed for. Beyond the Gertrude Jekyll-style garden with its formal hedges and water features, two slopes of grass and rhododendrons in full flower framed a distant view of the sea.

The breakfast was good too and she found she was eating more than she'd expected.

As Kate tucked into American pancakes, peaches and maple syrup, Elaine told her why she'd returned to Devon. 'I grew up round here. Went to school in Axminster - it's been knocked down now. I was branded a failure and hated every minute.' She looked up from eating her croissant to check that Kate was listening. 'Then I dropped out of school, started taking drugs, had affairs - a lot of affairs, mainly with married men - and started using my real assets.'

Kate stared back, 'So what changed? How did you get out of all that?'

A slow smile spread across Elaine's face. 'I was rescued by a knight in shining armour.' Kate's disbelief must have shown on her face. 'No, you're right. My first husband thought he was one of those. It bored me silly, him always wanting to please me. But one of my lovers came from a wealthy American family and the rest, as they say, is history.'

This was a disappointing route to success for a woman Kate was starting to admire. 'So you inherited Pierce Enterprises?'

Elaine's mouth tightened a fraction. 'No.' She wiped the crumbs off the corner of her mouth and the smile was back. 'Pierce Enterprises is the result of a lot of hard work - my hard work, together with resilience and staying power. Once I got over what turned out to be a disastrous relationship I started investing in me rather than pleasing other people. Self-sufficiency is very close to charm and I learned never to rely on anyone.' Any earlier hint of annoyance had been swept away as Elaine stood up to emphasise what she was saying, but Kate felt she was listening to a well-rehearsed speech. 'No, Pierce Enterprises is a result of my taking risks and investing where my rivals feared to go.'

Her arms dropped to her side and she glanced at Kate as if she'd just remembered who she was. 'And of course, because of that I've been able to help some good causes. Make life a bit better for those not quite so fortunate. I set up quite a few charities…'

'One of which,' Kate finished for her, 'being Kidpower.'

Elaine sat down again and leant closer. 'That's right. Kidpower. Also Martha's Dream, The Magic Garden Project for people with dementia, the new children's hospice in Exeter – and a few more. But Kidpower is the charity I'm most proud of and Terence, your father, was making such a difference there.'

'Like what?' Kate really was keen to know.

'He didn't tell you much about Kidpower then? Well, he was our leading fund-raiser as well as a mentor. He had so many important connections and was brilliant at persuading wealthy people that Kidpower really does get misguided teenagers back on track. But his greatest gift was his empathy with youngsters in crisis. They'd talk to him about their problems when their parents or social workers couldn't get a word out of them.'

The mention of her father's name brought back all her heartache tinged with guilt that she didn't know anything about that side of him. She also felt hurt. Dad had never listened to her in the way Elaine was describing when she was a teenager. Kate had a sudden, overwhelming desire to find out more about his life. 'I'd like hear more about Kidpower. Maybe it's something I could help with, in Dad's place? He would have liked that.'

'I'm sure. Look, I'll take you there sometime. You can look round and meet the Director, Lyndon Crud. He and your father didn't always get on but I know he admired the work Terence did with the young people he supported.' Elaine glanced at her watch. 'But this morning I'm off to London for a lunchtime board meeting. I thought I could drop you off at the Royal Free so you can see your grandmother. She'll have to know about Terence eventually.'

Kate went cold at the thought of breaking the news. She knew it would be better if she told her grandmother rather than leave her to hear it from a stranger – but she wasn't sure she was ready. Before she could think of a good excuse, her mobile rang. It was DS Sunday. She wanted Kate to meet her at the Coroner's office.

\*

The Coroner's Office was situated at County Hall and involved the usual checks at reception and signing in for a security badge. Jacqui Sunday had left a message to say she was held up so Kate waited outside the Coroner's Office. To fill the time she took out her iPod and googled 'Kidpower'.

The website was a bit ostentatious for a charity - full of flashing images and loud music. On the home page a bright orange banner filled the screen to reveal the back view of five hooded figures. They twisted round and flung back their hoods. Their shouts of 'KIDPOWER IS HERE FOR KIDS!' filled the waiting area as the four young men and a girl continued to shout and gesticulate wildly.

She selected '*About Us*' from the sidebar and read:

'*We at Kidpower believe the best way to stop crime is to prevent young people getting into trouble in the first place.*

•*We identify and help young people as early as possible by providing a range of support from mentoring to therapy.*

•*We work in the poorest areas along the Jurassic Coast in Devon and Dorset and are specialists in working with young people to empower them to tackle their problems, including depression, drug and alcohol abuse.*'

She scanned through the rest of the website. Apart from the rather chilling introductory video of the hoodie teenagers, the website looked respectable. There were quotes from teenagers telling how Kidpower helped them kick the drug habit and escape from the world of crime; a wordy but inspiring mission statement; and some small print at the bottom of the screen stating that a minor royal was Kidpower's President. She was drawn to the tab headed '*Opportunities to become a Kidpower Mentor,*' but all it said was, '*No vacancies at present*'. There is now, she thought ruefully.

The name of Lyndon Crud, Director of Kidpower, turned up quite a lot in different search engines. She selected one of the entries. The round-faced man with the trimmed black moustache filled the screen. His overstretched smile revealed the need for better dentistry and there was something reptilian about his piercing black eyes. She read on to find that, in addition to his charity work, Lyndon Crud also worked as a therapist offering hypnosis as well as a magician.

'*Lyndon Crud is one of Britain's most popular crowd-pulling acts, a long-standing Equity member, professional comedian and magician. He provides just the magic needed to kick-start a new company business plan or put the inspiration back into flagging team members. Half an hour of Lyndon's unique corporate magic show could change their lives and your company's performance for ever.*

He might lack the looks and charisma of Derren Brown but there must be something about him to justify the high fees Kate saw he charged for his private therapy work. Judging by the number of testimonials from people he had helped give up smoking, lose weight or overcome phobias, he was held in high regard.

Elaine Pierce had said that Lyndon Crud and her father didn't get on. Looking into his rather forbidding face on his website, she wondered why but her thoughts were interrupted as Jacqui Sunday rushed up, full of apologies for arriving late.

The two of them were soon sitting in a cluttered and stuffy room full of boxes and files while Vera Thomas, the Coroner's Officer fetched them a drink. They'd started to run out of conversation by the time Vera Thomas returned. A motherly looking woman in a baggy beige dress, she was carrying three mugs of tea on a tray and an official-looking folder under her arm.

She handed one of the mugs to Kate, 'I believe you are Mr Trevelyan's daughter? Thank you so much for coming in.'

Then she passed Jacqui the other mug and asked about the progress of a recent murder case before lowering her bulky body down to the armchair next to where Kate was sitting.

Kate took a sip of the tea and grimaced as she found it full of sugar. The room was overpoweringly hot, so she asked Vera if she could open a window.

Vera Thomas shook her head. 'I'm sorry. It's painted over. I keep asking for an electric fan but our finances don't seem to run to it.'

Kate shuffled uncomfortably in her chair as Vera rearranged her papers. Eventually she looked up. 'This must be very hard for you, my dear. I believe you identified your father's body yesterday? Are you the next of kin?'

'That's right. There's my grandmother, my father's mother, and a few cousins living in Devon who I haven't seen since my childhood.'

Vera Thomas smiled encouragingly. 'Well, my job is to gather evidence for the Coroner and prepare for the inquest into your father's death. I'm going to ask you some questions which the Coroner may find helpful at the inquest. I want you to be as comfortable as possible on this sad occasion so please ask me if there is anything you don't understand.' Then, glancing across at Jacqui, she continued, 'Now, I know DC Sunday has been looking after you but we can talk alone if you would prefer it.'

Kate reached across to stop Jacqui from leaving. 'I'd like DC Sunday to stay.'

'In that case I'll ask her to explain for the record what her role involves.'

Jacqui looked a bit surprised to be asked this. 'Because Mr Trevelyan died in an intensive house fire the cause of which may be arson, my role as a Family Liaison Officer is to support Kate throughout the police investigation.'

Vera nodded encouragingly. She then asked Jacqui some more questions about the fire, recording her replies on her laptop. The policewoman didn't know much about it, but just kept repeating that the Fire Inspector's report wasn't finished yet.

That clearly wasn't good enough for Vera Thomas, who raised her eyebrows and looked hard at Jacqui Sunday. 'But surely the police have some idea of the cause, even if the fire was accidental?'

Jacqui looked uncomfortable and Vera Thomas looked less benign. She ignored Jacqui and turned to Kate. 'I believe you lived with your father? How did he seem in the weeks before the fire?'

'I live in London but I've been staying with my father for the last few days while I've been working in the area.' She ignored the second question as she couldn't see what it had to do with the fire.

'Did you see a lot of your father while you lived in London?'

Kate managed to stop herself from saying, what the hell has that got to do with you? Instead she said, 'No, but we kept in touch.'

'So you didn't see much of your father just before his death?

'No.'

'You weren't particularly close, then?'

'Yes, we were,' Kate snapped. 'Look, I don't understand what this has got to do with my father's death...'

Vera Thomas peered at Kate over her glasses. 'You were about to leave England to work in the USA, I believe.'

Kate felt her cheeks redden, but she wasn't going to lie. 'That's right. I was going to work in the States, but that doesn't mean we didn't get on.'

'Did your father seem worried or preoccupied about anything?'

'No he was just getting on with his life.' She wasn't expecting to be questioned about her dad's state of mind. First Jacqui didn't know anything about the circumstances of the fire and now this woman was interrogating Kate as if she was complicit in her father's death.

Vera Thomas shuffled her papers and said, 'The police were investigating some recent events that had apparently traumatised Mr Trevelyan. She looked hard at Kate. 'He didn't talk to you about any concerns or seem anxious in any way?'

It was the first Kate had heard of any such events and she looked at Jacqui for some explanation. Jacqui shook her head.

The Coroner's Clerk continued, 'There's also a report provided by Mr Trevelyan's GP, Dr Laurence. Apparently he was treating your father for anxiety and panic attacks. He had prescribed Restoril and referred him to the Community Health Team.'

Kate knew Restoril was a strong sedative and was starting to see where the questions were leading. 'Are you suggesting my father had fallen asleep because he was taking Restoril? That he slept through the fire?'

'We have to explore all possibilities, Dr Trevelyan. The Coroner has requested toxicology reports to find out if Restoril or any other substance was present in your father's body.'

The meeting wasn't going the way Kate had expected. All this talk of the fire being an accident because of her dad's state of mind was rubbish, but she was perturbed by the implications the Coroner's assistant was obviously making. It was true; she hadn't spent much time with him, even when staying with him at Brathcol. If her father was being treated for anxiety, she obviously hadn't noticed.

Then there was Jacqui. Why hadn't she told her about 'the incidents' the police had investigated? All she'd said was she'd spoken about crime prevention at the community school.

She glared from one woman to the other. 'It sounds like you've already drawn your own conclusions! So tell me, how did my father die?'

Vera Thomas referred to her folder. 'The pathologist found that Mr Trevelyan died from respiratory distress. He had irreversible damage to the lining of his lungs.' She looked up at Kate. 'As your father was unconscious all the time he was in hospital, I don't think he would have been aware of his burns or the lung damage.'

That was reassuring, but Kate didn't like the implication that the fire was her father's fault. She'd been shocked at the fire damage at Brathcol but didn't believe her father's state of mind contributed to the fire. Quite the opposite. He bordered on the obsessional about tidiness and safety. She remembered the firebombing incidents she'd seen on the news. Ladram Heights was just up the road from Otterford.

'You don't think the recent riots and petrol bombing might be linked to the fire?'

Vera Thomas shook her head. 'It's too early to say, but in my experience not very likely.'

Then, looking straight at Jacqui, Kate asked her, 'What about the Fire Inspector's report? When are you likely to have it?'

Jacqui looked across at Vera Thomas, who replied, 'I believe the police forensic team are still investigating.'

'Is there any evidence the fire was started deliberately? Whatever happened to the investigation into arson you mentioned?' Kate interrupted.

'It hasn't really started yet, Kate.' Jacqui pulled her chair closer to her, 'Look, it's only natural you're upset. Have a talk to Dr Laurence. Maybe he can give you some tranquillizers to help you cope with the shock of your father's death.'

Kate stood up. She certainly would see Dr Laurence, not for tranquillizers but for some information about why he was treating her dad for depression. Kate had heard enough. Without bothering to say goodbye to either woman, she swept out of the untidy office, hoping it would be a long time before she saw either DS Jacqui Sunday or Vera Thomas again.

# 11

Jacqui Sunday knew a lot about the Trevelyan family. She might be the newest Family Liaison Officer in the Force but she intended to be one of the best and that meant doing thorough preparation for each of her cases. So far she'd only been allocated families of accidental deaths to support. But their grief was just as painful, just less complicated from the police point of view. Some of her police friends from the Met thought she was being sidelined because of who she was, but Jacqui thought political correctness was often a good excuse for a moan. She didn't mind bidding her time until her Chief thought she was ready for homicide support and until then she was going to do everything by the book and give each of the families she was working with her best shot. But she couldn't help hoping the Trevelyan fire turned out to be murder.

From her research she knew that the Trevelyan's were a well-established Devon family with impressive tombs in the graveyard of Otterford church. Terence was the only son of a well-respected local farmer, who preferred a career as a teacher to working on the land. From all accounts he'd been good at it and been appointed as Director of the new Ladram Heights Community School against stiff competition. There wasn't much about the Trevelyan family in police records until about six months ago when the occasional fight or drug possession had escalated resulting in frequent police call outs to the campus for disturbances and violent behaviour. Jacqui thought it was associated with the gang activity becoming more common in and around Ladram Heights. Nothing like the gang scene she'd known in London but it still needed stopping. Her boss, Chief Superintendent Ian Ross didn't agree, so very little was being done.

Jacqui had been out to interview Mr Trevelyan after the most recent incident. He'd been subject to unpleasant threats of personal attacks and had wanted to start a multi-agency group to manage the gang situation but Chief Superintendent Ross didn't want to know. The Ladram Heights Gazette had made the most of it, filling its front pages with interviews with angry parents accompanied by shadowy photographs of hooded students standing in front of gang graffiti. Jacqui found the hate campaign the local rag had fuelled against its community school director distasteful and some of Mr Trevelyan's staff were trying to get him sacked. Whenever she'd been out to the school she'd found him courteous and helpful. But it was no surprise to hear Vera Thomas saying he'd been taking tranquillizers.

All Jacqui knew about his daughter, Kate, was that she lived in London, didn't have a mother and was following in her father's footsteps as a successful academic – but if her father's death turned out to be from arson, Jacqui would have to be selective in what she said. A Family Liaison Officer's role was to support the close relations of victims of sudden and unexplained deaths, but she was also there as a detective. At the moment she was failing in both tasks. Dr Trevelyan had just lost her father and had every right to be rude and upset about the way the investigation was going, but until Jacqui managed to get hold of the Fire Inspector's preliminary report there was little she could do to move it on.

The glass fronted room used by CID was hot given its eco-friendly design. It was really a glorified greenhouse and the smell of body odour was overwhelming. Feeling in need of a coffee and a chat, Jacqui went in search of the only friend she'd made on the force since she'd arrived from London six months ago. Hannah Lucas, the other female detective in the team, held out a box of Ferrero Rocher chocolates as Jacqui approached.

'Dive in, honey. I'm celebrating my second successful date with Eric the Viking.'

Jacqui laughed and helped herself to a couple of chocolates. Hannah was always full on with her enthusiasm whether it was work related or to do with her love life. In this case it was both. Eric was a traffic cop based in Exeter. He was a mate of Jacqui's ex-husband and she'd heard all about how he got his nickname. Her good mood vanished as someone pushed past her and a hairy hand knocked hers out of the way and scooped up most of the remaining chocolates.

'Just what I need to go with that mug of tea you were about to make me, Sunday.'

She glared back at Inspector Hunt and would have told him where to get off except he was the officer liaising with the Fire Inspector over the

Trevelyan house fire and she wanted to know what was happening with the investigation.

'Do we have anything back on the Trevelyan house fire yet, Sir? Any idea how the fire started, his daughter, Dr Trevelyan would like to know?'

He ignored her question and continued to hold out his tea-stained mug. 'Sir?'

'A bit soon to expect anything isn't it, Sunday? The place will still be drying out. Didn't you learn anything in the Met, with all those riots?'

She could have told him her experience with London gangs had taught her complacency was dangerous but she was used to his sarcastic comments. She knew the only thing he disliked more than women detectives were ones from the Met.

For a quiet life she was about to take his mug when he grabbed her arm, 'Sounds like you need a reminder about your loyalties. The Trevelyan woman wants to know how the fire started does she. For all you know she might have started it herself.' He was so close to her face than she could smell his lunch, some of which was still congealed in the bubble of spit gathering at the corner of his mouth. 'Remind me. How long ago was it since you were at Police College?'

Jacqui didn't wait around to hear any more. She shook off his arm, grabbed her car keys and headed out of the room.

As she reached the door he shouted after her, 'You might be interested in a bit of scandal that surrounded the Trevelyan family in the eighties.'

Jacqui resisted the urge to turn round. It was just what he wanted. Confident that she'd read all the relevant records pertinent to the Trevelyan family she decided to ignore her Inspector and trust her own judgement.

# 12

Micki woke to the usual early morning chanting from the demonstrators. He dressed and went downstairs to join Luca and the other men on the afternoon shift. They were all sitting round on the floor with the curtains drawn. Pa had lit a candle to read *The Guardian* but it went out as one of the men in the room moved across the floor to get another beer. Micki put his hands up to his ears and shrugged his shoulders at Daz, one of the youngest builders in the house. Shaven-headed and muscular, he was only slightly older than Micki and the only builder who he counted as a friend. Daz didn't smile back but slammed his flask and packed lunch into his hessian bag. The lid of the sandwich box flew across the room and hit Micki on the side of his face, where his bruises from yesterday's roughing-up still hurt.

Daz threw his bag down and rushed to Micki's side. 'Are you alright?' and when Micki nodded, went on, 'Sorry, Micki, but they make me so angry. They're only doing this because the Miecza gang were out last night. Those demonstrators think because they see the word Miecza and other gang graffiti dabbed all along Salterton Avenue, and we live here, that we are part of the gang. Who's going to call their gang 'sword' anyhow? It's just English kids causing trouble.'

'Sword?' Micki asked.

'It's English for Miecza. I thought you were an expert at BBC English.' Daz scoffed. 'These gangs. They've got nothing to do with us. I don't know why we take it. Why we sit here like chickens, waiting for the bricks to come through the windows.'

'Because we all need the money, Daz,' Pa replied, 'and we don't want to sink to their level by fighting back.'

Micki was surprised by Daz's outburst. He was usually pretty relaxed about all the hate against them out on the street, but after the TV coverage last night showing the locals blaming immigrants for the petrol bombs it must have got to him too. Micki understood how he felt, he experienced it every day at community school. Always being blamed or mocked for his accent.

He winked at Daz. 'If we sit here long enough they will be arrested and we will have Ladrum Heights to ourselves.'

'Yeah, and chickens might fly,' Daz snapped back.

'Chickens? You mean pigs?'

Daz was always teasing him about listening to Radio Four to improve his 'BBC English' and Micki was rewarded with a grin as he threw an empty beer can at him.

'So, you are better at English now, little Micki.' They both started laughing.

'Not so loud,' Pa warned.

They sat in silence until the shouting outside stopped.

Daz had been pulling faces behind Pa's back. 'Can we talk now, Luca?'

Pa sighed and Micki thought how much he seemed to have aged in the last few months. 'You all right, Pa?'

Pa grinned and ruffled his hair, sounding more like he used to. 'It's me who should be asking you that, Micki. I was thinking of staying off work today so we could go out somewhere together but I've been warned I'll lose the work if I take any more time off.'

He would love a day out but Micki knew that he couldn't risk losing the money to send home to his grandmother, Opi, and Misha, his little sister. 'No Pa, you go. I've got homework to do.'

Daz snatched up the computer magazine Micki had been trying to read, peered at it and waved it in the air. 'Homework? What homework?'

Micki grabbed back his copy of PC Zone. His real homework lay unopened in his school bag. He kicked the bag further under the table. He was ashamed of the remedial reading and maths books inside. He wished he could persuade the teachers it was his English that was poor, not his brain. He was thirteen, not three. He'd read more difficult books before he started elementary school in Krakow. He caught the look of helplessness on his Pa's face. Luca hadn't wanted to come to England any more than he did. They both missed Opi and Misha. Micki used to find Misha a nuisance but now he often wished she was with him. He knew going home was impossible; that Luca wasn't allowed to continue to work in Poland and the building work here was the only work his pa could find. He just wished he didn't have to stay in England as well as his father.

'OK, Micki,' Pa said at last, 'if you're sure you are all right. I'll bring you a treat when I get back.'

He grabbed his rucksack and gestured to Daz. 'Out of the back and over the fence,' and turning to Micki, 'Goodbye, son, I'll see you later.'

Micki felt lonely when they'd gone. He read his magazine through twice but couldn't concentrate. He thought about missing community school but if he did Mr T would tell Pa, and Micki didn't want that.

Just as he was going out he noticed a piece of paper on the front door mat below the letterbox. It was addressed to him in Connor's illiterate handwriting, warning him not to tell what he'd seen outside Brathcol yesterday or the same thing that happened to the headmaster might happen to his dad.

\*

He thought he'd avoided the demonstrators. He knew the precautions: never wear earphones, so you can hear them before you can see them; be careful going round corners; don't look them in the eyes... But as Micki made his way to community school his head was full of thoughts of Mr T and what might have happened to him, so he nearly walked straight into a whole group of them.

'*Out, out, out!*' '*Immos go home!*' '*British jobs for British workers!*'

He'd had enough grief so he turned in the opposite direction and legged it towards the coast. The sea breeze felt good against his face and he was soon running through the countryside, along lanes with high hedges and no pavements. He'd never been so far out of Ladrum Heights and he liked it already. It felt more like his home outside Krakow, except for the sound of crashing waves.

The caravan park was full of holiday makers so he avoided the entrance in favour of an overgrown road. He ended up outside a padlocked metal gate with a faded plastic sign, '*DANGER. KEEP OUT,*' half covering another rusty metal sign, '*Pastures Hosp. . .*' and '*National Health Ser. . .*' He could see the roof and chimneys of a big old house beyond high wooden fencing. A bright orange butterfly was flying over nettles and thistles, darting between path and flowers. Micki watched it until it flew past his head and over the fence. He missed having adventures. He was fed up of always having to look out for danger and being kept out of places, so when he saw a gap in the fence he squeezed through it.

On the other side was a stone building like the ones in the grandest parts of Krakow, but this one was almost derelict. There was a nude statue of an ancient soldier holding a spear looking down at him. Micki was fascinated by the symmetry of the huge windows and wide stone sills and the coat of arms above the covered entrance. The doors and windows were boarded up with more 'DANGER – KEEP OUT' signs. On one of the windows the boarding had come away just enough for him to squeeze through. He landed on a dusty mosaic floor with a resounding slap.

Away from the window the building was dark and smelt like a mouldy grain store. Micki felt in his pocket for the lighter he'd stolen from one of the builders and the last of his supply of spearmint chewing gum. Good, the lighter worked and the gum filled his mouth with saliva and helped to mask the musty smell. He felt his way along a corridor, experimentally at first then striding out with more confidence until he lost his footing and dropped the lighter.

He scrambled around but couldn't find it. The solid floor felt cold against his fingers. As his eyes adjusted to the dark he made out a fallen door he'd tripped over and beyond that a dark space. He could make out doors on either side of the corridor and when he tried the handles, they opened. Some rooms were empty but in others he could make out the shapes of furniture.

Micki returned to a door half-way along the corridor. The inside of this room was lighter than the others; more boarding had come away from the window frame. Inside, a desk, chairs and a sofa were stacked upside down on top of each other. The room felt less scary than the others, more like an office. He tore down the remaining boards from the window, revealing an old notice board on the opposite wall. Unlike most of the windows he'd seen from outside, this one was missing its iron bars.

Ever since he'd arrived in England he'd been made to share a room with Pa and six other builders. Micki had wanted a room of his own more than anything – and now he'd found one.

He upended the sofa and pushed it to join the desk under the window. There was a long metal cupboard on its side and he tried to drag it closer to the sofa. It was heavy but he braced his back against the wall and pushed hard with his feet and it moved, tearing through the rotten carpet and making a scraping sound on the stone floor. On its journey across the room some of the drawers burst open, spilling their contents across the floor: an old radio which no longer worked, some bars of chocolate which tasted stale, an empty plastic lunch box which smelt musty when he removed the lid and some trainers too big to fit him. There was also a small book with a leather cover.

He wiped the mildew off its front cover. It was a diary, written in large clear handwriting. He started reading.

*19th or 20th of February 1987 (not sure what day it is)*

*This is my fifth try at writing a diary. They found all the others. I'm losing track. I no longer know how long I've been here. The drugs make me stupid and sleepy, so maybe that's why. Today I've decided to fight back. I've been pushing the pills under my tongue and hiding them in my toothpaste. Then it's been easy to flush them down the toilet when nobody was looking.*

*I've no friends here. They keep ganging up on me. I can't sleep for the wailing – it goes on all night long. I don't know why they can't drug the other patients here to keep them quiet like they try to do to me.*

*

*1st March*

*A better day today. I heard a seagull calling outside the window. They're so high I can't see out, but I listen to the rain, to the cars driving up, sometimes I can hear the sea. Reminds me of home. I miss it so much but maybe I don't have a home any more. At least I won't if that woman gets her way. I worry that no one will remember me? I know we're near the coast here but the seagulls usually keep away. I don't blame them. Who in their right minds would want to come here?*

*My hair is annoying me. It looks awful but not really long enough to wear off my face. No scrunchies here though, a torn elastic band will have to do. But it feels itchy. They keep refusing to give me a haircut – but if they don't cut it off for me I will have to find some scissors and do it myself. Of course, we're not allowed scissors. I could always ask Elliot. He's a sweetie. Said he'd look after me. Make sure the others don't hurt me.*

*

*2nd March*

62

*They found my pills. I think Dr Sands has it in for me. She seemed so nice at first but when they told her I'd been hiding my medication she told them to use injections. The more I struggle to stop them the more it hurts. The injections leave me so out of it I can't stop the others when they come to hurt me. Cigarette burns at first then pulling out my hair. Now they have stamped on my hand and broken my finger. And my hair still looks awful. I'm desperate to come home. Please help me.*

Micki couldn't understand all the words but he could tell they were written by someone very unhappy who was forced to leave their home to live in a place they detested, like him. He wanted to be home again too in his garden full of cherry trees and secret dens. Back in his Mama's kitchen full of the smells of coffee and his grandmother's baking. The place where he used to make houses out of the best pitch pine for his pet rats and change their straw every day. The rats never lived long, but while they did, he fed them smoked pork and kielbasa and bits of doughnuts smuggled from the tea table. Home was where Pa always gave him more money than he needed to feed his pets. Unlike here in Ladrum Heights, in a house full of builders who ate like pigs and only left him child portions because he was small and only just thirteen. No wondered he had spots, his voice wasn't breaking and he couldn't get a girlfriend.

Micki looked down at the book in his hand. The diary was a real find. It was like having a friend who understood. Reading and translating it was hard work though and his eyes hurt from the effort. He would have to read it a bit at a time. Not at the hostel or community school where someone was bound to ridicule him for reading it and probably tear it up. No, he'd come back to this room to read it. He'd bring pictures for the wall and supplies of chocolate and cola. It would be a place where he could read his books and magazines without interruption. No one need know. He'd come every day and work his way through the diary and find out what happened to the person who wrote it. Maybe he - or she - was still alive. He hoped so.

# 13

Kate climbed the stone Georgian steps to the office, still angry about her meeting with Vera Thomas. She'd arrived in the CCR car park with no clear idea what she was doing there but hoped that immersing herself in her work would stop her wishing she'd spent more time with her father. She passed some junior researchers on their way out for lunch and they called, 'Hi Kate.' She hurried past them to her own office to avoid having to make conversation. It was the first time she'd been back to CCR since her father's death and she didn't want to talk about it. She just hoped Jake had told everyone so she wouldn't have to.

Inside her office everything was just as she'd left it. Her reference books were in alphabetical order, her research papers stacked in piles corresponding to their start date and the progress charts for the ongoing research projects all up to date. It was as if yesterday had never happened. The tidiness overwhelmed her and she had to stop herself from throwing papers on the floor and ripping books off the shelves. Instead she went over to the window and looked out at the sea, breathing slowly and steadily, to get a grip.

She started to look through her post. A report on the effects of junk food on criminal behaviour; a letter from Channel 4 about a television programme they wanted her to feature in; an article on domestic violence against men waiting for a peer review; and last month's performance chart with her name highlighted as top earner. The usual stuff, but now it all seemed meaningless.

Vera Thomas's comments about her father had been going round her head all the way back from Exeter. He'd never mentioned any incidents involving the police. That Coroner woman had been misinformed. Her father couldn't have been under so much pressure that he needed medication and she didn't know a thing about it. She told herself it was rubbish but found she was surfing through the search engines for her father's name and was shocked to find a couple of hits. They were mostly short articles about student unrest and fights off campus between local students and the children of migrant workers. Derek Droney, a journalist from the Ladrum Heights Gazette, the local paper, had run a vox pop feature asking readers if foreign families should return to where they came from. There were also a number of letters from the public criticizing her father's handling of the situation at school.

Kate stared at the screen feeling stunned. Maybe she didn't know as much about her father's life, as she thought. Well, at least she would be working investigating the anti-migrant hostility herself now. It was a bit late, but she could find out what was behind all the aggravation her poor father had suffered and try and do something about it. It might help her come up with the evidence to prove the fire was arson that the police seemed unable to find.

She looked around her office expecting to find some crime statistics from Devon and Cornwell police. This was usual procedure at the start of any community crime research. The contract papers for the anti-migration research that Jake had been so keen on her to lead weren't there either.

But she couldn't concentrate on the research for thinking about Nan. She didn't even know her son was dead, not to mention the fire. Kate was dialling the Royal Free Hospital when Ginny, her administrator, walked in.

'Hi Kate, I thought I heard you come in.' She mouthed 'sorry' as she saw Kate was on the phone.

Kate's conversation with the hospital was brief. She was told her grandmother was too weak to be told about her son's death and if she planned to visit it would be better to put it off until tomorrow.

Ginny was still standing by Kate's desk looking horrified. 'Your father's dead?'

Kate didn't know what to say. It looked like Jake hadn't told anyone about her father's death. 'I'm sorry, Ginny. It's my dad ...' she took in a long breath before continuing. She was going to have to start telling people. 'He was killed in a house fire the night before last.'

Ginny rushed forward to give her a hug, 'That's terrible, Kate. We wondered where you were yesterday ... but we didn't guess it was anything like this. That's so awful.'

Kate's eyes were moist as she hugged Ginny back. The human contact felt good. Her own mother had died recently after a long battle against cancer. The warm embrace seemed to say Ginny understood.

'Don't be daft. How could you know? I should have rung and told you but I thought Jake would break the news.' Kate was still finding it hard to believe he hadn't told anyone?

'Kate, are you sure you should be back at work?'

Kate nodded. Just at the moment it felt the best place to be.

As Ginny turned to go Kate asked, 'By the way, have you seen the Ladram Heights anti-migrant research papers?'

Ginny shrugged 'I think Jake was in here earlier looking for them.'

'Is he in now?' She was annoyed that he hadn't thought to tell Ginny about her father – but she still wanted to see him.

'He's with clients but they should be finished soon.' Ginny hovered at the door, reluctant to leave. 'Can I get you a cup of tea of anything.'

'No. I'm fine. I'll collar Jake later.'

'If you're sure?'

'Definitely. Oh, and Ginny, thank you for the hug.'

She gave Ginny five minutes to clear the corridor then followed her out of the office. She wasn't going to put off seeing Jake any longer. She'd expected him to be in touch after he'd left her last night but maybe she'd upset him by going off with Elaine. She still didn't know why she'd done that.

Outside Jake's door she took a deep breath, raked her fingers through her hair and marched in, ignoring the 'Conference in Progress' sign. All three men inside the room looked up as she entered. Jake was in the middle of showing his two clients a PowerPoint presentation, both arms raised up in one of his familiar persuasive gestures.

'Kate?' The enthusiastic look in his eyes evaporated as he saw her.

'Can I see you for a minute?'

He glared back at her, then indicated his audience. 'I'm in the middle of ...'

Kate wasn't going to be put off, although one of the men was closing the file on his knee. She'd negotiated enough research contracts to recognise that she had just spoilt Jake's pitch.

'I'm sorry, but I need to talk.'

Jake strode across to her and grabbed her elbow, steering her back towards the door. He turned to the two men and smiled as if interruptions happened all the time, 'I'm so sorry – I'll be back in a minute.'

'God, Jake, what are you playing at? I thought everybody would know, I counted on you to tell them…'

Jake didn't even look embarrassed. 'You dragged me out of my meeting to tell me that?'

'Ginny was so embarrassed! But never mind.' She took a deep breath, she'd meant to win him over but now she just felt cross with him. 'Just tell me where the papers are for the contract you were so keen for me to lead…'

'I've given them to Denise. Look, I didn't expect you back so soon. I thought you'd be taking some time off.'

Kate blinked back furious tears. 'Well, thank you - but I've already started the preparation. I listed some key respondents, identified venues for meetings and started gathering background statistics while I was waiting at the hospital.'

'Great, so Denise can take all that over.'

He was heading back towards his office as she shouted after him, 'Denise isn't a senior investigator and she doesn't have my experience. I thought this contract was important for the company! Didn't the Home Office insist that I lead the research?'

Jake paused, his hand on the door handle. 'I don't think that's a good idea. You're too upset at the moment to be thinking straight.'

'No? Well, right now I'm trying to cope in the best way I can. Work will help me do that.'

'I'm sorry Kate, but you're wrong – you're in no fit state to manage anything.' He jerked open the door and returned to his meeting, leaving her staring after him.

'My home has burnt down, remember! How do you expect me to be?' She was shouting and hoped his clients could hear.

As she stormed back to her office, she knew exactly what she was going to do. She would lead the research team and Jake wasn't going to stop her. It was too good an opportunity to find out more about the troubles in Ladram Heights and why someone had set fire to Brathcol.

Denise's door was locked but fortunately her key fitted. Inside the room was far less tidy than her office and it took over ten minutes to find the Ladram Heights research papers.

Back in her own office, she started to ring round the list of Ladram Heights's people of influence, introducing herself as the lead criminologist and arranging appointments. Even Jake wouldn't want the embarrassment of pulling her off the contract after she'd introduced herself to all these important VIPs.

She was putting the phone down when Jake came into her office.

'Look, I'm sorry I wasn't more sympathetic. It's just that death ... well, it's one of those things I'm not good at handling. I didn't do too well last night either, did I?'

So she wasn't the only one to regret that she'd chosen to go home with Elaine Pierce. She got up and to give him a hug. 'Death messes up everybody. I'm OK.'

'Really?'

'Coping, I guess. The one thing I'm dreading though is telling Nan. I've put it off too long already.'

She felt better as he held her close and whispered in her ear, 'I've a meeting in London tomorrow. How about I give you a lift to the hospital and you can tell me all about it afterwards?'

She accepted his offer, hoping he was going to invite her to stay overnight. But he untangled his arms and moved away. 'See you tomorrow.' Leaving Kate feeling very alone and reluctant to return to Elaine Pierce and her mansion.

# 14

Kate Trevelyan sits opposite me, tucking into a large plate of lasagne, chips and coleslaw. She's returned from the office in a much happier mood - you'd never believe her father has just died. Comfort food, she calls it. Just as well I had some in. I'm hoping we have more time to talk tonight. I've chilled the Pinot Grigio specially, now I know it's her favourite wine and she'd said it was just what she needed. I've just refilled her glass and she sweeps it up and announces she's off for a relaxing bath.

It appears that she's not as badly affected by her father's death as one would expect. Not as besotted with poor Terence as he believed. He could never see what's obvious to me: that Kate is very much a career girl first and daughter second. Still, she's not quite the paragon of criminology he was incessantly going on about. I know at least three academics who strongly disagree with her views on restorative justice and her approach to treating domestic violence is very controversial.

She is quite bright, though, and it hasn't taken her long to work out the fire was no accident. How convenient of Vera Thomas to ignore her views; I can see the interview has upset her. It won't take long for that family liaison policewoman to see Kate for the selfish and unreliable young woman she is, either. No one will take her claim about her father's death seriously and the locals are ready to do whatever it takes to stop her research into the anti-migrant hostility.

Then there's the boyfriend. It seems he's back in favour now he's taking her to London tomorrow. Any clear-headed young woman knows that dating your boss is the fast track way to wreck your career. A shame she turned down my offer of a lift, though; it was an opportunity to see how frail the old bat really is.

# 15

They didn't talk much on the way to London. Jake was going to the Home Office, something to do with their investigation into the hostility against migrant workers, but seemed reluctant to discuss it with her. Kate was preoccupied, thinking about the best way to break the news of Dad's death to Nan, so she didn't question him much. She had hoped he would show a bit more affection. Another hug wouldn't go amiss. But he was in professional mode and, during such conversation as they did have, made it clear he was still her boss.

Just before he dropped her off at the Royal Free, he said, 'I don't expect you to work on the Ladram Heights contract now. Not after what's happened. You're too close. It's best if you return to the London office. Take all the time off you need first. You'll have lots to sort out,' and as she slammed his car door and stood on the pavement, he shouted after her, 'Good luck with your grandmother.'

Kate soon forgot Jake's unusually quiet demeanour as she wove her way along hospital corridors, avoiding patients in wheelchairs and people chatting. She seemed to be spending more time in hospitals during the last three days than she had during the rest of her lifetime.

She slowed down as she reached Nan's ward. She hadn't rung ahead to tell them she was coming and now she hoped Nan wasn't in too fragile a state after her operation. Kate didn't think she could face anything happening to her grandmother as well. She never found out what made Nan move to Bermuda. At the time she'd been too absorbed in her own teenage world. But she'd missed her like mad. Although she loved her dad, life was never the same with just the two of them.

It seemed she needn't have worried. Nan was propped up on pillows in a small side ward. She looked older and frailer but better than Kate had expected, despite all the machines and tubes. She was well enough to wave Kate over, and before Kate could bend down to kiss her cheek, reached out to hold her hand. When Kate saw how thin Nan had become she was full of doubts about breaking the awful news.

She was still wondering what to do when Nan said, 'It's all right, my love. I know about your Dad.'

All the numbness that had built up inside her since she'd first heard of her father's death dissolved with Nan's words. She'd been worried that she hadn't cried much. Now hot tears flowed down her face and she buried her head in the bed covers to hide them.

As soon as she could she whispered, 'I'm sorry. I'm so sorry, it was awful.'

Nan touched her shoulder. 'A young policeman's been round. He told me about the fire. He didn't seem to know what had happened to you and I was so worried you'd been hurt too.'

Kate took a couple of deep breaths to try to control her sobbing. She looked up to check Nan wasn't too distressed. Her grandmother's cheeks were wet with tears but she smiled back at Kate and beckoned her closer.

'Oh Nan, I had to identify his body ... it wasn't him any more but he didn't look hurt.'

'They shouldn't have asked that of you. It's not right.'

Kate swallowed hard, more in control now. 'It was not as bad as I thought. He looked peaceful.'

'And Brathcol? Has everything been destroyed?'

Nan seemed to have slipped back down in the bed and as Kate tried to lift her more upright she said, 'I think so. But I'm going back to see how bad.'

Nan said something about recovering their possessions that Kate couldn't understand. Her words were slurring, her eyelids closing.

As if she'd been summoned, a nurse carrying a tray of pots of pills came into the room.

'Mrs Trevelyan needs her sleep. It's probably a good time for you to go.'

Kate was about to tell Nan that she was going to stay on in Devon and would be staying with Elaine Pierce, but she was already asleep. So she gave the nurse her mobile number in case they needed to get in touch, and left.

As she waited outside the hospital for Jake to collect her, she wondered why she'd decided to returning to Devon. No one expected her to carry on working and her London flat was just up the road and much handier for visiting Nan while she recovered. But she'd seen how well the nurses were caring for her grandmother, and Nan seemed to share Kate's own concerns about what was going to happen to Brathcol and everything they owned. Back in Devon, she could help the police speed up the investigation and her work on the anti-migrant situation might help them discover what was behind the fire.

During the journey back she asked Jake about his meeting but he seemed reluctant to discuss it, reminding her that she was supposed to be taking time off work. Then asked if when she returned to London she'd like to go to the cinema to take her mind off what had happened. He'd downloaded her favourite music on the car's sound system. She must have dropped asleep. When she woke up they were on the outskirts of Exeter and passing the Pussy Paws cats' home. That's when she remembered Sinbad Seven, her dad's cat. Sinbad One, the cat of her childhood, had stowed away on the yacht of a family friend – hence the name. Sinbad Seven was a new and barely housetrained bundle of fur and would have been terrified in a house fire. Dad would never forgive her if anything happened to Sinbad Seven. She sat upright, now fully awake, as soon as Jake dropped her off she would return to Brathcol. She had to save the cat.

# 16

Kate parked her red MX5 a few yards from the entrance to her dad's house. An empty police car and a white van were parked inside the gates but otherwise everywhere looked deserted. The smell of smoke was still strong and her eyes started to sting as soon as she got out.

Three men in white forensic overalls and a female police officer were sitting away from the house under one of the Monterey cypress trees having a tea break and laughing over something in the newspaper. No one noticed Kate as she searched the shrubbery, calling out for Sinbad as loudly as she could without attracting attention - but there was no sign of the cat.

The house she'd grown up in was cloaked in a cloud of dust and looked more like a gothic mansion from a Tim Burton horror film. Her father's old Mercedes was parked outside. The full horror of what had happened didn't hit her until she looked inside the car and saw his old driving gloves still on the passenger seat. She tried to open the door to retrieve them. But it was locked.

As she moved closer to the house she could hear giggling and, thinking it was the forensic team returning, whipped round ready to explain to them what she was doing. Instead of people in forensic kit, a man with a ponytail and long waxed coat emerged from the side the house. He was walking backwards and was busy taking photographs. A moment later he was joined by a redhead who was laughing so much her dangling earrings rattled against her neck.

'Hey, I've got another headline,' the women giggled, 'How about frying tonight?'

That was all Kate needed to lose all the self-control she'd been holding on to. She rushed at the man, knocking the camera out of his hand.

'What the hell do you think you're doing?'

He picked up his camera and examined it for damage, then shoved it into his oversized pocket. A grin was spreading across his unshaven face as the afternoon sun glinted off his gold front tooth.

'There's no need for that, doll. I'll take your photo too if it makes you feel better.'

Kate found she was pummelling his chest with her fists for all she was worth, hitting him harder and harder, making him pay for all the anguish of the last couple of days. He tried to move his camera out of the way of her fists as a digital recorder, assorted pens and flash drives spilled out of his pocket and clattered onto the pavement. That made him laugh even more but he gripped her wrists and held her away from him.

Then, shading his eyes from the sun and staring hard at her face, said, 'What the devil have I done to upset you?'

'Bastard!' was all she could manage as hot tears flooded down her face.

He produced a screwed-up handkerchief from his other pocket and tried to pass it to her, together with a tatty identity card.

'I know who you are. You're the daughter. You used to live here. I'm Derek Droney from the Ladram Heights Gazette. Look, your dad was an important man round here. I'll pay good money for your side of the story. You might want to get in touch with me when you've calmed down.'

She glared back at him, knocking the card and handkerchief out of his hand, then stamped them into the pavement.

As he swept down in a mock bow to gather them up, his mobile phone started to play the James Bond theme. He put the phone to his ear, signalled for the woman to follow him and grinned at Kate. 'Got to go, girl, there's more trouble in Ladram Heights. Those demonstrators are on the rampage again. I'll love you and leave you. Sorry about your loss and all that, but I meant what I said about getting in touch. There's more to this fire than you think.'

He ambled off towards an old E-Type Jaguar parked further up the road, followed by the redhead. Kate was about to go after him to photograph his car registration number when she remembered why she'd come to Brathcol. She still hadn't found any sign of Sinbad Seven.

Closer to the house the progress of the fire was obvious. Charcoal burn marks extended out around the windows. A shudder ran through her as she realised they were the patterns made by the flames. All the windows were blown out and the back door was missing. There was nothing for it, she had to go inside. The heat hit her like an invisible hammer. The air smelt acrid and abhorrent, filling her mouth and nose. Everything around her was scorched and stained. She tried moving forward and her feet sank into the soggy carpet, throwing her off balance. She reached out to steady herself and jerked back in pain as her outstretched hands made contact with the hot wall.

She made it as far as the drawing room and looked inside. It was unrecognisable, even worse than the other rooms. This must be where the fire had started. She was finding it hard to breathe and couldn't see more than a couple of feet ahead of her. Turning back to go outside, she gasped as the daylight showed up smudged outlines of handprints around the walls. Tears were blurring her vision as she remembered all the good times she'd spent in the old house. She still hadn't found Sinbad but if the cat had been trapped inside it wouldn't have had any chance.

The sound of voices signalled that the forensic team had finished their tea break - unless the cocky journalist had returned. She didn't want to meet them now and there were still more grounds to search outside. She remembered Sinbad Seven was fond of sleeping in the old barn her dad had turned into his art studio.

Once clear of the house she sprinted across the lawn to check it out but there was no sign of the cat. Dad's paintings were intact though. She hadn't rated them much when he was alive but now they were priceless. She picked up a couple of the smaller ones, intending to come back for the others.

The only place left to check was the garden shed. It was far enough away from the house to be undamaged but still smelled of smoke. As soon as Kate entered she knew something was wrong. The usually pristine shelves stacked with Dad's gardening equipment had been trashed and the lawn mower, shredder and the mountain bike that he'd bought for her fourteenth birthday were all missing. Vera Thomas couldn't put this down to Dad's mental state. Someone had deliberately trashed the place and must have set fire to the house during a burglary. Maybe Dad had caught them at it?

With her anger building, she turned to leave - and dropped Dad's paintings when she saw what was in front of her. What was left of Sinbad – his head with fangs bared, his bloodied torso and half his tail – was nailed to the inside of the door.

# 17

Kate's frustration was rapidly reaching the point where she was going to say something she'd regret later. On the other end of the phone she could hear Jacqui discussing what she'd just told her with a colleague. The woman had obviously never heard of putting a hand over the telephone to block the sound.

'Dr Trevelyan believes the garden shed has been broken into and some items taken.' Then after a long pause, 'Yes, her father's shed is on the crime scene.'

'Just to be clear, Kate, you have actually been back to your father's house?' Jacqui was sounding anxious and the person she was talking to didn't sound very pleased.

Kate snapped back, 'Of course I have. I've just left there. I'm trying to tell you the shed had been trashed and some expensive gardening equipment's missing. But the worst thing is how they've killed the cat. It was horrible. The fire must have been gang-related – a burglary gone wrong. Surely your investigators have worked that out by now?'

This prompted more conversation away from the phone that Kate couldn't quite hear. Then Jacqui said, 'Whatever possessed you to go to the fire scene? Any forensic evidence has just been compromised.'

Kate ended the call and closed her eyes. The image of Sinbad Seven flattened against the shed door came back to her and she blinked hard to try and erase it. She was stupid to think she could trust Jacqui in the first place.

*

When Kate arrived back at Elaine's the house was empty which was disappointing as she needed someone to talk to. The fire, her dad's death, Nan's illness and Jake being less than helpful all felt like iron weights dragging her down. She was finding it hard to think. She slumped on Elaine's sofa in her palatial drawing room and put the TV on to take her mind off her thoughts. After flicking through the detritus of mid-evening television she turned on some music instead but that didn't help either. With a headache bearing down, Kate resorted to what she usually did when things weren't working out – writing a 'to do' list. She'd only written 'Book appointment with insurance company' when the sad prospect of all the arrangements she had to make overwhelmed her. She stood up to pour herself a gin and tonic, instantly regretting her decision to stay in Devon.

She was just about to turn off the drawing room light and go to bed with her drink when the lights flickered and went out. She tried to switch them back on, but there must have been a power cut. The radio was dead, as was the television.

Blackouts were common in rural Devon, they didn't usually last long. But the house seemed very dark. After waiting a good ten minutes, she tried ringing Elaine to ask for help but the call went straight on to voicemail. There was nothing to do but grope her way upstairs to her bedroom, although Kate didn't think she'd sleep. She knew she'd see the dismembered body of the dead cat as soon as she closed her eyes.

Feeling her way up the grand staircase, Kate stumbled spilling her gin and tonic. At the top of the stairs she used the door handles as a guide as she felt her way to her bedroom. The other bedroom doors were usually locked, so she was surprised to find that she was opening a door into a bedroom. Elaine's security must have been affected by the power cut.

She was still standing in the doorway when the hall light behind her flashed back on. The room was overwhelming. Two small palm trees in alabaster pots were positioned as if guarding the entrance; beyond them tropical plants were everywhere. The aroma of lilies made her feel light-headed. In the centre of the room was a huge circular canopied bed. The walls were covered in jungle print paper. Tigers bearing their teeth, snakes poised to strike, rhinoceros charging through the undergrowth.

Fascinated, she moved nearer to explore the wallpaper wondering how anyone could sleep in a room like this. Close-up, she could make out the shape of a hidden door in the wallpaper.

'What are you doing in my bedroom?'

Startled, she sprang round to find Elaine Pierce striding towards her, her face contorted with anger.

When in trouble Kate found it best to resort to something close to the truth, 'Sorry, Elaine. The power went off. It was creepy, especially in the dark. I was trying to find a way to my room.'

'Really?' Her angry expression had gone so quickly that Kate thought she must have imagined it.

She smiled back at Elaine. 'It's a pretty impressive bedroom though.'

Elaine ushered her out of her room, checking the bedroom door was locked after them. 'We'd better get you downstairs and into the light, then. I didn't take you for someone who was afraid of the dark.'

Back in the drawing room the television was showing a comedy show and canned laughter filled the room. Elaine grabbed the control and turned the TV off. 'I'm surprised the backup generator didn't work. The security system's supposed to be fail safe; I'll have to get the company out to fix it. Anyhow, I don't know about you, but I'm hungry.'

Kate had almost forgotten about the bedroom incident by the time they sat down to a meal of pesto and pasta, washed down with good Chianti. As they ate, Elaine asked her about Nan.

'Doing so much better than I expected. She knew about Dad, the police had told her, so despite my best intentions she ended up comforting me.'

'I'm so glad she's not badly affected by her accident. Will she be well enough to come to Devon soon?'

'No sadly, she's not that well. I think she will be in hospital for a few more weeks.'

'Such a shame.' Elaine reached across and touched her arm. 'So there's no one to help you with the funeral arrangements or the house insurance?'

'I guess not.' But Elaine's question had reminded her of all the things associated with a death that she had yet to deal with and stirred up the images of horrible things she'd done and seen in the last three days.

The older woman was looking at her intently, 'There's something else worrying you isn't there Kate?'

Kate found herself telling Elaine all about her visit to Brathcol, of seeing her father's gloves inside his car but not being able to reach them, her desolation at the damage to the inside of the house – and the very worst of all, finding the carnage of what was left of Sinbad Seven's butchered body.

# 18

Micki was on his way to community school but wished he wasn't. After the school had rung his Pa's mobile to tell him Micki was absent yesterday, Luca had threatened to escort him there. So here he was waiting at the bus stop. The only good thing about it was a girl he liked was waiting just ahead of him. She was in his year group at school and he liked the way she always broke the rules, never wore uniform and managed to get away with it. Today her red tartan tights matched the stripes in her hair.

Up on the top deck she sprawled across the seat in front of him, repositioned her earphones and turned up the volume. A red-faced mother with a chubby toddler on her knee got up from her nearby seat and moved further down the bus.

As she passed Micki, she hissed, 'Some people have no consideration for others.'

The girl responded by turning the volume louder. Micki stared out of the bus window, not wanting to be involved.

*BANG BANG BANG*!

He looked up and saw the girl thumping the window. She was trying to attract the attention of a group of purple-clad youths emerging from the side of some shops.

*BANG BANG BANG*! She tried again.

'Hey, Connor. You idiot! Can't you see me?'

Micki immediately slumped lower in his seat as he recognised Connor's face, but they weren't looking in the direction of the bus. The girl was getting more frustrated and moved back down the aisle, banging on the windows as she went. Connor's gang had closed in together to form a tight circle, their arms round each other's backs. Each of them had purple cropped hair with a thick blond stripe running through it: from above they looked like a colony of badgers. Connor turned round and flashed two fingers in the air towards the bus as it swung round the corner. Something knocked against his foot and he looked down. It was the girl's ipod. She was level with his seat so, picking it up, he held it out to her. And was rewarded with a smile that changed her whole face as she snatched it back.

'You're new round here, ain't you? I've seen you round school.'

He coloured slightly and tried to think up a good reply in his best English.

She sat down next to him and grabbed his arm. 'It's OK, I've seen how they diss you cause you're foreign.'

The bus was slowing down but the girl was still talking. 'I don't think it's right, what they do to you. I'll tell Connor, he's my boyfriend. I'll see he treats you all right.'

Micki's panicked. He looked round to see if he could get off at the next stop. He wasn't used to attractive girls showing an interest in him and didn't know what to do - and he certainly didn't want to meet Connor. Best to make a quick exit.

He managed to splutter, 'See you around,' as he pushed past her and headed down the stairs. Then jumped off the bus - too fast to notice where he was. For as far as he could see light posts and windows were plastered with '*MIGRANT WORKERS OUT*' posters. He guessed he was about a kilometre and a half from the community school and a quick search through his pockets confirmed he'd spent the last of his money on the bus fare.

*

Kate woke from a disturbed sleep as memories from the last three days flooded back. Seeing Dad's body in the morgue; how Brathcol had become a burnt-out ruin, then the horror of finding Sinbad Seven.

She knew she had been upsetting people since her father's death including Elaine and felt bad about being discovered in her hostess's bedroom. She'd been too exhausted to fully appreciate the splendour of Hawke Towers and its lush grounds. But this morning, after her much needed lie-in, she felt more like tackling all that lay ahead of her. There was the funeral to arrange for a start. She had no idea what else had to be done after the death of a relation but obviously Nan couldn't see to it. Nor, it seemed, could she leave the investigation into Dad's death to the police who hadn't got back to her about the dead cat and the damage to the shed. But as she fastened the robe Elaine had left in her room she felt she'd had enough of 'death' and needed to get back to her usual routine. Once she was involved in her work again things would feel more normal.

As she entered the impressive kitchen a petite brunette, who she hadn't seen before, was loading the dishwasher and straightened up as she entered the room. 'Hello, Miss Kate. Miss Elaine said I was to get your breakfast.'

Kate sat down at the circular table. 'Thank you.'

In between the many suggestions of things to eat, Kate discovered that the young woman's name was Brita and she came from Latvia. Miss Elaine had helped out her family and now she was helping her. After a delicious breakfast Kate went upstairs to dress. It was a lovely day and she thought she'd make a start on interviewing local politicians about the migrant workers.

*

Five figures with purple hair striding towards Micki spread out sideways like something out of a Western.

'It's one of em fucking immos.'

They were grinning unpleasantly. Someone grabbed him from behind and Connor's voice whispered in his ear, 'Well if it isn't my little friend, the one who hangs around Otterford.'

Connor spun him round and gestured across his throat. 'You're dead.'

The others laughed. Micki hoped if he ignored them they'd leave him alone. He edged closer to the rubbish bins, hoping to make himself more invisible. There was no one else around. Curtains and blinds in all the nearby houses were drawn shut.

The gang moved in on him, then stopped. It was as if they'd reached the edge of an invisible protective line drawn around the dustbins. The sweat started to trickle down the back of Micki's neck.

The big one next to Connor lunged right up to him and spat in his face. 'Go back home where you belong, you bastard. We don't want you here.'

The one next to him shouted out, 'Yeah, we like to keep the streets clean,' then started to stamp his foot. The others joined in.

Stamp stamp stamp. 'Out! Out! Out!'

The gang were closing in on him. Their fists punched the air and their boots stamped into the floor. Boots he'd soon be feeling.

Just as the chanting reached a crescendo, a girl's voice demanded, 'Hey, man, what's going on?'

Connor turned towards her. Micki swallowed hard as he recognised the girl on the bus.

She came up to Connor and took his arm. 'Come on, man. Leave him alone. He's not worth bothering with.'

Connor shook her hand off and moved closer to Micki. There was a glint of metal and Micki felt a sharp pain across his face and then the warmth of blood. He slumped to the pavement and put his hands across his face. Then the boots went into his ribs and he knew he'd pissed himself and hoped she wouldn't see.

'Connor, don't...' The girl's voice ended in a scream.

He thought he heard the squeal of car tyres. Then everything went blank.

# 19

Kate's morning was going well. Two out of the three councillors she'd approached seemed keen on the research she was carrying out. They'd even offered to organise small focus groups of their members to share views about the migrant situation in Ladram Heights. She was glad to be working again. She'd had to be at her most professional to persuade them that CCR was a reputable outfit and the research was needed. But it felt great when she won them over. Even Councillor Church, the curmudgeonly man who refused to be interviewed had agreed to think about it. Kate was glad she hadn't lost her talent for getting information out of people without them noticing. After five minutes she knew the Councillor's passion was coaching Honiton United football team.

She was developing a persuasive argument to put to him when they next met. Something about how the migrant workers excelled at football and would make brilliant additions to his team if he could help her with the research. So she nearly didn't see the mugging.

But some instinct made her stop and reverse when she caught sight of the youths with their purple Mohican haircuts out of her rear view mirror. They were kicking the hell out of someone on the ground. She spun her Mazda MX5 around but they'd scattered by the time she'd parked and was out of her car. Their victim was groaning on the pavement. She went to assess his injuries and then helped him to his feet. He was just a kid with short shaved hair and thick dark eyebrows, no more than eleven or twelve. He looked a bit undernourished. There was blood all over his T-shirt from a cut on his face and he was so groggy he could hardly stand. It was an effort to support him, despite his slight build. She eventually got him into the car's passenger seat. He brightened up and said something foreign. When he registered she didn't know what he was saying, he said in English, 'Is this yours?' At least he was talking – a good sign, even if she found it hard to understand his accent.

Fresh blood was trickling down his face. She felt a kind of dread creep over her. There was only so much hospital corridor smell she could take in three days, but he obviously needed medical attention. 'We're going to see a doctor and maybe we can get hold of your parents.' She tried to reassure him but he seemed too busy admiring the dashboard of her car to listen.

By the time they arrived at the hospital Kate had managed to persuade the boy to let her ring his home, although he still wouldn't tell her his name. She got through to someone called Daz who initially sounded suspicious and was about to cut her off until she described the boy who had been hurt. Apparently his name was Micki, his mother was dead and his father was out at work. As Daz didn't have a car, she told him she would stay with Micki at the hospital and then bring him home.

*

The doctor sutured his face and told Kate that his bruises would be painful for a couple of days but there were no bones broken. While the boy was waiting to be examined, he told her in faltering English that his name was Micki Hamereski and he lived in Ladram Heights with his father Luca. Then he subsided into silence.

But as the painkillers took effect during the journey to Ladram Heights, he became more vocal. Kate was relieved to see the colour returning to his face. Micki had begun to call her Dr K after he heard her name, which she found cute. As they approached Ladram Heights he stopped staring out of the window to ask if she lived there too.

'Not now, but I used to live in Otterford village when I was a child. It's not far away.'

Micki seemed to be thinking that over, eventually saying, 'I don't live here either. I'm waiting for Pa to finish earning money so we can go back to Krakow. That's my home. We came here last year after Mama died. We needed money to pay hospital bills and to feed my sister Misha.'

Kate felt an affinity to the slight figure next to her. He'd also just gone through bereavement and she felt privileged that he was taking her into his confidence. 'I'm sorry your mother died, Micki. You must miss her.'

He looked straight at her, his eyes darkening, 'Yes, I do ... she was always ... '

His voice trailed away and Kate put her hand out to touch his arm. She knew exactly how he felt and had a strong urge to comfort him.

Tears gathered in her eyes and she breathed in hard to stop them. Tears weren't going to help him. Instead she confided, 'My father's just died too. I wake up, then remember he's not here any more. I wish I'd spent more time with him.'

She thought he might be embarrassed but was rewarded with a brief smile. 'Yes, I think that too. When I knew she was going to die I missed school and spent as much time with Mama as I could. It was only because Pa is a doctor and he worked at the hospital that he found out and made me stop.'

Kate felt privileged that he was talking to her about his mother. He seemed to have gone through a lot of hardship for someone so young.

She was struggling to think what to say next when he broke the silence, 'What about your pa, Dr K, was he ill too?'

Kate found she didn't mind talking about her father to this skinny, bright-eyed boy. 'No, he died in a house fire.'

His face lost all its colour. 'I think I knew your pa. He was our head teacher.' He glanced across at her to gauge her reaction. 'I saw about the fire in the newspaper. Mr Trevelyan was good to me. When the other teachers put me in the bottom class and talked to me like I'm an idiot, he tried to help. I knew him from Kidpower, too.'

'Kidpower?' The charity that her father and Elaine Pierce were keen for her to join just before he died.

Micki nodded. 'I called him Mr T. He used to take me out on trips and talk to me about being bullied. I'm sorry he's dead.'

'Thank you, Micki.' She was touched by his sensitivity but curious to know more about what he'd just said. Somehow, knowing he was one of her father's mentees made her feel closer to the boy. But before she could ask him anything else, he indicated they'd arrived at the builders' hostel where he lived. She stopped outside and Micki snatched at the door handle in his hurry to get out of the car.

A man was scrubbing the front door of the hostel. Micki shouted something in Polish and he dropped his brush and rushed over to him. At first Kate thought he must be Daz, he looked too young to be Micki's father, but on closer inspection she saw the dark shadows under his eyes and the his look of resigned exhaustion. His eyes scanned her as she stood waiting to explain what had happened to Micki. Despite his unshaven face he had an elegance that didn't belong in a donkey jacket and builder's boots and there was a definite resemblance to Micki in his angular profile. Micki had told her he was a doctor, which didn't make sense when he lived in a builders' hostel.

She held out her hand. 'You must be Micki's father. I'm Kate Trevelyan.' But he brushed her aside and started to usher Micki inside the house.

Kate tried again. 'He's OK, Mr Hamereski. He was attacked by some yobs but I took him to the hospital.'

She wasn't sure if he could understand her or was even listening, as he cradled his son in his arms and continued talking to him in a stream of Polish.

Then he turned round and spoke to her in good English. 'I'm sorry for my rudeness. Are you from the police?'

Before she could reply Micki shouted out, 'No Pa, this is Dr K. She helped me. She's not police.'

'Micki's tired and in a lot of pain, Mr Hamereski. Let's get him settled and I'll tell you what happened.'

As she followed them into the house Kate noticed the remains of eggshells and congealed yoke sticking to the front door which was obviously what Mr Hamereski had been cleaning off.

Inside the entrance hall she could hear shouting coming from the room next door and had to raise her voice as she said, 'The doctor sutured the cuts and gave him some painkillers for his bruised ribs. He might need to take some more.' Kate rummaged in her handbag to find the prescription the doctor had given her and handed it to Micki's father who was looking intently at her. 'Well, now Micki's safe, I'll say goodbye…'

He seemed to give himself a shake, then smiled. 'No, please. I'm forgetting my manners. I will take Micki to his bed, then I will come back and make us both a drink and you can tell me what happened.' He was quite good-looking, she thought, when he stopped scowling.

Micki's eyes were closing as his father guided him up the stairs but he managed to mutter, 'Thank you, Dr K. You my friend now and I'm all good.'

This was a good opportunity to slip away but Micki's words made her want to stay, so she edged into a large open-plan room to wait for his father's return. The room was full of men dressed in jeans and T-shirts who ignored her and carried on cheering at a football commentary on a small radio. She was glad when Mr Hamereski returned and ushered her through to a kitchen area at the back of the building. The floor was littered with black bin bags and empty beer bottles.

'How is he?' Kate asked, suddenly feeling exhausted herself.

'He's asleep.' He scooped up the pile of men's magazines from one of the chairs and indicated for Kate to sit down. 'So you're a doctor, like me.'

'I am, but not a medical doctor, I'm a doctor of criminology.' Then looked up at him to make sure she heard him right. If he was a doctor, what was he doing building houses in Devon?

He continued to stand, making her feel uncomfortable. 'Tell me, how did you come across Micki? Was he fighting again?'

'No, I don't think so. He was cut by a knife and beaten up.' She realised as she spoke that she didn't really know what happened to him. 'He was hurt and frightened. He was obviously in need of medical attention so I took him to the hospital.'

He pulled out a chair and sat down, then buried his head in his hands. He was so close she noticed the flex of his muscles and the fine dark hairs on the back of his arms. Then looked away and scanned the kitchen before he noticed her staring at him.

She jumped when he suddenly raised his head. 'It's my fault for bringing Micki to England. I dragged him away from his friends and made him stay here in Ladram Heights where he gets bullied all the time.'

Kate stood up abruptly and held out her hand. He frowned, took her hand and held it firmly. 'Don't go. Not before I find a way to thank you.' He squeezed her hand more firmly and looked her straight in the eyes. 'Can I buy you a meal? I would invite you here but the house is usually full of men,' he indicated the room, 'and the kitchen is impossible to cook in.'

She nodded and gave him her mobile number. There was something attractive about Luca Hamereski, but she was certain that she would never hear from him or Micki again.

# 20

After another restless night of dreams about burning buildings and dismembered cats, Kate finally woke to the ringing of her mobile. It was Jake.

'What the hell are you playing at, Kate? Some sort of punishment because I didn't commiserate enough about your dad or tell the rest of the office he had died? OK, I'm sorry, but there was no need to take all the Ladram Heights background papers from Denise's desk. Or to interview key locals after we'd agreed you were going to take some time off – that was crazy.' In the silence that followed she felt too groggy to respond. 'Kate, are you even listening to me?'

'Yes, I can hear you.' She couldn't believe he was shouting at her. 'OK, I disobeyed your orders, but I thought you were wrong.'

'Wrong? About what?'

'I know the background to this contract better than anyone and as you pointed out yourself, I grew up round here. You were wrong. My father's death hasn't affected my competence to work. You said I was the best person to lead this contract and I still am.'

'We'll talk about that later. For now I want you to listen. I shall be out of signal range soon.' He still sounded impatient.

'Why? Where are you?'

'On the early morning train to London.' That explained his bad mood; Jake never did like early mornings. 'I have to attend an emergency meeting at the Department of Justice. They're considering cutting the funding for the Ladram Heights research and I'm going up to fight our corner.'

'Well, if anyone can sort it, you can. Look, I know I shouldn't have taken the papers without telling anyone but I was hoping we could ...'

'Listen Kate,' he interrupted her, 'this is important. You'll have to take my place at the West Country Enterprise Forum. It's all organised. All the influential entrepreneurs and policy makers will be there. You need to get them on our side.'

'Enterprise Forum?'

'It's being held at the head office of Pierce Enterprises. Starts at nine, so you'd better get a move on. Denise can't make it, she's running an event in London, and as you are conveniently placed in Ladram Heights you'll have to take my place.'

*

She made it to Ladram Heights just after nine fifteen. From the packed car park it looked a popular event, despite the shift in the weather. The brilliant sunshine of the last few days had changed to heavy rain. Kate pulled the collar of her linen jacket up round her neck as the rain bounced off the roof of her MX5. Her headache was crashing in and she tipped the contents of her handbag out on the passenger seat in the hope of finding her migraine tablets, but all she found amongst the dirty tissues was an empty packet.

Shimmering spirals were clouding her vision as she followed the receptionist's directions to the conference room. It was already full of about thirty business men and women, most in smart suits, chattering in small groups or helping themselves to coffee and croissants. Kate tried to blink away the visual distortions, she might not be feeling great but she had written the original specification for the research, so at least she knew what she was talking about.

She took a seat at the huge conference table next to an Asian woman wearing a multi-coloured headscarf who smiled broadly as Kate sat down, and introduced herself as Councillor Dominic.

Kate smiled back and was about to explain who she was when the woman said, 'We're all waiting for some criminologist from London. They're all the same, these people, expecting us to sit here wasting our time while they make their money.'

Reddening, Kate decided not to challenge this opinion. Instead she replied, 'I'm Kate Trevelyan from The Centre for Criminal Research, one of those criminologists – and the motorway was very busy.'

The woman grimaced and shook Kate's proffered hand. 'Sorry, but your research isn't proving very popular. We're all getting a bit fed up with outsiders telling us what to do. I'm one of the few round here who do support the work you're doing. It's about time someone took a stand against these demonstrations. The protesters aren't local and I don't believe we should blame everything on immigrants.' She fingered her hijab. 'As you can see, I'm an immigrant.'

The councillor was giving her a business card when a striking, athletic looking police officer came over. From the silver pips on his shoulders he must be the Divisional Commander.

'You're the only person I don't recognise,' he said to Kate, 'so you must be Professor Williamson? I'm Ian Ross.'

Of course, they were expecting Jake. 'No, I'm not,' she corrected him. 'Professor Williamson had to go to London ... I've just been asked to take his place.' She hesitated as she realised the room had gone quiet and everyone seemed to be paying close attention to what Chief Superintendent Ross was saying.

'And you are?'

'Dr Kate Trevelyan. I'm heading the research into the anti-migrant demonstrations.'

'Well, Kate, I'm sure you will make a very good substitute.' He held out a well-manicured hand. 'Welcome to Pierce Enterprises.'

She looked round. 'I thought Elaine was going to be here.'

'She was. The CEO usually hosts this event but she's been unavoidably detained too. She's asked me to get it started.' He looked amused. 'Do you know her?'

'I'm staying at her house at the moment.'

'Good friends, then?'

When she didn't reply he scanned her from top to toe, the amusement in his amber eyes making her feel uncomfortable.

'Professor Williamson must have a lot of respect for you, leaving you to lead such an important meeting in his absence.' She nodded, although she didn't think it was respect that Jake felt for her at the moment. 'Well, I look forward to hearing more about your research, although I am surprised Ladram Heights has been selected for it. Our rates of violence are the same as any other coastal town in the area and we already have a number of successful initiatives to tackle our street disorder.'

Kate reddened. 'And the demonstrations?' she asked.

'There's nothing to them.' His smile was still in place but the amber eyes had hardened.

Kate was used to defending her research from sceptics. 'I've met people who are scared to leave their homes because of the demonstrations. The incidence of violent crime along the Jurassic Coast should be low for this demographic, Chief Superintendent, but it has escalated recently and the Ministry of Justice is particularly interested in what's happening in Ladram Heights. It's a new town in which the Government has invested a lot of money and tax payers have a right to have answers.' Then, remembering she was here to win people over, added, 'But I am very keen to find out more about the initiatives you mentioned.' Noticing the clock on the wall beyond him, she said, 'For now though, I think we need to start the presentation.'

Chief Superintendent Ross went back to his seat and introduced her somewhat offhandedly. People were looking at her expectantly. Kate, starting to relax, stood and, looking directly at him, began her speech.

'Ladram Heights has experienced a three-hundred-per-cent increase in street violence over the last twelve months mainly due to anti-migrant ill feeling. Like you, we at The Centre for Criminal Research want to find out why that is and, more importantly, what can be done to stop it.'

She went on to explain how the methodology of the research would be based on work from the United States on cultural strategies and promoting community cohesion.

There was some loud groaning in response and someone shouted 'Speak English, woman! We don't need academics using ridiculous words telling us what to do.' The speaker was a thickset man with a moustache and dark glasses. 'Here in Ladram Heights we solve our own problems and are doing a very good job, thank you.'

Kate quickly switched to talking about the practical side of the research and made a mental note to find out who the rude speaker was and find out what problems he was talking about. Avoiding the mention of focus groups and other jargon, she looked round the room trying to make eye contact and explained that, together with her research team, she would be interviewing police, hospital staff, youth workers, local politicians, council officers and, of course, local business people. But the research team also wanted to talk to recent immigrants and anyone who had been a victim of violence or had taken part in a demonstration. They would be looking at every side, everyone's view counted. She was starting to explain that any information given would be in complete confidence when her words were drowned out by shouting from outside the room.

A group of youths wearing purple jackets with matching spikes of purple hair pushed their way through the door. She recognised the attire if not the faces of the gang that had beaten Micki up yesterday. One of them came straight towards her, jabbing his finger in the air in an obscene gesture and stopped level with her chair.

'We don't need no fucking researchers telling us where the violence is coming from. It's them foreigners, them Polish bastards that come over here and take our jobs. Get rid of them and we'll all be happy.'

A few of the audience started to applaud. Kate felt more angry than scared.

She faced the youth. 'You're right, there has been a big increase in the number of migrant workers in Ladram Heights doing the jobs that locals won't do. Many of them have been victims of violence and we will certainly want to talk to them.'

She pointed towards the entrance where the stamping was getting louder, 'Maybe I should start by talking to your friends?'

The youth was close enough for Kate to feel his spittle hit her face as he continued to swear at her. As she moved her head away she sensed rather than saw the knife in his hand as he raised his arm. Reacting to instinct rather than logic, she picked up the jug of water in front of her and emptied it over his head, feeling a surge of satisfaction as the water dripped down his face and dark patches appeared on his purple jacket. As he spat out the water he hissed, 'I'll get you for that, you bitch.'

She was saved from working out what she would do next by Chief Superintendent Ross, who grabbed the youth's arms and pinned them behind his back.

'Come on, sir, it's time for you to dry out. You shouldn't get involved in things you don't understand.'

Ross looked straight at Kate as he handed the struggling man over to two uniformed officers. 'And you might find that applies to you too, Dr Trevelyan.'

The calmness Kate had felt when she faced up to the hostile youth was ebbing away. Flashing, spiralling helixes were crowding her vision. Her migraine was kicking in. Somehow she needed to regain her professional cool and finish the presentation. At least she had everyone's attention now. One or two people were applauding. Afterwards she couldn't remember what she'd said or what she'd missed out, although her request for people to wait behind to arrange to be interviewed was followed by shuffling as most of her audience got up and hurried away.

The sound of solitary loud clapping halted the exodus. Elaine Pierce was standing in the doorway, barring their way. In a voice of calm authority she said, 'I think we should thank Dr Trevelyan for making the research so understandable and dealing with our questions so patiently. Be in no doubt that her work is essential for Ladram Heights's future. We need to stop the sort of behaviour we have all just witnessed before it's too late. I will certainly be interviewed. So, I am sure, will everyone else here.'

Kate was relieved to see some of the people rather sheepishly return to their seats, and those who had remained began to clap.

Elaine walked over and lowered her voice. 'I'm worried about you. You look as if you're about to collapse.' She turned to Superintendent Ross who had joined them. 'Ian, where are your manners? Dr Trevelyan has come to Ladram Heights to help us. She's had to suffer a badly-organised reception and a personal attack. Please say something encouraging.'

'Of course, Elaine. Doctor Trevelyan, you are very lucky that Elaine Pierce wants to support your work. She owns most of the successful businesses here in Ladram Heights and if you want to find out what's happening and who to interview, she's the lady you should be talking to.'

'Bang on,' interrupted the thickset rude man. 'I was coming over to tell you and that Professor Williamson where to shove your research, but if Elaine Pierce thinks it's OK, it might have some merit.'

Elaine treated the two men to one of her disarming smiles then turned to Kate, 'Meet Lyndon Crud. You wanted to know more about Kidpower, well here's your man.'

But Lyndon Crud was already walking towards the door. Then Ian Ross turned and guided Elaine away. His parting words to Kate were, 'Ladram Heights is a very close-knit community. You'll have your work cut out, but I hope it works out for you.'

Elaine slipped her arm out from his and walked back to her. 'Remember, I'm here to help you whenever you need me. But for now, you need to rest. I'll ring Brita and tell her you're coming back to the house.'

Then with a small wave of her hand and a glint from her sapphire ring, Elaine returned to Ian Ross, leaving Kate standing in the emptying room.

As she signed up the few people willing to be interviewed, she couldn't help feeling the morning had been a complete disaster.

# 21

Micki stopped and listened. He was sure he heard something moving further down the corridor. His mouth felt dry as he gripped his torch with both hands and swung the beam in an arc along the walls around him. Nothing. He was being stupid: there was no one there. He slowed down and listened again just to make sure. He was starting to regret coming back to the old hospital but nothing would make him go back to community school in case he met Connor. He'd promised Pa he'd stay in bed and rest but by lunchtime he was bored.

Up to now he'd felt safe moving around the dark corridors of the old hospital. Then he heard the sound again - like a match being struck. He jabbed out his torch and was plunged into total darkness. All he could hear was his own breathing. But he wasn't alone in the corridor, he was sure of that.

He knew the layout - that must give him an advantage. He could picture the corridor and all the doors leading off it. His hands were sticky with sweat but he managed to slide them inside his rucksack. The knife felt cold and smooth against his fingers. He'd decided to stand up to Connor. He wasn't going to be a coward any more.

He heard a shuffling sound - it was getting closer. This was the moment. He snapped the torch on with one hand and gripped his knife with the other. A slim figure was exposed in the beam. As he struck out he felt a sharp pain in the side of his knee. He spun round to see what had hit him and lost his balance, dropping the knife.

'There's no need to bloody kill me.'

Micki recognised the girl's voice but to make sure he shone the torch across her face, lighting up the green stripes in her hair.

'Or to bloody blind me. I've only come to see what you're up to.'

Micki's heart was thumping but he was relieved to see the girl from the bus.

She was holding out his knife with the handle towards him. 'What were you were doing with that?'

He might as well tell her. 'I take it everywhere. It's to stop Connor and his friends getting to me.'

'Really, so that's why you've not been to school. That won't stop 'em. You'll just make it worse. You gotta ignore it. Give 'em time. They'll move on to someone else. It's what they do.'

She was grinning at him as he snatched the knife back. His fingers were so wet with sweat he could hardly hold it. He was starting to relax until he thought that if Girl was here, maybe Connor was too?

'Who are you that you know so much about it?'

She circled around him, 'I'm Girl. Or at least that's what Connor calls me. It's better than Mattie or Matilda Murray, and I know who you are.'

He was considering what to reply when he noticed the blood trickling down her arm.

'Did I hurt you?' His voice sounded squeakier than he intended.

'You? Nah.' Girl inspected her arm then wiped it across her jeans. 'I've had much worse.'

Micki held out his handkerchief. She ignored it. He grabbed her arm and wrapped the handkerchief round it. She tried to pull away but he hung on until he'd secured the makeshift bandage. Then offered her some chocolate from his pocket: he'd used to use it to tame stray kittens he rescued from back streets of Krakow. There were some similarities between this girl and a stray cat, he thought. 'Here, take it.'

He was rewarded with a brief smile as she snatched up the chocolate. 'This is more like it. So what is this place, then?'

Micki looked away trying to decide whether to trust her.

'I said what is it here?'

'A hospital for mad people.'

She moved a bit closer to him. 'Yeah, right. Where are they then?'

Micki was feeling more in control of the situation. 'It closed down years ago.'

'How you know?'

'Daz told me about it. He says there are ghosts.'

Girl stuffed what was left of the chocolate down the front of her top. 'Come on then, let's find some.' Before he could reply, she'd grabbed his torch and shot off down the corridor, leaving him in darkness.

He could hear her shoes clank against the metal stairs. 'Wait.' The hospital was his secret haven and he wasn't sure he wanted to share it.

When he caught up with her she was trying to peer through some circular windows set high up in a pair of metal doors.

'Come on, help me. I can't get these open.'

Micki added his weight to hers and the doors burst open, throwing them together onto a cracked linoleum floor that smelt of cat litter and turpentine. Girl lay on her back with her arms outstretched. They'd fallen over a box full of candles and she stood a couple of them up, took a lighter out of her pocket and lit them, exposing a huge old ballroom.

'This is brill.'

Micki lay down next to her gazing around the room. It was. Each corner hosted a ragged cluster of deflated balloons and above their heads hung a huge multi-sided globe of silver. A grand piano was propped up close to where they were lying, a candelabra balanced on the lid.

'This must have been where the old nutters danced.'

'They weren't all old.' He told her indignantly.

'How do you know?'

'Because I've read about it. I found an old book in my office.'

She look at him scornfully. 'Your office?'

'A woman doctor's. It was once her office. It is full of clues.'

'Clues. You Sherlock or something?'

He waited for her next cutting remark. Instead she nudged up closer to him and rested her face on her hands. She was very close and he could smell the spearmint on her breath from the gum she was chewing.

'I used to hide all the time when I first came to Ladram Heights. They called me names too, 'cos I came from Plymouth.'

He took some gum she was holding out to him. 'Where's that?'

'It's a city, dimmo. It's where I grew up. Where my mam dragged me around flat after flat, until Harry got sent down.'

Micki could see the edges of her irises were speckled with gold. They stood out against her dark pupils.

'Was Harry your pa?'

She twitched her nose from side to side. 'God, no. A sort of uncle, a friend of Mam's. But he looked after us. Then the council made us come here. We were some kind of experiment – we had to come 'cos they threw us out of our old flat when Mam smashed it up when she was off her head. Well, her or one of her boyfriends did. But they don't want us here - nobody likes us either.'

Micki was trying to make sense of what Girl was telling him. So Polish builders weren't the only people unpopular in Ladram Heights. She seemed to think they had something in common. He could live with that.

He was still thinking of his reply when she jumped to her feet. 'Come on. Show me your office.'

Girl headed towards the other end of the ballroom and jumped up onto the stage shrouded in faded velvet curtains, then disappeared through the drapes.

'Come here, and bring your torch.'

He followed her at once, eager to show her the den in the office. Huge boxes were stacked unevenly around the stage. Girl was already balancing on one and trying to open another. She turned towards him and overbalanced. The top box fell over on top of her in a clattering rush.

He dashed over to her, 'Are you OK?'

There was no answer. Micki shoved the boxes aside and ignored the pain as a large splinter sliced into his thumb.

'Girl,' he called again until he could make out the red stripes of her top. He clawed at the packing cases and heard her giggling.

'Had you scared, didn't I?'

He didn't reply, just moved aside more packing cases.

Girl crawled out between them, clutching two cans. 'This one's full of drinks, there's booze an all.'

Micki grabbed the can of cola. When he opened it, he was sprayed with sticky brown liquid. Girl started laughing and this time he joined in. Somehow being brave didn't matter any more; he just felt good sitting on a dirty floor, surrounded by packing cases, in wet jeans and being laughed at by someone who was so full of life.

He held out his hand to her. 'Come on, I'll show you the book in my office, we can come back here later.'

They were soon in what he called his office, where Girl moved around like a caged lion cub trying each of the chairs then opening all the cupboards and rummaging around in the old boxes. The back of Micki's neck suddenly got hot as she moved towards the corner of the room where he'd relieved himself and he rushed forward to divert her away.

'You wanted to see the patient's book. It's over here.'

He wanted to trust her, to share his find with somebody. 'OK. It belongs to a woman who was locked up in here. She was supposed to be a mental patient, but I don't think she was. She says Dr Sand her doctor was keeping her in hospital against her will to stop her telling everyone about the treatment that was going on in here. If she's still alive I'm going to try and find her.'

Girl pointed to the diary. 'Go on then, read it.'

Pleased that she was interested, Micki cleared his throat and started to read.

*8th of April, 1987*

*'My Darling,*

*PLEASE COME AND GET ME.*

*The sun is out today but the bright light hurts my head. I think it's because of my treatment. I've become a creature of the dark.*

*It's two weeks since you came to see me and you won't recognise me now. I'm not the same happy person I used to be. I know Doctor Sand told you not to come again until she rang you – one of the other patients heard her tell you. But please come. I need you more than ever. You mustn't believe what she says. I think she's trying to destroy me. She's jealous of your love for me - like that other old bat. She's old and withered and no one loves her.*

*She's forced me to have a new treatment and it makes me feel much worse. Of course I'd heard about ECT before they took me down. Now I know that all the bad things they said about it are true. First they strap you down by your wrists and ankles. I've got marks where the leather straps cut into my flesh. I keep shouting for them to stop but the nurse puts her hand over my mouth to shut me up. Then they injected me. After that, I can't shout except in silent screams in my head. I knew all about it, every terrible second of it. The taste of rubber as I try to spit out the thing they shoved under my tongue; the cold of the metal plates strapped to my head and the burning smell like the dentist's drill as they shot the current through me. I'm so glad you can't see me. If you'd been there I think you would have killed Dr Sand. I wish I could.*

*Now I'm terrified they will come and do it all over again tomorrow. Dr Sand says I must co-operate or I'll never come home.*

*I don't think you can love me any more. How could you when you leave me here to suffer.*

*I'm so scared.*

*Please come and rescue me before it's too late.*

They both sat quietly for a moment until Girl said, 'That sounds dreadful, like some kind of torture. And her doctor sounds like a maniac.'

Micki agreed.

'Whose diary is it?'

'I told you, she was a patient here a long time ago.'

'Is this her?' Girl picked up the diary from the floor. In contrast to the other pages filled with large, scrawled writing, this one was colourfully illustrated with rainbows, flowers and butterflies. In the middle of the page was a photograph of a young woman in a flowery dress with a tumble of red hair and making a V sign to the camera. The word 'Sara' was written in the middle of the page in bright red ink. From the hesitating way she turned the page upside down he realised she couldn't read. 'What's this mean?'

'I think that's her.' Micki said, suddenly realising it must be the person who had written the diary. 'It's Sara's book.'

'Yeah? How do you know?'

'Says so here.'

'Yeah, 'course.' Girl said and made a grab for the diary. Micki held on to it and it tore in half. Before he could say anything she was gathering up pages and handing them back to him. 'I didn't mean to tear them. I want to know what the rest of it says.'

There was no point getting angry, keeping Girl's friendship was more important to Micki than this old book. He looked through the different sections and could see they were no longer in the right order. He put them in a plastic bag he'd found under the desk. 'Don't worry. I'll take the pages home and repair the book. Then we can come back here and read some more.'

They sat in silence for a couple of minutes before Girl said, 'Do you think she ever got out?'

Micki didn't know. Maybe Sara had died in the hospital. He looked round, expecting to see her ghost. Girl stood up and brushed chocolate crumbs of her jeans. 'And after that, we can try and find this Sara. It'll be our secret.'

# 22

An afternoon spent by Elaine's pool followed by a massage had done Kate the world of good. For the first time since her dad's death she'd managed to sleep for a few hours without any nightmares, aided by her migraine tablets. She woke with a new sense of purpose and was looking through Derek Droney's article on the fire at Brathcol, which was brief and insignificant and the notes she'd written to prepare for the talk at the West Country Enterprise Forum, which were even briefer.

Elaine came into her bedroom to say she was back from her meeting and to find out how Kate was. 'You're looking a lot better. Have the migraine tablets done the trick?' She picked up the packet of pills from Kate's bedside table, 'Are these good?'

Kate nodded and noticed Elaine glancing down at the papers she was reading. 'It's good to see you working again. Are these to do with the research?'

'They're the notes from my presentation this morning, although after my rubbish performance I think I need to tear them up and start again. Not surprisingly, I didn't get a huge response to my invitation to local business leaders to arrange to be interviewed.'

Instinct made Kate cover up the notes she'd been making about the fire. She held up the newspaper with Derek Droney's article. 'Now the police have washed their hands of Dad's death I'm trying to find out more about his life before he died.'

Elaine placed a hand on her shoulder. 'Don't torture yourself. Maybe getting immersed in your research would be better for you. I've had a few phone calls since your talk this morning. People wanting to sign up for interviews. I'll pass them on to you.'

Kate murmured her thanks, still deep in thought. She was wondering why the brief article that Derek Droney had written was so uninspiring when he'd implied the fire might be suspicious. His account of the latest demonstration in Ladram Heights was much more colourful.

*

The Ladram Heights Gazette shared its HQ with its sister publication in Sidmouth and was within walking distance of the promenade where Kate had told Elaine she was going for an early evening stroll to clear her head. The woman at reception made her wait while she rang to check if Derek Droney would see her. Kate was beginning to have second thoughts about this visit when he came running down the stairs, taking them two at a time. The annoying grin she remembered from their last meeting was plastered across his face.

'Dr Trevelyan. What a pleasure. You've seen sense at last then?'

She ignored the hand he held out. 'I've come to see if you really do know anything about the fire at Brathcol or if you are making it up to fabricate a news story.'

He didn't seem at all put out. 'Friendly as usual, then? I'm just about to get a coffee. Care to join me?'

Kate wasn't thirsty but she could see it was the best way to humour him and headed towards the entrance. 'OK. Lead the way. But I'm paying.'

He caught up with her at the automatic doors. 'You'll be able to afford a lifetime's worth of coffee when you get the insurance money from your father's house. It was quite a pile.'

She could do without the smug reminder. The insurers had been leaving messages for her to contact them urgently, messages that up till now she'd ignored despite promising Nan she'd sort it. She strode ahead of him out of the building and down the road until he called her back. He'd stopped outside a cafe next door to the Gazette. It was so small she'd walked past it.

He held the door open for her. 'It's where all us newshounds go. You'll like it.'

Inside the green plastic tables and chairs were cramped together, fully occupied by elderly couples and a group of workmen in overalls. The walls were covered with assorted tie dyed tablecloths and a single plastic red rose decorated each of the tables. As the sweet smell of joss sticks and cinnamon reached her nose, she was sure she didn't expect the coffee to be up to much either. After asking Derek Droney what he wanted she strode over to the counter and ordered a black Americano for him and a latte with a shot of hazelnut for herself.

He was right, it was popular and they were forced to sit closer together than she would have liked. The pockets of his leather gilet swung around him as he reached across to load his coffee with sugar. She tried to see what he kept in them that weighed so much.

'Great coffee, thanks, Kate.'

Her latte was delicious but she wasn't going to tell him. Instead she straightened up and tried to look severe. 'Good. Now perhaps you'll tell me what you meant when you said there was more to the fire at Brathcol than I thought.'

He raised an eyebrow. 'Oh that. Nothing, really.'

'It didn't seem like nothing when you were trespassing all over it to take those photographs.'

He leant in towards her. 'If I remember rightly, you weren't too keen to know about it.'

She suddenly felt very tired and hopeless. She couldn't do anything right, even getting information out of a second rate journalist. She never really helped or understood Dad when he was alive and she was still failing him now he was dead. If she thought talking to this man was going to help her understand what happened to her father, she was wasting her time.

'Forget it.' She got up to make her way out through the crowded cafe. Derek got to the door first and stood holding out a handkerchief. She hadn't noticed the tears that were pricking her eyes. The handkerchief looked dirty; it was probably the same one she'd stamped all over when they'd first met. She took it anyway.

'Look, I'm sorry. I know you are having a bad time and the police are being difficult. I'm not getting very far with my enquiries either. I think we can help each other. Won't you come and sit back down? ' He actually sounded contrite.

She'd dabbed at her face and handed him back his now soggy handkerchief covered in mascara. 'Why should I expect you to know anything about the fire? Nobody else seems to.'

'Oh, the fire was definitely suspicious but I haven't got any proof yet.' She gave him a look of disbelief but sat down again. He pulled his chair closer to hers. 'Look, can I trust you?'

Kate frowned. 'I know you've got to protect your sources.'

'No, it's nothing like that. I just don't want to alert the powers that be until I'm ready. For what it's worth, your father didn't have anything to do with my enquiries. He just happened to be working for Kidpower. That's where I think the story lies, not with him. Not until the fire.'

'So what's changed? Why your sudden interest?'

'I saw some of the young criminals from Kidpower hanging round outside on the night it happened. Otterford isn't their usual sort of haunt so I was curious. I'd been out there covering the Summer Fair at East Budleigh.' His grin was back again but this time Kate found it less annoying. 'It was a punishment from my editor. I was supposed to be spotting local celebrities.'

'And did you spot any?'

Derek laughed. 'No, but then that's not the sort of story I want to write.'

'I'd have thought it would be just up your street.'

He feigned surprise. 'Watch it.'

Kate managed a smile. At last she had some information to pass to Jacqui Sunday. 'So you think the youths you saw had something to do with the fire?'

'Probably. But I doubt they were working alone or the police would be on to them by now. What I'm really interested in is Kidpower. I think it's a front for something illegal. Something big.'

The implications of what he was saying sunk in. 'You can't think my father was involved and they killed him?'

'To be honest, I don't know. But I don't think so. From what I hear he was trying to improve things at Kidpower. Maybe that was the trouble.'

'That's what Elaine Pierce thinks.'

He pushed his chair away from Kate, knocking into the woman sitting behind him. 'A friend of yours, is she?'

'Not exactly. I think she was a friend of Dad's. She's invited me to stay with her for the time being, seeing as I've lost my home. She thought Dad was an asset to Kidpower too. She's genuinely upset by what's happened. Apparently, he was under a lot of pressure at the Community School for helping the immigrant students. It didn't go down too well with some of the locals. I thought you might know about it.'

'I do. I wrote the copy on it.'

At least he was telling her the truth about that. She hoped she could believe everything else he was telling her.

*

Derek waited until Kate had gone then returned to the cafe where the tables were emptying. Bit of a surprise having Terence Trevelyan's daughter turning up like that. She'd turned out to be much more gracious than he'd expected, quite a looker too. He hoped he'd done the right thing telling her about the louts outside Brathcol. But he did have his suspicions about the fire, although he hadn't seen Connor and his mate do anything. They were just hanging around, which was what they spent most of their time doing. He suspected something had happened to make Kate Trevelyan suspect the fire had been started deliberately. She just wasn't ready to share it with him yet.

Derek Droney took his phone out of his pocket and made a call. Then ordered another coffee and waited. It was a no smoking cafe, so he reached for his matches and took a couple out of the box. He chewed them for a bit then split them in half and used the ends to clean his nails. Bye the time he'd worked his way to his right thumb, the man he was expecting arrived. The couple at the next table looked up at him as he moved towards Derek and hurriedly shifted their chairs closer together as Lyndon Crud squeezed past their table and sat down to join him.

# 23

Pa had taken time off work to explain Micki's absence from school and tackled Miss Blundell about the bullying. As a result she had agreed that until it was sorted, Micki could work on his project at home. So he'd spent the last couple of days patching Sara's diary back together and trying to read it. She'd used a lot of long words and it was hard to understand. He thought she must have been suffering from the ECT treatment. Some days she just wrote one word like 'Bastard' and then stabbed at the paper so hard the pen made big holes. Micki hoped they changed her treatment like she wanted so she could get better.

He was in the middle of reading the diary when Miss Blundell called round to see how he was getting on. She seemed impressed when he showed her his project folder with the photographs he'd taken of Pastures' Victorian gothic architecture with its tall pointed windows and endless spires.

'I'm glad you've found something to bring out your talents,' she said. 'How are you getting on with the rest of your project? Have you found more out about mental hospitals in the nineteen eighties and how they differ from today?'

'Not yet.'

'Well, I might be able to help you there. You can try the library in Exeter and it might be worth checking out newspaper articles from the eighties.' Micki wasn't very keen on libraries. 'Oh, and my Aunt Dora used to be a nurse at Pastures Hospital. Would you like to talk to her?'

'Yes, please. That would be brilliant.' Much better than a stuffy library; he was already thinking up questions he could ask.

'As you've worked so hard, I'll see if you can visit her later today. I know she'd like to talk to you. She loves young people.'

Micki was delighted. 'Does that mean I can stop writing up my project?'

Miss Blundell laughed; it made her look a lot prettier. 'Well, you can today if Aunt Dora can see you. But you might want to take notes to write up later.'

She made a phone call, then wrote down the address of her aunt's care home.

As she was leaving, she turned round suddenly and said, 'By the way, Micki, the hospital building has been condemned and will be demolished soon. Don't go inside, it could be very dangerous.'

Micki smiled back but made no promises.

*

Ms Blundell even gave him some money for the bus to Sidmouth. It was worth the climb up Salcombe Hill to the Fairview Rest Home; it lived up to its name and the view from the top was fantastic. He stopped to watch the tiny fishing boats scurry across the estuary, then followed the signs to reception. At first the nurse behind the desk didn't seem very pleased but once he gave her Miss Blundell's letter explaining why he was visiting, he was shown into a big room smelling of disinfectant and coffee. There were lots of easy chairs and sofas all facing the sea. It was somewhere he wouldn't mind living. He liked old people.

Aunt Dora turned out to be much more lively than he had expected. She insisted on giving him some rather fusty-tasting biscuits, but she seemed happy to talk to him about her time at Pastures.

'I spent some of the best days of my life in that place. Us nurses were all good friends, you know. Had to be really, life could be tough at Pastures and they didn't keep their staff for very long.'

Micki wasn't sure what she was talking about but decided to dive straight in with his questions. 'Did you work with a Dr Sand?'

The old lady closed her eyes. He hoped he hadn't upset her. Or maybe she'd just dropped off to sleep. He was considering giving her a prod when her head jerked back. 'She was a fine psychiatrist, one of the best. Such a shame she was taken so young. She was always friendly to us nurses, didn't look down on us like some of them doctors. She was a real moderniser as well. The hospital was a much better place when she was working there.'

This wasn't what he'd expected to hear. According to Sara, Dr Sand was a very wicked woman.

'She brought in therapeutic communities.' The old woman had started talking again but he wasn't interested in therapeutic communities, whatever they were. 'Then there were the ward meetings with patients and doctors and them Sensitivity Meetings, where they shared their views on the patients' treatments. Patients were encouraged to go outside the grounds more and that was years before Care in the Community. There was a lot of opposition from the management though, especially when she insisted on censoring patients' letters. They didn't like the time that took so she did most of it herself. But she was right. Some of the things the patients wrote could be very hurtful for their families.'

He'd almost stopped listening until she mentioned the letters. Sara had been very upset that Dr Sand had read her letters. Now he was impatient to know more. 'What about the patients, especially ones who were locked up and were given ECT, did you treat those?'

The old lady shuddered and wrapped her arms more tightly round her thin body. Her eyes glazed over. 'None of us liked working in Lavender Block, that's where the most violent patients were kept. I only spent a few months there and couldn't wait to get out.'

He was really fascinated now. Sara had mentioned Lavender Ward in her diary.

'Did you treat any of Dr Sand's patients in Lavender Block? A young woman called Sara?'

'What, dear? Oh yes, some of them were hard work. There was one in particular. She might have been Sara. She had a butterfly tattoo on the inside of her wrist. She made a horrible mess of her arm trying to cut it out.'

Micki was finding it hard to hear the old lady and moved closer, ignoring her faint smell of wee and talcum powder, to find out more. The tattoo might be a clue if it was mentioned in the diary. Micki held up his sketches of the ECT treatment. 'Did she have to have this?'

Aunt Dora seemed to be ignoring his question and just kept staring at the drawing. Seeing the picture seemed to bring back bad memories. 'We all thought she was lovely at first, despite being so refined and very different from most of the others in there. She always looked glamorous and they weren't allowed any make up or tweezers or anything like. She always managed to get the staff to do just what she wanted by being nice. But if you didn't....' She shuddered. 'At first I thought she was a treasure, always sorting out spats between the other patients and helping with jobs around the ward. Dr Sand thought so too and used to give her special privileges. Then it all backfired. She started being difficult. She'd take over the TV lounge like it belonged to her and only let her favourite patients use it. She was much worse when she'd hidden her meds. She'd give you presents one minute and spit in your face or worse the next. I started to hate working there; there were so many fights. And then there was the suicides. There's nothing worse than finding a poor mangled body.'

He was writing notes in Polish as quickly as he could and hoped he could read them later. Was she talking about Sara, or Dr Sand? She was probably confused. He'd have to see what Girl thought. She hadn't been back to the hospital since she'd torn up the diary. When he told her what he'd found out, maybe she'd come back there.

# 24

Micki didn't think he'd ever see Mr T's daughter again but here he was sitting opposite her in the Clock Tower Café, letting the tang of vinegar chips linger in his mouth. He'd been busy writing up his notes from his visit to Aunt Dora and was delighted when she knocked on the door of the hostel. The café was perched on the edge of the cliff and looked a bit like the toy fort he used to have when he was little. He'd half expected red coated soldiers to emerge from behind the turrets. Dr K said it was her favourite cafe in Sidmouth and sent him upstairs to look at the wood carvings while she found them a table with a good view next to the cake counter. He liked this café with its many windows: every way he turned he could see the sea. The upstairs room was full but when he stood back from the top of the stairs he saw the wood carvings of sea creatures all round the top of the walls. The dolphins dancing were his favourite, but he quite liked the old fisherman with his net.

On his way back downstairs he patted the bulge in his pocket to check Sara's diary was still there. He hoped Dr K would be able to tell him what some of the long words meant.

Back at their table he waited for the right moment to interrupt her but she was busy talking about her work. 'I'm so lucky to have a job I love. Crime happens all over the world and sometimes researching why it happens and how to stop it can be very emotional.'

He liked watching her. She was so animated, using her hands to reinforce every word as her voice got faster and louder. She even made the work she did sound exciting.

'I've worked in places where families are so scared to go out, they barricade themselves in their homes. When I was in New Orleans during their last heat wave - people starved to death because of it.'

She must have seen his 'so what' look. Her face relaxed and she laughed back at him. 'I know you've been suffering in Ladram Heights, but it was a lot worse there. It was the mothers who sorted it out in the end. They worked with the police when they were too afraid to come into the area; they forced the drug dealers to stop dealing outside the schools and held midnight vigils to reclaim their streets.'

'We could do with mothers like that round here,' Micki said, thinking of his own mama.

Dr K looked horrified. 'I'm sorry, Micki. I didn't think. I'm sure your mother wouldn't let you get hurt if she was still alive. You must miss her?'

He did, but he didn't want to talk about it. 'You said you'd like to know more about Kidpower?'

'I do, Micki. I know when my dad worked there he thought he was helping young people like you. Was he?'

Micki could understand why she wanted to know about her pa's work but he knew he had to watch what he said. If Connor found out he'd been talking to her, the police would be hauling his body out of the sea.

Dr K looked uncomfortable at his silence and held up her hand to attract the waitress. 'I'm talking too much as usual - and it's time for some pudding.'

He nodded his agreement and reached in his pocket to take out Sara's diary. Before he could pass it over the waitress came to their table. She was skinny with dark curly hair and winked at Micki as she scooped a notepad out of the pocket of her skin-tight jeans.

'Are you ready to order?'

Micki recognised the accent at once. 'Hey, you're Polish!'

She beamed back at him with equal recognition. 'From Gdansk; I'm working my butt off to pay to go to university.'

'Do you like it here?' They'd slipped into Polish but he remembered Dr K wouldn't understand so repeated his question in English.

The waitress screwed up her face. 'Some things. I like the red cliffs and the beautiful scenery. The television is better here but I don't like the weather, it rains too much. I also like the beer.'

'Me too,' Micki agreed then glanced at Dr K to see if she approved. Daz often sneaked him bottles of English beer and he was developing a taste for it.

It was great to meet someone from Poland; someone he could have a proper chat with. She told him her name was Danuta and offered him some free cake next time he came to the cafe.

'How about some cake for now?' Dr K suggested.

He followed Danuta to the display of cakes in the glass case. He hadn't had many treats since he left Poland, so he pointed to the largest one.

Danuta winked and said in Polish, 'I'll get you something special. I can't stay and talk any more, I have people to serve. But I would like to talk to you again later.'

He returned to his seat and watched her as she glided round the tables taking more orders and joking with customers. He was conscious he was blushing and hoped Dr K hadn't noticed.

He was still thinking of telling her about Connor setting fire to her pa's house. She was upset that the police thought the fire was Mr T's fault. 'Dr K, I know there are gangs at Kidpower and they are English, not migrant workers. They cause the trouble, not us.'

'That's what I think too, Micki, but I've got to see it happen or at least find people who will talk to me about it.'

Helping Dr K could be his way of fighting back but before he could say any more Danuta came towards their table with a huge slice of cake and a large ice cream. He whistled as she placed it down in front of him.

'This is for my favourite customer. It's got extra fudge bars and brownies on and lots of cream. Enjoy.'

Micki tucked in: it tasted great. He was making up for the all the meals of tasteless packet soups or undercooked fish fingers. He'd nearly finished the cake before he remembered his manners and offered Dr K one of the brownies.

'No thanks, Micki. I'm enjoying watching you devour it.' As he wiped the cream away from his mouth she laughed and handed him a tissue. 'I've enjoyed today, you're great company and I feel better than I have done since my father died. I guess we've both lost people we love.'

Micki could see she was upset and wanted to get up and give her a hug but thought she might be offended.

She blew her nose and smiled back. 'Would you like to come out with me again? We could go sailing if the weather's fine.'

He punched the air. 'That would be brilliant.' This sounded much better than his usual thing of watching sport on the television. Then he thought of Luca. His pa could do with a break, too, and from what he'd said at breakfast about Dr K, Micki knew he liked her. 'Can my pa come along? We used to go sailing a lot.'

She was really smiling now. 'Great. We'll make a day of it and I'll bring a picnic.'

He was about to ask her if they could go next Tuesday, his pa's next day off, when a silence fell. Dr K sat upright and stared at the door. He was about to turn round to see what was happening when she whispered urgently, 'Stay where you are Micki, Just act normal.'

Not understanding at first, he turned round, then whipped his head back to stare down at the table. The figures collecting in the doorway were dressed in purple jackets with balaclavas pulled down over their heads. The one at the front had low-slung purple trousers and his fingers were tucked inside his yellow braces as if he was about to dance a jig. Micki recognised the braces first, then the stance of the wearer. Connor O'Brian.

The gang strode over to the counter. Micki froze as they brushed past his table. One of them grabbed Danuta's arm and twisted it so hard she dropped the tray she was carrying, sending hot tea down her leg and over an elderly lady customer. They both shrieked with pain. Her attacker jerked her closer to him.

'Call yourself a waitress?'

Micki rose from his seat.

'Sit down, Micki,' Dr K whispered. 'I'm going to try to get help.' She slowly drew her iPhone from her bag.

The gang started banging on the counter with their fists and shouting to the beat, 'Out! Out! Out! Get them foreigners out!'

Customers were crowding the doorway, trying to leave. Connor shoved them back towards the tables. He bent down to face a couple sitting next to a toddler in a pushchair. 'You English then?' he demanded, poking the man in the chest.

'You bet, mate. I'm with you,' the father shouted back, jumping up and steering the pushchair and his partner out through the door.

Connor slammed the door shut and jammed his bulk in front of it. 'No-one else leaves.'

Micki saw Doctor K start texting. Then she wrapped the iPhone in her scarf and whispered, 'I've asked the police to send help and now I'm taking photos.'

Micki held his breath. He resisted the impulse to check they hadn't seen her. If he turned round they would recognise him.

The youths were still hammering on the counter. Out of the corner of his eye Micki saw Connor grab the man sitting at the next table by his coat collar. The man wriggled to break free and squealed, 'I'm English, I'm English.'

Then someone screamed and Micki turned to see that two of the gang were holding Danuta spread-eagled over the counter. Two of the gang were tugging at her jeans, while Connor walked towards her and started undoing his trousers. Dr K leapt up dropping her phone. Micki picked it up and kept filming. She grabbed the chair ahead of her and used it to charge into the back of the youth holding Danuta down. He turned to grab Dr K but she was too quick for him and sidestepped out of the way, pulling Connor's balaclava off as she went past him. He tried to follow her but slipped in the pool of tea and fell over another youth, landing hard on the floor at her feet.

Dr K grabbed Danuta's arm and pulled her upright. Then, kicking out at both gang members, she dragged Danuta into the ladies toilet and slammed the door. Connor charged at it like an enraged bull but the door wouldn't give way. He was about to try again when the sound of police sirens made him turn away, shouting, 'Leave the bitches. I think they get the message.' Then, with his face pressed up to the locked toilet door, snarled, 'Don't worry, we know where you work. We'll be back to finish the job.' Then he spun on his heel, turning all the tables over on his way to the door. 'The pigs are here, let's go.'

When the last of the gang had run from the café, Micki went over to the toilet door. 'It's OK, Dr K. They've gone.'

As he tried to force the door open he was grabbed from behind and pulled round to face a uniformed police officer.

'You again!'

Micki expected to be arrested. It was the same police officer that had cautioned him him last month for shop lifting.

Then he heard Dr K's voice: 'Let him go, officer, he wasn't involved. The gang has gone. You might catch up with them down the street - but if not, I can identify them.' She held out her iPhone.

The officer grinned back at her, 'Bring it with you to the police station, you can make a statement at the same time.'

After the police had checked that both Danuta and the remaining customers were all right, they took down details of what had happened.

When it was his turn he told them what he'd seen without mentioning Connor by name, and just kept repeating that Dr K was a hero. The police officer seemed to agree with him.

As Dr K gave him a lift back to the hostel on her way to the police station, he decided he was going to do everything he could to help her - and next time they met, he'd show her Sara's diary and tell her about seeing Connor outside her father's house on the night of the fire.

# 25

The police officer had been delighted with the images on Kate's iPhone. Fortunately, Micki had the sense to keep filming the attempted rape and had managed to capture the moment when she removed one of the gang's balaclavas. Her hopes to catch up with Jacqui Sunday at the police station and of getting an update on the investigation into the Brathcol fire were dashed when she found out that Jacqui was off duty. So she left a message asking her to ring her back as soon as possible.

It was only seven in the evening but Kate felt wacked. She lay back on Elaine's sofa when she arrived back at Hawke Towers and scrolled through the photographs and video of the assault. There should be enough there for the police to make an arrest, and they might find out the gang knew something about her father's death. Despite her tiredness she felt much more positive about finding out who had started the fire.

'That looks interesting.'

Kate jumped as Elaine's voice spoke close to her ear. 'Sorry, you were so absorbed in whatever you were watching I didn't want to disturb you.'

'Hi, good day?' She closed her iPhone down.

Elaine poured out two gin and tonics and brought one over to her. 'I spent the afternoon at Kidpower. The Youth Offending Team brought some teenagers across to start the mentoring programme. If you really want to know about Kidpower you should come to a new intake session, the next one's tomorrow. Lyndon gives an excellent talk about the benefits of mentoring, then afterwards I'll take you to meet him. He's not as bad as he looks.'

'That would be great,' Kate said, pleased that Elaine had mentioned mentoring. Since her lunch with Micki she'd been thinking about how she could help him. 'I've met a youngster who goes there. Dad was one of his mentors and this kid seemed to find his input very helpful.'

'Hopefully they all do.'

'Well, that might be asking a bit much.' She swirled the ice cubes round in her drink. 'There is something else you could do to help.'

Elaine sat down opposite her. 'Ask away.'

Not one to miss an opportunity, Kate carried on, 'I'd like to replace my father as this boy's mentor. He got on really well with Dad and I think we've hit it off too. But I guess it would involve some training?'

'Nothing too demanding, you'd find it no problem at all. What's the boy's name?' Elaine said, picking up Kate's iPhone, 'Is he on here?'

'It's Micki Hamereski. And no, he's not on there. I was checking some photographs I took of gang members who tried to rape a waitress earlier today.' Kate said holding out her hand to retrieve her phone.

'Goodness, Kate. Was anyone hurt?'

'Fortunately not, and the police have got some video evidence now. I managed to remove one of the gang's balaclavas so he should be easy to identify.

'Good for you,' Elaine picked up Kate's half empty glass and went over to the cocktail cabinet to refill it. 'You were asking about mentoring. I think I know Micki, he's Polish isn't he?'

'Yes, I think he's the son of one of your builders on the Ladram Heights estate.'

'Even better.' Elaine raised her glass up to Kate's. 'Here's to your new mentee – Micki Hamereski.'

*

Kate's gone off to bed but it's much too early for me, especially after hearing all about her so-called heroic actions at the café. Hard to know who is the most foolhardy: Connor, for trying to rape a woman in front of witnesses - or Kate, for taking on a gang of violent young men?

She's obsessed with helping this Micki Hamereski stay out of trouble. I think it's a guilt thing, remorse for letting her father down and not being there when he needed her. Now she thinks she can fill his shoes. He was helping the Polish boy and now she wants to take his place. Says it will make her feel closer to Terence. What rubbish. Still, she's left me a problem that needs sorting and she's conveniently left her iPhone with the evidence on the coffee table.

Wiping the video was no trouble, now for the police.

The woman at the switchboard recognises my voice, but I don't want to be put through to the big man Ross this time. His underling will do.

'Inspector Hunt? It's Elaine Pierce.'

He responds with some sycophantic slobbering. He's obviously seen me with his boss. I move the phone away from my ear while he prattles on.

When he's finished admiring my achievements I say, 'You're just the man to help me. It's my friend Kate Trevelyan. Yes, that's right – daughter of Terence Trevelyan. The fire was a terrible tragedy. I'm very worried about her mental state. She's taking her father's death very badly, imagining all sorts of conspiracy theories.'

He isn't very impressed with Kate and goes on about her wasting police time.

'DS Sunday has been most understanding.' I say, 'She was very good and didn't dismiss Kate's story about the damaged shed and the dead cat out of hand. But I'm sure you realise it isn't true. It's very sad, Kate's saying it was a pack of dead dogs now and there were swastikas all over the house. Yes, it is quite impossible – you agree?'

Oh, so when the forensic team arrived there was no sign of any damage or dead animals. No, I'm not surprised. You're not treating Mr Trevelyan's death as suspicious any more, so Kate will be able to go ahead with the funeral arrangements. I'll let her know. And she won't be seeing DS Sunday again. Well, I'm sure she's very busy dealing with real crime. Thank you so much, Inspector. I'll tell Chief Superintendent Ross how helpful you've been. I'll make sure to send you a little something from the Pierce Enterprises corporate hospitality list. Would you prefer a season ticket to the football or rugby?'

Now I've just got to find someone to destroy the video footage that she left at the police station showing Connor's stupid face – and he should be safe, for now.

# 26

Micki was standing in the entrance of Exeter Library ready to continue his search for more information about Pastures Hospital. He'd rather reluctantly taken up Miss Blundell's suggestion, but the library wasn't at all like he'd expected. It was big and modern with sofas to sit on and a cafe for drinks. There were the usual shelves of books that he'd walked around to try and find books about hospitals, but had failed to work out where they were. The counters to get your books stamped had been replaced by electronic boxes and there was no one to ask for help. Eventually, he spotted a young woman putting books from a trolley back on the shelves in the crime section and asked her to help him.

She told him to wait while she fetched someone. This librarian, who was old, could remember a scandal about a doctor at Pastures Mental Hospital and took him round to a different room with a lot of computers. He was surprised how much there was on the internet about Pastures and she helped him find a number of articles. Micki was excited to discover the scandal was about Dr Sand. It seemed she'd written a book about her patients that had made her famous and led to lots of TV appearances, but the book had also made her a lot of enemies. The librarian left him to search through the articles while she went in search of a copy of Dr Sand's book.

So he started to read.

*Cosmopolitan Book Review August 1987*

*'The Sociopathy of Evil: Patients who Kill' – by Dr Julia Sand, reviewed by Sally Ann Mills.*

*Could you identify a Psychopath?*

*Her book 'The Sociopathy of Evil' is based on her eighteen years' experience of working in mental health, including five years at the ground-breaking Pastures Hospital. Dr Sand, who looks much younger than her forty-four years, told me how mental hospitals have improved since the sixties. But Britain is locking up more mentally ill people than ever before, when what is needed is more therapy and caring for the mentally ill in the community.*

*In her view, everyone needs to understand more about mental illness, including the extreme behaviour of some of the patients she writes about in her book. Serial murderers are rare, but psychopathic behaviour is hard to detect and more common than people think. Psychopathic children are growing up with no sense of guilt. Without help they will become adults who are expert in manipulation and who never develop fulfilling relationships. Dr Sand illustrates this by introducing the reader to some of her patients. Most of them have experienced repeated punishment or abuse in their childhood and all have gone on to kill.*

*'The Sociopathy of Evil' is a fascinating glimpse into the relatively unknown and frightening world of the psychopath, written in an interesting and accessible style - but don't put it on your Christmas reading list unless you want to have nightmares.*

He couldn't understand all the long words but had written them down in his note book to ask Miss Blundell or Dr K. But he knew enough to know that some of Dr Sand's patients must have been dangerous.

The librarian returned with Dr Sand's book and asked if he'd like to borrow it. He said he would and asked if he could he have a copy of her photograph on the back cover for his crime wall. She gave him a puzzled look but took the book away to copy it, telling him the library would be closing soon so he'd better be quick. Micki didn't have time to read all the articles but he'd found one that was about Dr Sand's death and thought that would be well worth having.

*Local Author takes her own life as her book rockets up the charts*

*The death of local psychiatrist and author, Dr Julia Yvette Sand, is being treated as suicide, after her body was found by her husband, solicitor Marcus Sand, on his return from a business trip. Dr Sand, 44, had been receiving death threats and hate mail after the publication of her recent book. 'The Sociopathy of Evil' is based on her experience as a psychiatrist at Pastures Mental Hospital near Exmouth, in which she describes the behaviour and treatment of some of her patients. Although the patients' real names were not used in the book, many relatives believe they can be identified. Senior management at Pastures Mental Hospital have criticised Dr Sand for putting her career before her patients. She was under suspension pending a disciplinary hearing.*

*A spokesperson from the Coroner's Office said the result of the autopsy may be delayed, while further tests are carried out. Police have confirmed a suicide note was found on the premises.*

*Exmouth Evening News, Tuesday, 18th January 1988*

The librarian returned with the book and photograph of Dr Sand and agreed to make copies of the two articles Micki had found.

Back at Pastures Hospital, Micki cellotaped the articles to his crime wall. Girl had been texting Micki all day asking questions about the 'mad woman' in the mental hospital. So after his morning spent in the library he was waiting for her in his office, eager to share what he'd found out. As he stood back to inspect his work, he hoped Girl would be impressed. She was so full of questions and now he'd be able to provide some answers. A big fan of detective stories, she always going on about TV programmes like Luther, Sherlock and some woman with an insect tattoo. From what he'd seen, it seemed that most TV detectives had a Perspex 'crime wall' with knives and guns and blood-drenched photos of victims together with identi-kit drawings of suspects. So he decided to make his own crime wall called 'Finding Sara'.

He added his drawings of patients undergoing ECT. They were strapped to beds, shaking with convulsions with something sticking out of their mouths to stop them biting their tongues - it was hard to believe this treatment was supposed to make them better.

To finish off, he'd written some notes about Dr Sand and Sara. Opposite the photograph of Dr Sand he cellotaped the photograph from the front page of Sara's book. Then he wrote their names above their photographs.

Underneath 'Sara' he'd written:

*Likes someone called Elliot*

*Bullied by other patients*

*Doesn't like her boyfriend or Dr Sand*

*Keeps cutting her hair and sometimes herself*

*Forced to have ECT*

*Could be difficult and upset people*

Under Dr Sand's photo he'd written:

*Liked by Aunt Dora*

*Hated by Sara*

*Might have used Sara's real name in her book*

*Successful Author*
*Mother of two children*
*Killed herself*

Then he connected the photo of the doctor and the one supposed to be Sara to each other by a red ribbon secured with drawing pins. He hoped his crime wall would answer some of Girl's questions and help them find out what had happened to Sara.

While he waited for Girl to come he read another entry from Sara's diary.

*9th May,1987*

*I think I'm in love with Elliot!!! He's so much fitter and better looking than you are – and much better at making love. Well, what could you expect if you never come to see me any more? That's not all, I've got rid of the butterfly – remember? The tattoo you wanted me to have instead of the scorpion. I've cut it out, and very bloody it was too. You should make that old bat let you out. It's time you proved you were a man and came and fetched me. So when you don't, I blame you for me having to stay in this place. It's all your fault.*

He waited another half hour but Girl didn't turn up.

Disappointed, he decided to read another extract from Sara's diary. As Girl hadn't come, she deserved to miss it.

*17th July, 1987*

*When I started being ill, Dr Sand (or Dr Death as we call her) insisted I had a full medical examination. She poked my breasts and looked up my vagina. It hurt so much. Elliot was on holiday or he'd never have let her do it. She tried to give me new drugs but I refused to take them. They stopped giving me ECT so there were some good things came out of it. Dr Sand said she didn't want to harm my baby but I don't trust her. I was right. When I refused to take my meds for the same reason they held me down and gave me injections. I wasn't going to give Dr Sand the satisfaction of causing an abortion. I found an old glass bottle and smashed the top off – then thrust it up inside me. I was very sick and I thought my stomach was going to come out. At first it didn't work, so I tried again.*

*Now I'm sitting in my own blood. Somewhere in all this goo is the fetus. I can't stop the bleeding but I don't care. I'm a murderer and it feels good.*

Micki dropped the diary and jumped away from it as if it was on fire. He could understand enough of the words to know Sara had killed her baby. He shivered as he thought about it. Shadows were forming round the room and rain was beating against the shutters. He still didn't know what to think of Sara, but she wasn't as much like him as he'd first thought. He'd never kill a baby or allow anyone else to. But then she must have been brave to hurt herself with the bottle – or mad.

He was desperate for some help to understand what he'd found out and if Girl wasn't going to help him, he'd try texting Dr K.

# 27

It was six thirty and time for the weekly new recruits' induction at Kidpower. Ten teenagers were jostling around the snacks and plastic cups of squash. Lily, the receptionist was squeezing between the rowdy teenagers with her precious crystal vase of flowers clamped to her flat chest. Why she felt the need for them in every room Lyndon Crud would never know. He smiled as she stumbled and nearly dropped the flowers trying to avoid the teenager's groping hands. She eventually made her way to her refuge behind the reception desk and glared back at him. He felt a hand on his arm and saw Elaine at his side holding out a lit cigarette.

'I don't know why you hired that girl.'

Lyndon took the cigarette trying not to inhale her perfume. Although he didn't like her taste in scents, Elaine Pierce's business decisions couldn't be faulted and she'd steered Kidpower through some difficult times and always came up with the funding. Standing with the sunlight behind her, she looked like a star of one of the early Hitchcock films. Her waist-nipped outfit and power shoulders would have looked old fashioned on anyone else, but on Elaine it looked sassy.

He took the glass of wine she was offering him and rewarded her with one of his rare smiles, 'She has hidden talents.'

Elaine raised her eyebrows in mock disapproval.

'I hope you don't mind me dropping in?'

He didn't really mind. It wasn't as if she was checking up on him. He knew that being a perfectionist was one of her many talents that got her such impressive results. 'No Elaine,' he said, gulping down his wine. 'But Dr Trevelyan hasn't shown up, you'll be disappointed to hear.'

It was clear to Lyndon that Kate Trevelyan was a troublemaker. Terence Trevelyan had been bad enough, always asking questions about how Kidpower was being managed and being very selective about whom he mentored and now his daughter was going to be around investigating if Kidpower was contributing to the local gang behaviour.

Elaine sipped her wine. As they strolled through to the training room filled with noisy teenagers she said, 'They're like young bulls waiting for the matador; but I'm sure they will be fine once you try out your mass hypnosis?'

'You shouldn't joke about my professional life.'

She smiled and the laughter lines increased around her eyes, 'Who says I was joking?'

Lyndon decided to ignore the question, 'No, the magistrate's court has had a blitz. It's the summer holidays and their sending everyone unfortunate enough to come in front of them down to us. With your connections I'd have thought you'd know all about it?'

'Perhaps I do - but changing the subject, I'm sorry Kate didn't put in an appearance, she has an impressive track record for criminal research.'

Lyndon sighed. 'She's not so much impressive as interfering, just like her father.'

'Lyndon, that's not a nice thing to say about someone who's just died.'

He was never quite sure if she was being serious. 'What was she supposed to be doing here?'

'She's running this Government sponsored research into our demonstrations and reporting back to Ministers.'

'She wasn't coming here asking about her father then?'

'Hard to tell.' Elaine moved aside to let two squabbling youths squeeze past. 'We don't want to upset her.'

Lyndon downed the rest of his wine in one gulp, 'I don't want to upset her, I just want to avoid her. Or more especially avoid her having anything to do with Kidpower.'

'Oh I don't know, maybe having Terence's daughter on the Board would be a real asset.' He started to protest but Elaine held up her hand to silence him, 'That way we can benefit from her expertise and you can manage the damage limitation you seem to think necessary for her involvement in Kidpower. Anyway it's too late. I've already agreed to her training to become a mentor. She wants to help little Micki Hamereski. In fact that's why she hasn't come here. She's meeting him at The Clock Tower Café and wanted to go for a run round Sidmouth first.'

Lyndon felt his cheeks flushing. He usually avoided upsetting Elaine she was too influential for it to be worth it, but there were limits, 'Just a minute Elaine, that woman is dangerous. She was too close to her father and she's got all sorts of Government contacts. She's the last person we want poking around into Kidpower affairs.'

'Sorry Lyndon, I don't agree. I like her, she's gutsy. I'm going to arrange a lunch for Kate so she can meet some of the other board members. I think we should be as helpful as ...'

Whatever she was going to tell him was cut short as she was jostled by three youths tussling over a magazine. One knocked her elbow splashing red wine over her cream satin shoes. She jerked him back by his t-shirt. He tried to pull away and Lyndon saw her grip tighten, 'Well?'

'Sorry, Miss,' he leered back at her then managed to free himself, laughing as he returned to his pals. Elaine looked hard at Lyndon expecting him to do something but he didn't feel like bothering. She'd dropped in uninvited, something he didn't encourage, especially on a new intake evening.

Elaine bent down to wipe the wine off her shoes, 'What was that young man called?'

'The one who bumped into you is Mason Talbot; he's already a father of two lucky bastards somewhere in Ladram Heights.'

'You're going to have fun with him.' She stood up and smoothed down her skirt. 'And talking of fun, I've got to get ready for a show.'

Elaine handing him the wine stained tissue and weaved her way through the young people to the door. She turned to blow him a kiss before leaving. He knew her 'show' involved pleasuring men she wanted to influence or control. He'd been to one himself, once. He remembered Elaine recorded all the action on a red camera she kept especially for the occasions.

Feeling old, he cleared his own way through the throng of teenagers to join the youth workers and volunteer mentors lining up at the far side of the room. Some looked slightly apprehensive. Lyndon felt most at home when he was centre stage; he knew he was good at controlling his audience.

Enjoying the feeling of anticipation, he stepped forward. 'Welcome to Kidpower. He didn't raise his voice, he knew just the right level to use. The chatter stopped immediately as he continued, 'I'm Lyndon Crud, your director.' He paused to let his words sink in, timing was everything, 'Thank you for listening.'

He looked around as he spoke to identify potential troublemakers. Mason Talbot had his back to him and was giggling with his mate.

'I know you don't want to be here - but you're here because of your bad behaviour and while you're at Kidpower you will behave yourselves. You will start by sitting down and shutting up.' Lyndon clicked his fingers and continued, 'And you will do it now.'

The room fell silent.

# 28

Micki hadn't known how he would feel about returning to the Clock Tower Café but it was where Dr K suggested they meet – and he liked the cakes. After his disappointment over Girl's no-show, he thought he deserved a reward for his efforts. He'd been badly shaken by the last entry in Sara's diary. He didn't think she sounded like someone he'd want as a friend, and his office in the old mental hospital didn't seem such a safe haven any more. Maybe he'd misunderstood what he'd read? Which was why he'd brought the diary to show Dr K and ask her to read it to him. In return he'd tell her about seeing Connor with the petrol can outside her Pa's house.

It was a lovely afternoon and, with a bit of luck, Danuta would be there and give him some cake or ice cream. The tables were mainly occupied by elderly couples or families with children who were running about and being noisy. There was no sign of Danuta. A young man wearing an apron was standing behind the cake counter and called out to him, 'Can I help you?'

He knew he didn't have enough money to order anything and nearly turned to leave until he remembered he was supposed to be being brave so that Girl would like him. So he marched up to the man and said, 'I'm looking for Danuta.'

The man came round to the other side of the counter. 'I know you. You and your friend helped her when those racist thugs invaded the place.'

Micki turned to make his escape. Coming here wasn't such a good idea.

The man called after him, 'Hey, don't go. You're from Poland, aren't you? Danuta told me. It's nice of you to come and see her, but she's not working today.'

Micki was already at the door. 'I'll go then.'

'Stay and have a drink first.' He must have read the hopeless expression on Micki's face. 'It's on the house. You can have a cake too.' He pointed to the chiller cabinet and its array of goodies. 'Please, I'd like you to stay.'

Micki hadn't eaten all day and couldn't resist. Soon he was sitting upstairs watching the seagulls dive for fish as the friendly waiter brought him a hot chocolate and big slice of carrot cake that melted in his mouth. As he ate he looked round the walls at the wood carvings. The otter was his favourite and he thought they must live nearby because there was a river named after them just up the coast.

The waiter told him that Danuta was shaken up after the assault but she wasn't badly hurt and would be back at work tomorrow when he was welcome to come in and have another drink on the house.

It wasn't until he'd finished his cake that he looked at the clock and realised Dr K was late. He was about to leave when he heard someone behind him say, 'Micki Hamereski, I thought so. What are you doing here?' It was Mr Crud, the man who ran Kidpower, and he was pulling up a chair to sit down.

Micki wasn't sure what to say but from the expression on Crud's face an answer was expected. 'I came to see if that waitress was OK,' he mumbled.

'The waitress who was attacked? How nice. Do you know her?'

Micki didn't particularly want to tell him, but said, 'I met her when Dr Trevelyan bought me here for a meal.'

'You're a friend of Dr Trevelyan?'

Micki was trying to working out how he could slip away when Crud reached across and pinned his arm to the table.

He said quickly, 'She's Mr Trevelyan's daughter.'

'Dr Trevelyan has annoyed a lot of people in Ladram Heights, including the police. She's probably not a good friend to have.' Micki shuffled in his seat and saw the waiter looking across at them as Crud continued, 'I've been thinking about your progress at Kidpower. You don't go there much, do you? You know I can send you back to the magistrates' court for further punishment. They could send you away to a Young Offender's Institution. Not pleasant, I can tell you.' He paused to let his words sink in. 'But I'm willing to talk to the police on your behalf. Maybe get your condition of attendance at Kidpower removed - but first you will have to show me that my belief in you is justified.'

Micki sat very still.

Crud was staring at his bruised face. 'Who hurt you?'

'Hurt me?'

'Did you get that at Kidpower? I can stop that happening again.'

So Crud did know about Connor. Micki started to back his chair away.

'I think you are having trouble at Kidpower.'

He struggled to free his arm. 'Trouble? No.' He swallowed hard. 'No. I'm fine, Mr Crud. There's no trouble.'

'I know that's not true, Micki, and I want to stop it happening.'

'No, you mustn't.' Micki was trying to stay cool but the memory of Connor slicing the knife into his face was making him tremble.

'It's all right, Micki. Connor will do what I tell him. I can stop him threatening you.' Crud suddenly released his hold on Micki's arm and smiled pleasantly at the waiter, who was coming towards them. 'Micki here was just telling me about the waitress who was attacked last week. How is the poor girl?'

The waiter still looked uneasy. 'As well as can be expected.' He mouthed, 'Are you OK?' to Micki behind Crud's back as he cleared the table but Micki could sense Crud looking at him from behind his dark glasses and nodded.

Crud took a map of Devon out of his pocket. As the waiter moved away, he opened out the map and smoothed it out on the table. He pointed to Lyme Regis. 'A lot of rich people live here and artistic ones as well – novelists, artists and media people. It's an expensive place but they can afford it.' He stabbed his finger down on the map. 'And here is where Kidpower's illustrious Chairwoman lives. Out here, above Lyme, with a spectacular view and an eight-foot-high electric fence all the way round.'

His hopes of escaping were dashed when Crud stood up and leaned over his shoulder, pushing him down into his chair. 'I want you to do me a favour, Micki.'

This didn't sound good. Crud continued, 'I need to get hold of some video footage that Mrs Pierce keeps forgetting to give me. Not a difficult task and one I wouldn't trust to Connor. You, on the other hand, will be perfect.' Micki could taste half-digested carrot cake in his mouth. 'She entertains a lot and she's having a party tonight.'

He started to protest but Lyndon's glare froze the words on his lips. 'I'll pick you up at ten from that hovel you live in with your father. Think of this favour I'm asking as a substitute for coming to see me every day at Kidpower.'

Micki couldn't remember leaving the café but found he was running down the steps towards the sea in what he hoped was the opposite direction to Lyndon Crud. He didn't notice the spray of the waves against his face or the seagulls squabbling over a dead fish carcass as he wished the last half hour had never happened.

*

Kate was still regretting taking the old coast road with its spectacular views but absence of petrol stations. She'd been grateful to the farmer who'd stopped to ask if she needed help, then insisted on giving her a lift to get some fuel. She knew she was late and hoped Micki was still waiting for her. But as she reached the entrance to the Clock Tower Café, Lyndon Crud pushed past her.

They stood staring at each other for a second until he smiled unpleasantly and said, 'I think your friend has already left.'

She dashed inside the café and searched around for Micki. The waiter recognised her and called out, 'The young man has just gone. He seemed a bit upset.'

Kate ran back outside, her anxiety growing. Crud had disappeared. She looked over the handrail leading down to the rocks below and giving her a panoramic view across Sidmouth. She made out a solitary figure running along the esplanade but there was no way she was going to catch up with Micki now.

# 29

Kate drove up and down the Sidmouth semi-pedestrian one-way traffic system in the hope of seeing Micki. She was about to give up and go back to Elaine's when she saw him waiting in a bus shelter.

Pulling to a halt she called out to him, 'Micki, what's happened?' but he seemed either too exhausted or too scared to answer her.

'Did that man hurt you?'

Micki gave her a rueful smile and shook his head.

'Have you got money for the bus fare?' He was still avoiding looking at her.

She threw open the passenger door. 'Get in. I'll take you home.'

He didn't need more persuasion and slipped in beside her. There was no conversation during the journey to Ladrum Heights and Kate respected his need for silence.

When they arrived at the hostel, Luca sent Micki to bed. Kate thought his lack of argument was more worrying than his silence in the car. Luca was astute enough not to ask any questions either and just kissed the top of his son's head as he went upstairs.

Unlike the last time Kate had brought Micki home, she felt quite relaxed waiting for Luca to come back down. The noisy men in the other room didn't bother her any more as she thought how much her relationship with Micki had changed over the last couple of days. It felt good to be trusted. She'd enjoyed his company in the café and her recent experience with the gang had shaken her more than she liked to admit.

Luca's voice cut into her thoughts. 'You seem to do a better job of protecting my son than I can.'

She could hear the desperation in his voice and regretted thinking he was a bad father for bringing Micki to live in such hostile surroundings. It was the locals who needed to change, not Micki and Luca.

'Will he be alright?'

'For now. But something's going on. I knew he was being bullied at school, but that happened to me too. I thought it was part of growing up and he would get used to it. Micki is very sensitive, takes after his mother. I thought it might do him good to have to stick up for himself. But not this. This is much worse than bullying.'

'I don't know what happened today and Micki won't tell me, but I think it's got something to do with Kidpower. I think the Director's been harassing him. I don't trust that man. I think he's got some hold over Micki.'

'I guess he'll tell us when he's ready.' As he came closer she could see the worry lines around his eyes; he looked exhausted. But then he smiled faintly and said, 'Please stay while I make you some coffee.' Then he started searching through the cupboards but only seemed to find empty jars. He held out an empty Nescafé jar. 'I suppose you're used to better than this?'

Kate shook her head. To make Luca feel better she said, 'No, but I'm especially partial to tap water,' and was relieved to hear him laugh. 'Don't beat yourself up. I've got more time on my hands than you have and I'm not a parent.'

'Oh, that's a big advantage. But you're an important person. A top Government researcher.'

She could feel her cheeks burning as he placed two glasses of water on the kitchen table in front of her and pulled up a chair. Their knees touched under the table.

'Micki talks about you all the time. You've made a big impression on him. Now he wants to be a criminologist - not a poorly paid lackey like his Pa.'

His closeness stopped her thinking straight and she blurted out, 'Well, Micki got on well with my father. I think that's why we get on so well.' Then realised what she was saying could imply Luca was a bad father.

But Luca just looked sad, 'Micki told me your father had died recently. I'm very sorry. Please excuse my insensitivity. You must feel his loss at the moment. It's very good of you to keep helping Micki.'

She leant in closer, 'Being with Micki helps me feel better and I enjoy his company. It's good to hear him talk so positively about my father. In fact I was thinking of taking over his place as Micki's mentor.' Probably not the best thing to say to someone who doubted his parenting skills, but Luca didn't seem to mind.

'This mentoring, what does it involve?'

'Oh, you know, someone to talk to who's not family, going on trips out,' she couldn't stop blushing, 'that sort of thing.'

He was looking at her very intently, 'I think that would be good for him.'

'You do? Of course, it might all come to nothing.' She knew Lyndon Crud wouldn't welcome her becoming a mentor for Kidpower.

'I thought we could start by going sailing in my dad's old yacht. Micki said you were good at it and might like to come along. See a bit more of Devon. He said you were free on Tuesdays.'

He grinned back, aware of her discomfort. 'So he's my diary keeper now?'

She picked up her handbag. 'I didn't mean ... you don't have to come. I just thought Micki could do with a bit more fun.' She was about to walk away when he got up to stop her.

'Is it a dinghy or something bigger?'

Kate looked up at him, 'You mean you would like to come?'

'I think I'd be a fool to turn down your offer.' There was the glimmer of a smile as he said, 'Don't you want to say goodnight to Micki?'

She knew she should go. Staying around was beginning to feel like a commitment she didn't need. 'It's a Wayfarer, and it is sea worthy.'

'I'm sorry, I'm being a brute. You are being very kind to Micki and in return I just insult you. Please accept my apology.' He looked hard into her face, searching for a response. 'You are right. We both need some fun. I shall look forward to Tuesday.'

She went upstairs with him to have one last look at Micki. Luca seemed to have forgotten she was there as he stroked his sleeping son's forehead. She knew she was witnessing something special; the closeness of a father and son. It must be great to have a child to look after, she thought. Without disturbing Luca, she crept out of the hostel, feeling a bit more positive for all of them.

As she drove back through Sidmouth in the moonlight, Kate decided to go for a run by the sea; something she hadn't felt like doing since her dad's death. She was still dressed in her work suit but she kept some old joggers and trainers in the back of her car. She changed in the toilets, feeling more light hearted. Tomorrow was going to be a better day; she was going to see Nan and she was looking forward to taking Micki and Luca out on Tuesday. She should start looking for somewhere to rent, she didn't want to outstay her welcome at Elaine's and Sidmouth would do fine. Then there was the look Luca had given her as he reminded her that he now owed her two meals out and he hoped they would be taking them soon.

# 30

Micki shivered in the passenger seat of Lyndon Crud's big car. On any other occasion he would have enjoyed sitting on soft leather seats and breathing in the waxy smell of the polished mahogany dashboard. But tonight he would have given anything to be somewhere else. Away from the mad instructions that Crud was shouting at him as they sped along steep-banked, narrow country roads.

'Are you paying attention?'

He nodded; he was trying to.

'When I pull up at the electronic gates I want you out of the car. You're not to be seen, or at least not seen anywhere near me. Got that?'

Micki clung on to the sides of his seat as Lyndon swerved to avoid a tractor, then pulled up sharply outside some impressive solid metal gates.

'She goes for the best sort of security, does Mrs Pierce, so this is where you get out and sneak inside before the gates close. Keep low or the security cameras will pick you up.'

Micki swallowed and looked at the door handle. He didn't think there was any automatic locking on these old-fashioned cars. If he jumped out now he could he get away but Mr Crud would be sure to find him. Before he could decide he felt a sharp sting across his thigh as Crud slapped it hard. 'Are you sure you're listening, Micki?'

He gulped and nodded again.

'You wait for twenty minutes then sneak round to the back of the house. Look out for the guard dogs. They should be inside because of the guests, but you never know.' At the mention of dogs Micki's breathing went into overdrive and he searched through his pockets for his inhaler but it wasn't there. Crud didn't notice his discomfort, just carried on talking. 'I'll go into her bedroom and leave the patio door open. There are some spiral stairs going up there from the garden.'

Lyndon reached across to open the glove compartment and Micki could smell his sweat mingling with his own. He was sure he glimpsed the barrel of a gun before Lyndon brought out a torch which he dropped on his lap.

'You slip inside and search all the cupboards. You're looking for a red Nikon camera it should still be warm. I don't know where it will be but she keeps it somewhere in her bedroom.'

Micki had no idea why Mr Crud wanted a camera or why he couldn't just ask Mrs Pierce for it. As if he'd read his thoughts Crud said, 'I can't get it because of the security at the entrance doors. I'll have to walk through it and a camera would show up. Besides it will be good for you, move you up the criminal ranks.'

Mr Crud leant across Micki to open the car door. 'We're here. What are you waiting for?'

He had no option but to go along with Crud's plan.

*

Kate arrived back at Elaine's glowing from her run and ready for a shower and an early night. She did not expect to join a queue of cars waiting to gain entry to the driveway. Or to encounter three large white vans with 'Gourmet Dinners' emblazoned on their sides outside the kitchen and girls in aprons unloading plastic boxes of what smelled like hot food. She was sure Elaine had never mentioned she was having a party.

At the front of the house, guests were arriving in the latest designer evening wear. Waiters in cute tuxedos weaved between them with trays of glasses filled with wine or champagne. They had '*stop me and order anything*' embroidered on their backs. A neat idea, but then everything about Elaine Pierce was stylish.

Still in her running gear, Kate felt distinctly out of place. As she pushed her way through the revellers to the main staircase she bumped into Lyndon Crud coming down. Sweat was oozing out of him and he looked about as pleased to see her as she was to see him. They faced each other like boxers waiting for the starting bell.

With no trace of a smile he said, 'Dr Trevelyan, I didn't expect to see you so soon. How is the research going?'

She snapped back, 'Very productive, thank you, Mr Crud.'

He looked her up and down, 'Surely you're not here to interview demonstrators?'

'I'm here as a friend of the hostess.'

'Really?' He raised an eloquent eyebrow.

She tried to think of something sarcastic to reply but was saved the trouble by Elaine coming over to kiss her cheek. As usual, Elaine's passage between her guests was accompanied by admiring glances. She looked glowing in a cream silk dress that showed off her curves. Kate felt dreadful, not only was she the only person not dressed up to the nines but she stank of sweat. As Elaine moved closer, Kate could see her pupils were extraordinarily large. She was wearing so much J'adore perfume that it drowned out the odour of Kate's perspiring body.

'I've been telling Kate she needs a little pleasure,' she told Crud, speaking very quickly, 'especially when all her friends are back in London.' She lifted a hand, weighed down with diamond rings, to brush a strand of Kate's fringe away from her forehead and Kate could tell she'd been drinking. 'I've been worried about you. You're hardly eating and always look so tired.' Elaine grabbed hold of Crud's arm dragging him closer to Kate. 'Don't you think Kate needs fattening up, darling?'

Crud didn't bother to reply just started edging his way backwards.

Deprived of Crud's arm for support, Elaine latched on to Kate's arm and propelled her round the room introducing her to the dressed up party goers. Kate immediately wished she was still wearing a suit and her makeup. The reflected light from the crystal chandeliers were illuminating her far more than she would have liked.

She forced a smile as Elaine turned to her and said, 'I've just noticed what you're wearing. Don't you think you'd better go up and change?'

Just when Kate thought the evening couldn't get any worse, she saw Jake making his way through the party guests towards them. His shirt was buttoned up wrongly and he looked sweaty.

'The party's going well, Elaine,' he commented as he handed her one of the two glasses he was carrying. Then, as an afterthought, he acknowledged Kate. 'Of course, you're billeted with Elaine. I'd forgotten.' He took in her sweaty sport's wear, 'I guess you're not staying.'

Kate stared back at him expecting more of a welcome. Unlike Elaine, he wasn't wearing anything to cover the musky smell of recent sex.

Elaine moved in closer, a tiger stalking its prey. 'Kate was telling me how well her research is going.'

Jake's face tensed. 'She shouldn't be talking about that.'

'Oh dear, why not?' Elaine walked a crimson polished finger along Jake's arm.

'Because it's confidential. Isn't it, Kate?'

Kate held her breath, trying desperately to remember what exactly she'd said to Elaine. She said, 'I'm sure I can't remember a thing about it.'

Jake put his arm around Elaine and guided her away. Kate watched as they joined the party guests, leaving her standing alone wishing Elaine's Persian mosaic floor would open up and swallow her.

# 31

It started to rain as soon as Lyndon Crud dropped Micki off just before the entrance gates. He was soaked long before he made it to the house with its windows all lit up like the Titanic. Cars were arriving, making their way along the drive. He waited for a gap in the vehicles so he could move unnoticed between the lines of trees. Closer to the house he could hear the bass thud of rock music, mixed with snatches of conversation, squeals of laughter and champagne corks popping, spilling out through the open windows.

He kept down low to dash across the lawn to the side of the house where it was quieter and darker. As he rounded the corner of the building he hoped there were no dogs out. But his luck was in and he soon spotted the spiral staircase leading to Elaine's bedroom that Crud had told him about. He stood under it sheltering from the rain, waiting for the time to pass. As he watched for Crud to open the bedroom door, he tried to think of good memories of family outings in Krakow to take his mind off what he was about to do. He didn't like the idea of going through other people's belongings.

A flash of light from the window above drew him back to the present and he jerked back against the wall. There was a sound like a door sliding open. Micki looked at the watch Lyndon Crud had given him and saw it was twenty-five minutes since he'd been dropped off at the gate.

In less time than he needed to blow his nose he'd scaled the stairs, slid open the door and stepped inside from the garden. He panicked for a moment when he couldn't find his torch until he realised it was already in his hand. He switched it on and swept an arc of light around the room. It was big and filled with exotic plants like the tropical house he used to visit in Krakow. His torch beam picked out paintings of human-sized insects and animals all over the walls. There were dragonflies as large as tigers peering out between the flowers. Even the circular bed in the middle of the room had bedding covered with butterflies. Mirrors lined the ceiling and the walls of the room, increasing his uneasiness as he kept seeing his own reflection projected around the room. All the furniture and fabrics looked very expensive and he avoided touching it in case he left a mark. He stepped forward and his feet sank into wall-to-wall carpeting. Without thinking he bent down to take off his trainers, then stopped as he realised he might need to leave quickly.

He swept the beam round the room, picking out a door across the room from where he'd come in. He opened it and light from the upstairs corridor spilled into the bedroom. He shut it quickly; people were close by. He could be discovered at any moment. If he was in the wrong bedroom Mr Crud would make life hell for him if he didn't return with the camera. But however much he looked around all he could see were the mirrored walls and his many reflections reminding him he shouldn't be in there.

Desperately he felt his way round the walls and found some comfort in the feel of the cold glass against his skin. As his hands swept across the glass he felt a button of some kind in the wall and pressed it. There was a grinding noise and the wall he was leaning against slid open. He stumbled into another room which flooded with light as soon as the door opened, and found he was surrounded by racks of clothes. It was the largest wardrobe he'd ever seen, like walking into a clothes shop. There were folded jumpers in pull-out drawers arranged according to their colour, shelves of boots and shoes, and lots of dresses on hangers. He looked through them all, taking care to replace everything exactly as he found it. But there was no sign of any camera.

He looked at his watch. So far he'd been inside the house for nine minutes. He went back into the bedroom to see if there were any other hidden doors. Once he knew where to look it was easy and he found there was a button that opened a hidden door in each of the four walls. One door led to the room full of clothes, a second to a gym with exercise apparatus and racks of weights like the one that Luca used to go to, but it didn't smell of sweat and was much tidier. The third room housed the biggest bathroom he had ever seen, with two walk-in showers as well as a sauna and bath. The last hidden room was nearly empty except for an iron bedstead and lino covered flooring. The room felt damp and smelt of sweat and rotting grass. Church candles that were half burnt down formed a circle around the bed and chains wrapped round with silk scarves were fastened to the corners of the bedstead. Open metal shelving covered three of the walls which were covered in weird objects.

One end looked like a torture chamber, with pliers and padlocks, at the other an assortment of plastic and rubber objects were plugged into the nearest wall.

He looked between the objects for the red camera that Crud wanted him to take but apart from the metal and plastic gear only found a circular mirror, a knife and some bags of white powder.

Micki was starting to panic and finding it hard to breath and turned back to the door he'd come in by. By the door was a desk and on the desk he saw a red camera. As he scooped it up, he noticed a thin black wooden cupboard on the wall above the desk and couldn't resist seeing if it opened. A light came on as he opened the door illuminating a display of photographs. It reminded him of his crime wall at the hospital. Most of the photos were old and brown, curled up at the edges. There were lots of shots of a family; mainly consisting of a young man and older woman, who was occasionally holding a small child. Then he saw another photo which made him drop the torch. Dr Sand was staring out at him from the cover of her book about psychopaths and next to it a new looking photograph of Dr K.

He pocketed the camera and ran.

# 32

Although Kate had gone straight to her bedroom, she couldn't sleep. She spent lonely hours looking out the window at Jake's Porsche in the driveway - long after the party had ended. It was almost a relief when her mobile rang after all that tossing and turning. When she saw it was Jacqui Sunday Kate answered it straight away, hoping she had an update on the Brathcol fire.

'Hi Kate. How are you?'

'Have you any news?'

There was a slight pause. 'Yes, in a way...'

'Go on.'

'We're closing the case. Forensics haven't found anything suspicious. They'll be clear of the house now so you can start clearing up and arranging things...'

Kate nearly dropped her phone. 'You can't do that. It's a clear case of arson. Someone deliberately killed my father.'

'I'm sorry, Kate.' At least Jacqui sounded embarrassed. 'We've talked it over with Vera Thomas and the Coroner. They both agree the fire was accidental.'

'You're not trying to blame it on my father again? Or on me for not looking after him properly?' Her voice was shaking with anger.

'These things happen, Kate. No-one's to blame. But we're closing our investigation and so you won't see me any more. I just wanted you to know. Oh, and to wish you luck.'

'I don't need luck,' Kate shouted down the phone. 'I need you to do your job properly. What about the burglary? The damage to the shed? And - the cat? Are you trying to tell me my father nailed it to the shed door before he set fire to his own home?'

There was a brief silence, followed by a sigh. 'There was no cat in the shed. No evidence of a break-in. It's natural when you've had a shock to sometimes get things muddled. You've been under a lot of stress, Kate, you're not ...'

Kate stabbed at her phone to end the call. She slumped back on top of her bed. It was typical of a rural police force. Why hadn't they brought in outside experts if such detection was beyond their capabilities? Well, she wasn't going to leave it there. Someone was responsible for her father's death and she was going to find out who.

She dressed in a hurry, not caring what clothes she threw on. It was only when she was parking her MX5 outside Ladrum Heights police station when she remembered she was supposed to be driving to London to see Nan.

*

Jacqui Sunday was looking out of the window of the police station when she saw Kate Trevelyan drive into the parking area. When she found out Kate had come to see Chief Superintendent Ross she rushed to his office to defend any complaint that she was certain was coming her way.

Ian Ross greeted her as if she had just won a police commendation award and directed her to the sofa's and coffee table at the end of his office, then asked if she wanted a drink. Declining his offer, Jacqui told him she had some misgivings about Inspector Hunt's closure of the investigation into the Trevelyan house fire. That as the Family Liaison Officer on the case, she hadn't been consulted, in fact she was still waiting to see the Fire Inspector's preliminary report. Chief Superintendent Ross agreed that Inspector Hunt's should have discussed the case with her and told her that her concerns would be noted. He was asking about how she was finding the rest of her work when the phone rang.

From the curt way he responded she wasn't surprised when he cupped his hand over the phone and said, 'It seems Dr Trevelyan wants to see me.'

As Jacqui stood up to leave he added, 'I know all about her daft allegations that her father's shed had been trashed by animal killers. She seems to be taking her father's death very badly. Ms Pierce, who she's staying with, is very worried about her mental health. I think you'll find Inspector Hunt was right, the fire at her father's is nothing to do with police work.'

As Jacqui hurried back down the corridor to avoid seeing Kate Trevelyan she had her doubts about what Chief Superintendent Ross had told her. When Errol, her ex-husband was playing around and told her he wanted a divorce she'd behaved erratically too, forgetting appointments, putting the dirty dishes back in the dishwasher with the clean ones, and overcooking food. She could understand Kate being upset and suspicious. In her shoes she would be too. And in her opinion, Inspector Hunt was far too eager to cut corners with investigations and avoid anything which increased the paperwork. She hadn't liked upsetting Kate and it sounded as if the Chief Superintendent was about to dismiss anything Kate said to him, which only made Jacqui feel worse. She had been meaning to visit Bill Brewford, the force analyst, as part of her training for the family liaison work. So she left the police station by the back entrance and headed into Exeter to Devon and Cornwell Police Headquarters, Middlemoor.

The traffic was particularly light and Jacqui was soon sitting on a wobbly stool, watching Bill Brewster at work. His tiny office was down in the basement and crammed full of box files and empty coffee mugs. Perspex screens illuminated with displays of crime statistics covered most of the walls and it was to one of these that Bill was now directing Jacqui's attention.

'I've extracted all our crime stats for the last three years so you can get an idea of the trends. But as you know recorded crime statistics don't reveal everything, so I've also included the local Accident and Emergency Department's records of injuries from violence, reports from the East Devon Pub Watch Scheme and a recent report I've done on drug related crime in the area. But what might give you a better idea of gang activities are the digital tracking records.'

'Digital tracking records, that sounds sophisticated. '

Bill looked across at Jacqui and grinned, 'It's my analysis of all our CCTV footage. It saves the cops at Middlemoor hours of staring at video footage. We used to have it everywhere in Devon, along the esplanades, shopping arcades, access to all our public buildings and social housing. Everywhere, that is, until the Government cut the funding. But there is still enough left to use to identify patterns of behaviour and location.'

Jacqui was paying close attention now. 'Are the images good enough to identify individuals?'

'Mostly, the images are a bit grainy though, especially at night,' Bill said using his laser light to highlight areas of the map. 'We've got a lot of footage from here, where most of the migrant workers live.' He moved the laser light onto a different map, 'And the red areas here are where the gang activity takes place. As you can see there's a lot of overlap.'

'The gangs are made up of migrant workers then?' Jacqui was starting to think the fire at Brathcol may be some sort of reprisal for Kate's research, or an attempt to stop it altogether.

Bill was shaking his head, 'I don't think it's that straight forward, but most of the senior brass round here seem to think so.' Including Chief Superintendent Ian Ross thought Jacqui.

He pointed his laser light back at the screen and the map showing the areas where gangs predominated changed to dark blue. 'The blue is where the newcomers from the city overspill live.'

'Overspill?'

'From Bristol, Plymouth and Exeter. The councils either ran out of housing stock or didn't want them around, so they relocated them to Ladram Heights.'

Jacqui was aghast, it was more the kind of political shenanigans that went on where she'd come from in London. Not what you expect in an Area of Outstanding Natural Beauty. 'So the gangs could be made up of migrant workers or families re-located from other cities?'

'It could be both, the digital tracking images are mainly of the migrants but sometimes they don't look right, more like someone dressing up and over doing the fake tan.'

She was intrigued now and wish she'd come to visit Bill at the beginning of the year when she was supposed to.

Bill was still talking, 'Then there's another complication, most gang disorder happens in the daytime and is usually fuelled by alcohol and drugs and off licenses are more likely targets than domestic homes.'

'Like the recent riots in Ladram Heights?'

'Just so. But recently the burglaries in Ladram Heights have become more organised and often result in arson, burning the house down to destroy the forensic evidence. And now the frequency of burglary related arson is increasing in affluent areas like Sidmouth, Otterford and West Hill.'

Bill scrolled through a number of maps which showed how the frequency of crimes had changed in the different parts of East Devon.

Jacqui asked him to go back to the map of incidents in Otterford. The tell-tale dots were clustered round Brathcol and had all taken place over the last month. But the Brathcol fire wasn't amongst them?

Bill was asking if there was anything else she needed to know as he had a report to prepare for the Senior Commanders' Meeting.

'Just one more thing,' Jacqui said, working out the implications of what she'd been shown. 'If someone reported seeing a dead animal and when the police checked there was nothing there, would there be traces of blood or other forensic evidence left behind?'

'You bet.'

'So you could tell if someone moved the evidence?'

Bill grinning back at Jacqui, 'Give me the address and I'll get it checked out for you.'

# 33

They had started their day out with a boat trip in Kate's father's old Wayfarer. Luca and Micki were delighted at the prospect of a sail, but Micki's new friend just screwed up her face and glared at Kate. Kate recognised the signs of a rebellious streak from her striped orange and purple hair and rows of piercings. She'd been a bit of a rebel at that age too so she didn't push it when the teenager refused to tell her what her name was.

'She's Girl.' Micki piped up.

So that was what Kate called her, although even then she didn't get much of an answer. Luca turned out to be an excellent crew; recognising her expertise and conceding to her superior knowledge of the local tides and currents. Micki was keen to take the helm and Kate tried to show him how to steer by 'going about' while Girl slumped in a corner complaining whenever the yacht keeled over. She had an annoying habit of flicking the ends of any loose ropes across Micki's legs to attract his attention, causing them to get in a tangle.

At first Kate had felt put out with Micki for bringing Girl along. She'd been hoping to find out what Lyndon Crud had spoken to him about in the café. Micki was so besotted with Girl that he'd hardly spoken to Kate, leaving her to spend more of her time with Luca. But she soon got over her initial irritation in Luca's company. Girl was turning out to be good for Micki. He looked more relaxed and obviously enjoyed her company.

Back on dry land, Luca insisted on hiring a car and paying for everything. In Tesco's he'd selected her favourite wine, cheese and chutney after replacing most of the bags of pickled onion flavoured crisps, chosen by Micki, for pistachio nuts and Gü chocolate pots.

When he asked if she knew a good picnic site she suggested the Donkey Sanctuary at Salcombe Regis because Micki loved animals. They were halfway there when her iPhone rang. A Mr Whitcher from the insurance company wanted to meet her at Brathcol and - apologising for such short notice, as he was going on holiday - it had to be today.

She was feeling nervous as they pulled up outside Brathcol and her sense of foreboding increased when a magpie flew in front of the car, nearly hitting the windscreen. Kate looked around for a second bird to fend off the bad luck that a solitary magpie could bring. But there were no more to be seen. The striped police tape had been removed from the entrance to the drive but the toxic smell still lingered in the air. In the summer sunshine the shell of the house looked more charred and desolate than ever. Micki looked excited and wanted to go inside to explore, but Luca had pulled him back and explained it was dangerous. She took them round to the sunken garden at the back of the house. It was one of her favourite places and held a lot of good memories of her childhood. From here the view of the building was hidden by the rich summer foliage of ash and beech trees. Micki and Girl lay on the grass enjoying the sunshine while Luca unpacked their picnic.

Kate's meeting with the insurance assessor was over quickly and she was able to join the others for the picnic. As she approached, Luca looked up and said, 'I think they've had enough of our company.'

Micki and Girl were sitting close together on the swing seat, half camouflaged by shrubbery. Suddenly, Girl jumped off and ran, leaving the swing spinning erratically. Micki tumbled to the ground, staggered to his feet and chased after her. Kate watched them, her mood lifting. It was good to see Micki enjoying himself. She sipped her wine, feeling happy despite all that had happened.

Luca was watching his son too. 'Micki has had to grow up so quickly,' he said. His voice was heavy with sadness.

She realised she didn't know much about him or Micki in fact, or the life they'd left behind in Krakow. Micki had never spoken about it. She'd assumed they'd moved to England for the work and the money.

'You must both miss Poland.'

Luca didn't answer straight away but looked away, 'Yes, very much. We lived in a small village called Krishta just outside Krakow. Micki was always making dens in the wood or playing football with his friends there.'

Kate thought how innocent and different that sounded from the life he was forced to live in Ladram Heights. She was working out the best way to ask him what he thought about Kidpower when the sound of loud giggling interrupted their conversation. They both looked towards the pond where Micki was on one knee handing Girl a bunch of bedraggled twigs and flowers. She kicked them away and rushed into the shrubbery with Micki following in hot pursuit.

It was a relief to hear Luca laughing. She wasn't coping very well with her own grief so what chance did she have sorting out other people's troubles.

'Well, he seems to have a new interest now.' Luca said, waving back at Micki. 'I'm just glad he's found a friend. He didn't want to come to England. I know he's unhappy here.'

Kate thought of the terror in Micki's eyes after he'd been attacked. 'Is that why he got into trouble and had to go to Kidpower?'

'That and losing his mother. They were very close. He misses our old life in a comfortable house where we had plenty of money to go out on trips and buy the latest electronic gadgets.'

'Her death must have been hard for you both.'

Luca looked into the distance before replying, 'She had a brain tumour - she was in and out of hospital for months. Micki thought she was going to get better but I knew she wouldn't.' He turned suddenly and looked straight at Kate, 'I was one of the medical team looking after her. I broke the rules to help her stay alive, that's how I ended up here working on a building site. I didn't tell Micki how bad it was. I guess I was having difficulty coping with my own feelings and thought I was doing the right thing.'

She could see it was a hard subject for him to talk about and could feel the now familiar ache at the back of her throat as she searched his face willing him to continue. But Luca only shrugged his shoulders, then filled up their wine glasses.

'Micki's become so remote. He was always such a chatty kid.'

'Maybe it's his age?'

He smiled at her and Kate saw where Micki got his mischievous look from. 'Yes, I can just about remember what it felt like to be thirteen.'

She smiled back. 'Micki is special. Not at all like the other youngsters who get sent to Kidpower.'

Luca's face clouded over. 'The place seems full of racists. Everywhere Micki goes he gets the fact that he's a foreigner thrown back in his face – on the news, at school or outside our house.'

She remembered the spattered eggs on the front door. 'That must be awful. The media don't seem to distinguish between people coming over legitimately, like you, and illegal migrants who shouldn't be here. I know my father was trying to improve things at the community school.'

'Your father did much to help Micki.' He gave her such a warm smile that she wanted to hug him. 'When he was arrested for stealing I probably didn't listen to him enough. Micki always seemed calmer after he'd been to see your father.' He passed her some cherries and pointed to the burnt-out house. 'How about you, Kate? How are you coping? Your father's death must have affected you badly too.'

She was tempted to share her grief – to tell him how her moods kept changing from ice cool to burning anger and how she increasingly found everyone around her irritating, especially Jake. Instead she said, 'Sometimes, but my research keeps me busy.'

He didn't look convinced. 'And your mother and the rest of your family? Do they live around here?'

'My mother is dead. I was brought up by my father and grandmother. Then my grandmother moved to Bermuda to run a women's refuge when I was a teenager. I don't really know why she went but I think it was my fault. They used to row all the time about me. Dad used to stop me doing things and Nan would spoil me. I think she thought he blamed me for my mother's death but we got on better after she'd gone – I did miss her though. She's in hospital in London at the moment recovering from a hip operation. And no, I don't have many friends round here, except...' She paused as she felt his fingers intertwine with hers. Kate rested her head on Luca's shoulder, closed her eyes. None of that mattered any more.

*

Micki sprawled across the swing seat watching Pa and Dr K talking, glad they were getting on so well. This was turning out to be a perfect day. Girl's head was resting on his bare leg with strands of her orange hair tickling him like feathers, causing a prickling sensation in his stomach. He watched stray strands of hair close to her mouth dance in time to her breathing as her chest rose and fell. It must be great to be able to go to sleep anywhere whenever you like. It had taken him weeks to block out the builders' swearing, guffawing and snoring in his shared room at Salterton Way. Even now he still woke in the night, thinking there was someone creeping around his bedroom.

The jingle of an ice cream van interrupted his thoughts and caused Girl to stir.

Pa got up and reached in his pocket. 'Anyone want an ice cream?'

Girl opened her eyes, stretched out like a kitten and shouted across to him, 'I'll have a Ninety Nine with everything. Micki will too.'

By the speed she sprang into action Micki guessed she had only been pretending to be asleep. Dr K went with Pa to get the ice creams and Girl bent over him and ruffled his hair. She smelt of damp grass and he felt his cheeks get hot. 'What are you up to, then?'

'Nothing.'

'I'm doing nothing too.'

He tried to sound casual. 'You've been fast asleep and missed all the excitement.'

'Excitement! I woke up for an ice cream. What was so interesting that you were doing then?'

He was starting to feel more comfortable about the scornful way she talked to him. 'Thinking about what I've found out, but I'm not going to tell you!'

She picked up a half full can of coke and held it over his head. 'Oh, no?'

Not wanting to get wet he said quickly, 'I know where Sara is.'

# 34

The day had been brilliant for Micki. He'd loved the garden at Mr T's old house, although it was sad to see it in ruins. Then when they'd returned to the builders' hostel Pa had allowed Girl to stay and left them alone together in the communal bedroom. She'd insisted they share some joints and he hadn't been keen on the marihuana at first, but now he felt on top of the world and Girl was giving him more heart-stopping moments by snuggling up to him. Micki was slowly building up the courage to kiss her. He was thinking the day couldn't get any better when Pa barged into the bedroom and spoilt it all.

'Put those out,' he shouted, snatching the reefer out of Micki's hand. 'They're illegal. Do you want to get us deported to Poland?'

'I don't care,' he snapped back.

Girl retreated to the corner of the bed and pulled her hood down over her face. As his pa went to open the window she sprang up and pushed past him, shouting back, 'Is that better?', slamming the door behind her.

Micki swallowed down his disappointment. 'She says you have to do cool things like smoking to stop them bullying.'

'I don't care what she says. If you carry on like this you'll end up in prison, where the bullying will be a lot worse.'

Pa's voice had an edge to it. Micki knew he was being unreasonable but he still turned on him. 'That will be a lot better than living with you.' All the anger that had been building up since his arrival in Britain was coming to the surface. 'You think I like being spat on and called names? And going to a school where the teachers are all ignorant and insulting?'

Pa's face softened. 'I don't like it here either, but we have to be here, we've no choice. He walked towards him with his arms outstretched to give him a hug. 'Micki, I'm sorry.'

Micki felt too churned up to respond and pushed him away. 'I don't have to be here. You brought me to this place to live with people who beat me up. What would Mama have thought of you?'

'She'd have thought I'd let you down by allowing you to steal and smoke marihuana and break the law. Micki, we've both let her down.'

153

A muscle at the side of Luca's neck was starting to twitch. Micki knew if he stayed around for any longer one of them would do or say something they would regret for ever. He couldn't understand what Pa was making a fuss about: it was only a bit of hash, after all. There was no reason for shouting him down in front of Girl. She was just getting interested in him and his pa had ruined it all. Now she'd be ridiculing him at school and refusing to answer his calls. He felt close to tears; everything in his life had gone wrong since Mama died.

'She wouldn't have died if you'd been a better doctor, we would never have come to this stinking place.' He felt a mixture of gratification and guilt watching his pa recoil at these words.

Micki didn't wait to hear any more. He barged out of the room, pushing past Daz who was hovering outside the door listening.

Daz started to protest. 'Hey, Micki, what's up?'

But Micki was through the front door and striding down the road. He felt hot, despite the rain battering against his face. How could Pa spoil things when they were starting to get better for the first time since they'd arrived in this hell hole? Being with Girl made everything bearable. So why had his pa gone on and on about her? From the look Girl gave him as she marched out of the door, he didn't think she would ever speak to him again.

The rain was lashing down and Micki had to sidestep discarded cans of beer and plastic McDonald's boxes flowing down the pavement in water from a blocked-up drain. He nearly collided with a group of children who were walking backwards with their anorak hoods pulled down over their heads. Micki recognised them from school and prepared to receive the usual insults. This time he was going to give back as good as he got. But the weather seemed to have diluted their passion for foreigner-baiting and they passed by with their heads down. A bus with steamed up windows went past, spraying his jeans with oily rainwater. He swore loudly in Polish, then started to run after it. A bus was the quickest way out of Ladram Heights. As he jumped on the platform his mobile rang. He nearly didn't answer it, expecting it to be Pa.

'Micki, how are you doing?' He recognised the breathless nasal quality in Girl's voice and punched the air with his free hand.

'Better for hearing you.'

'Can you come down to the Parade?'

'Why?' The Parade was what she called the area of scrubby shops where he'd been beaten up and now avoided.

'You want to help Dr K, don't you? Well, here's your chance.'

Micki felt a prickle of excitement gather at the back of his neck. She had forgiven him. 'OK. How?'

'If you want to know, you gotta come to see for yourself. You know where the offy is, the one you got beaten up in?'

'Course I do, how could I forget.'

'Then come over. Come quick. They're already gathering.'

'Who?' Micki could hear a lot of shouting in the background and someone calling her name.

'You'll see. You'll come then?'

'OK, but...'

'I gotta go. See you.'

The line went dead. The bus was only five minutes away from The Parade.

*

Kate was taking a long slow bath and enjoying soaking up the fragrances of frangipani and ylang ylang in her favourite bath oil. It was a week since Dad had died and a lot of things had gone wrong since but she felt surprisingly buoyant, although the locals were still hostile to her research and Jake still wasn't returning her calls. Elaine Pierce was starting to ask intrusive questions ever since she'd told her she would be moving out at the end of the week, and the police had made zero progress towards finding out who had started the fire at Brathcol and given up.

She thrust her head back into the foamy bath water, still thinking about the picnic at Brathcol, and the warmth of Luca's hand, and came up smiling. She hadn't felt so good since she'd arrived back in Devon. When she'd suggested the day out to Micki, it was because she enjoyed his company and wanted to help him. But instead, she'd found that talking to Luca had helped her sort out her own pain over her father's death. He was also fun to have around. When she'd first met him she'd found him cold and intense and could quite understand Micki's resentment. But now she knew his wife had died after a painful and lingering illness and he'd lost his job as a surgeon for fast-tracking her

155

treatment, she felt differently about him and was looking forward to seeing him again soon.

The bath water was getting cold and she shivered as she heard the rain beating against the window and the shriek of seagulls, signalling it was going to be a rough night. She stepped out of the bath and wrapped her robe round her. She'd told Ginny that she'd join her and the rest of the team for dinner in Sidmouth and had already laid out the dress she would wear. But she didn't feel ready to face Jake or join in the discussion about the lack of progress they were making in their research. On the plus side, Kate had a long chat with Nan on the phone and arranged to visit her tomorrow and then there was Luca. She hung the dress back in the wardrobe and stretched out on her bed thinking back on their conversation and how good talking to him had made her feel. It was true, she'd never really missed her mother. How could you miss someone you never knew? All Kate knew was that she'd died giving birth to her. She'd often asked about her when other children's mothers collected them from school but it seemed to be a taboo subject. Nan discouraged her from asking in case it upset her father. She'd felt more upset by her dad's sadness which had always been a shadow in the background of their relationship. Maybe now she could find out more about her mother; what sort of family she came from or even what genetic traits she might have passed on to her.

She was still lying on the bed thinking when the phone rang.

'It's Luca.' He sounded breathless.

'Is everything OK?'

'I'm worried about Micki ... We had a row. He's run off.'

Kate thought he'd probably gone to meet his new girlfriend and said, 'I'm sure he'll be back soon.'

'No, I don't think so, Kate. I really upset him. I was worried about his behaviour and said his Mama would be disappointed in him. I shouldn't have said it.'

She was paying more attention now, imagining Micki's angry face masking all his hurt. She said, 'I'm sure he will get over it and come back soon,' but she was picking up the panic in his voice and starting to feel uneasy too.

'I've tried to ring him. He won't answer.'

'Well, that's normal for a teenager.'

'It's not usual for Micki. He always answers in case I'm in trouble - and then there's the riots. It's on the news at the moment.'

She turned on the TV and saw images of demonstrators with placards pushing against police officers in riot gear and recognised the shops were Micki had been attacked. Luca was still talking. 'They want us out and they'll use any means to get rid of us.'

'And Micki's out there?'

'Yes, I'm going to look for him. I just wanted to check he hadn't come to you.'

'Don't go out there alone, Luca. I'm coming over. I'll be there in half an hour. Wait for me.'

But as the sound of angry demonstrators drowned out the empty phone line, she didn't think he would.

# 35

'Stay off the streets. Police are warning residents of Ladram Heights not to go outdoors as the anti-migrant demonstrations become more violent. Cars have been set alight. Emergency vehicles are being blocked from gaining entry, with shops and homes also being the target for fire-bombs. Several people have been injured already and the situation is described by Devon and Cornwell Police as extremely serious. Extra officers from Plymouth and Exeter have been brought in to assist with dispersing the rioters. If you live in Ladram Heights, lock your doors and stay at home tonight.'

Kate jammed her foot down hard on the accelerator pedal as she listened to the local news on her car radio. It sounded as bad as Luca feared. As she arrived at the edge of Ladram Heights she saw the roadblock - a row of police vans and officers positioned across her route. They were stopping all the traffic and turning everyone back.

She cursed, then remembered a short-cut through a local farm and spun her car round. On the farm track the route was uneven and muddy, especially for a low car like hers. She winced at the sound of her exhaust scrapping against the ground but she was making good time and was nearly at Salterton Avenue, near enough to see flames and smoke on the horizon and to smell burning through her open car window.

She was starting to relax when a large shape appeared in front of her windscreen, causing her to slam on the brakes. As the car slid sideways she saw she had nearly driven into a herd of cows. She jumped out of the car, heart thumping. Two boys aged about ten were standing around herding the animals across the road. The cows at the front of the herd had stopped to eat some grass from the verge halting their progress, but the boys were deep in conversation and didn't seem to have noticed.

'Can you move the cows out of the way please? I'm trying to get through and it's an emergency.'

They looked at each other then back at Kate and carried on talking. She grabbed one by the arm. 'Please move them. I've got to get through.'

He made a face at her. 'You've frightened our cows, that's what you've done, and we'll move them when we're ready.' At that they turned their backs on her and continued to talk loudly but did nothing to encourage the cows to move.

She tried shooing the nearest cows into the field but they just looked up from eating the grass and stared at her.

'Told you so,' the nearest boy yelled.

Kate stormed back to her car and revved up the engine, creating a gap. With her foot hard down on the accelerator and wheels squealing she drove through the herd, covering the boys with slurry.

It was only when she managed to park inside the police barricade that she thought of ringing Micki and saw she had missed several calls from him. She tried to ring him back but there was no answer.

Worried, she left her car and headed towards the mayhem where sounds of banging, shouting and breaking glass were getting louder as she ran. She soon reached the back of the demonstration and jumped up on to the seat of one of the few wooden benches that hadn't been overturned to get a better view. The march had already passed the builders' lodgings and was moving towards the parade of shops where she'd first met Micki. There were so many protestors that she couldn't see the front of the crowd and their insistent chant of 'Out! Out! Out!' was hurting her ears. Police officers in their orange fluorescent jackets were interspaced between the protestors and Kate wondered if Jacqui was amongst them. Some officers had stopped a group of teenage boys about Micki's age from spray painting 'out' on the sides of parked cars, but they weren't doing much to control the ringleaders at the front, if the numbers of upturned cars were anything to go by.

In the distance the sirens of emergency vehicles were getting louder and Kate wondered how many people had been hurt and how long it would take the ambulances to get through the crowds. The air, thick with acrid smoke, made her shudder.

The demonstrators at the back were mainly women, some with children who were crying. Most of them were trying to manoeuvre out the way of the jostling protestors. Kate was propelled along with them, away from the direction of Micki and Luca's hostel. There was no sign of either of them. Something sharp rammed into the back of her legs and she spun round to face her attacker.

'I'm so sorry. Are you hurt?' The woman who'd hit her with the front of her pushchair was tiny, and her curly flame-coloured hair was plastered against her face. She was struggling to keep her pushchair upright against the surge of the crowd. The child was partly protected in his blue-rimmed plastic cocoon but looked very hot and red from screaming. His small hands gripped the arm rests so tightly his knuckles were turning blue.

Kate, surprised to encounter politeness in the midst of the mob, said, 'No, I'm fine. But what about you?'

The woman moved closer but Kate still had to bend down to hear what she was saying. 'This wasn't supposed to happen. I'd no idea the crowd would be so big… I'd never have brought him if I'd thought there'd be trouble…'

'Are you trying to get home?'

'I am now. I've been coming on these marches every week – they're supposed to be peaceful. I came to show the council and the police we want action against these immigrants taking our jobs.' But she didn't sound very convinced as a bottle came hurling between them, smashing at their feet, its glass scattering over their shoes.

Kate helped the woman steer her pushchair to the outside of the crowd and left her trying to console her toddler.

As Kate got closer to the front, the protestors were mainly men, most with masks covering their faces. She was shoved out of the way as they hurled traffic cones. From the smell of burning, the ones right at the front had already started throwing petrol bombs. She was still looking for Micki when she heard shouting coming from the direction of the shopping arcade where he'd been beaten up. Kate pushed her way through the press of bodies and saw an elderly woman lying on the pavement with a couple of youths bending over her. One looked up and she recognised him immediately. He was the gang member who'd tried to rape the waitress in the café. He'd lost his balaclava in the struggle in the café and was clearly identifiable on the video on her phone.

He stood upright and, looking at the gathering crowd, shouted, 'It was one of them foreigners. Look, he's mugged her. Left her for dead.'

Kate was close enough to see his scowl as he looked in her direction. The old woman was inert on the ground but before Kate could do anything to help he was pointing to the end of the row of shops, the nearest of which was well alight.

'Over there, that's the bastard what did it.'

She followed where he was pointing. A figure in a blue sweatshirt was huddled against a shop doorway further down The Parade. It was the same doorway that she'd found him beaten up in just over a week ago.

*

All the anger and defiance had gone out of Micki as he sheltered in the doorway, watching the crowd moving in on him.

He had done as Girl asked. He'd come to The Parade to meet her but she never turned up. He was too busy trying to find her in the crowd that he hadn't realised he was in danger but when he'd seen the demonstrators fighting with police and throwing fire bombs he'd taken cover in the doorway.

He was about to try and slip away when he saw her making her way towards him through the crowd. Girl had been waiting for him after all. She came running across to him, skimming round the gang, grabbing his arm to pull him back into the shadows of the shop doorway.

He could just hear her whisper urgently in his ear, 'Connor's gang work for Kidpower and Crud pays them to cause bother. Stick around and you'll see how it works.'

He expected her to stay and watch too, but after a quick glance over her shoulder she backed away from him. He shouted after her but she'd disappeared into the crowd. It was now raining heavily and his sweatshirt was soaking and sticking to his skin. He wrapped his arms round his chest, uncertain what to do next. He searched his pocket for his phone but it wasn't there. Earlier, when Girl didn't turn up, he'd thought of ringing his pa but he would still be angry. So he'd rung Dr K instead, but she didn't answer.

Now his was way out was blocked in one direction by the demonstrators and by Connor's gang in the other. He peered round the corner of the shop entrance to find an escape route and recognised an old woman standing in the middle of the street trying to calm her dog. She lived a couple of houses away from them in Salterton Avenue and often stood outside her doorway swearing at Micki when he passed. He hoped the old bitch was getting very wet. Then he saw Connor strutting towards her, waving his arms like a celebrity as he shouted orders at his gang.

The youths spread out around him. They surrounded the old woman and their boots went in.

Her scream was sharp and shrill, followed by another.

Micki instinctively stepped towards her. He didn't like the old woman but she didn't deserve the kicking she was getting. The dog had run off.

Connor grabbed the woman's shopping bag and slammed it into her face, knocking her flat as she tried to get to her feet. The others joined in, kicking her as she lay prostrate on the ground.

Micki stood under the street lamp, unable to move. The demonstrators had reached The Parade and were coming closer to him. Then Connor broke away from the rest of the gang and pointed at him. Micki backed into the doorway again as the crowd moved in; he could read the words 'Migrant Workers Out' and 'Send Them Home' on their placards. Then Dr K pushed her way through the crowd towards him and he gave a great sigh of relief.

Suddenly Connor darted back to the old woman, shouting and prodding her – but gently this time. Then, just as quickly, he straightened up and pointed straight at Micki. 'There he is. That's the bastard what did it. It's one of them foreigners. He mugged her and left her for dead.'

# 36

The demonstrators started to move in on him. Micki dodged around the nearest two gang members and charged round to the back of the shops searching desperately for somewhere to hide. Nothing, only a pile of old cardboard boxes stacked up against the six-foot-high brick wall. Micki had seen Connor and the gang use these as makeshift seating when they were dealing drugs. He jumped on top of the boxes and felt them slide away under his feet. But they provided enough lift for him to grab the top of the wall, lever his legs over and drop to the ground below.

Except for tearing his hands on the razor wire on the top of the wall, he'd escaped injury. But from the advancing shouts of the mob, it wouldn't be long before they reached his side of the wall. For a moment he thought of waiting to tell them it was Connor and his gang that hurt the old lady – not him. Dr K would back him up, if she was with them. But as he heard dogs barking, and the shouting getting louder, he couldn't take the chance that they would take any notice of her either.

He ran away from Salterton Road towards the building site his pa worked on. At first he thought he was getting away. He was a good runner and fitter than most of the braying crowd behind him. Then he stumbled over some old tyres and slipped in the mud. His hands hurt so much it was hard to push himself back onto his feet. He set off again but his legs felt heavy and he knew he was slowing down.

He thought he'd escaped them when he reached the building site. Then he heard the squeal of tyres and a convoy of cars stopped abruptly on the road just yards away from him.

He looked up beyond the crowd to the darkening sky and thought of Mama telling him to be brave when he'd visited her at the hospital. 'Why, Mama? Why do they hate me? What have I ever done to them?'

No point thinking of that now. Micki knew where the gaps were in the perimeter fence and there were plenty of places to hide on the other side. He was soon inside and sprinting through stacks of bricks and cement blocks, past the huts where he'd sometimes took Luca his lunch. There was scaffolding ahead of him. He'd been up the scaffolding before with Daz. It was a bit scary but easy to climb.

Something shot past his head, making him lose his grip on the iron rail - one of their banners, alight with orange flames. Another missile landed by the side of the hut next to him and flames started to lick up its side. It was followed by a torrent of burning banners. The demonstrators were inside the perimeter fence. They were coming towards him. No choice now, he had to carry on.

The metal was slippery from the rain and hard to grip because of the pain in his hand. The smoke from the hut, which was now well alight, was rising up around him making him choke.

Don't look down, he told himself. Keep on climbing.

At the top of the scaffolding, the wind was stronger. It was a struggle to hold on.

When he did look down there were fires everywhere lighting up the ground and illuminating the mob below screaming and shaking the scaffolding. He held on tight and closed his eyes. Something hit him at the back of his head and he nearly lost his grip.

He tried to block out what was happening. Think of Mama. Was she watching him now? She'd been so brave and he wanted to be like her but he wasn't.

His rain-soaked jeans suddenly felt hot between his legs where he'd wet himself and he felt disgusted and useless. No wonder Girl preferred Connor. He opened his eyes to look down at the mob but couldn't recognise anyone. There was no sign of Dr K and if Girl was there she would be disgusted with his cowardice. He'd told her he didn't mind the taunting and name calling, that he was tough and could take it. But as he looked down on the distorted faces screaming for him to jump, he knew it wasn't true. He didn't want to admit it, but she must have known what was going to happen – always at Connor's beck and call.

He wanted to forget about being brave and be back in Krishta with Misha playing under his feet and Opi baking. He closed his eyes again and thought of Mama - if only she hadn't died. I'm sorry, Mama. I'm not brave like you. I can't take it any more.

He released his grip on the scaffolding, enjoying a second of exhilaration before plummeting towards the ground a long way below.

# 37

At first Kate didn't recognise the body half buried by sand on the ground directly ahead of her. She had been hit in the leg by a missile which had made her lose sight of Micki, and only the sudden roar, then a mighty cheer coming from the direction of a building site, had drawn her on. An excited crowd was standing round looking down at something and, as she dashed forward, a man in the crowd ran alongside her and kicked the body in the head. Kate lashed out at him, feeling a satisfying crunch as her fist made contact with his face. Then, when she recognised the body, she wanted to keep smashing the man's face but someone behind her grabbed her arms and she was thrown down in the mud beside Micki.

He was lying face down with his legs splayed out at an unnatural angle. Blood was spreading out around his head and mixing with the sand. She crawled between the spectators' legs to get closer and put her hand on the side of his neck. It was warm but she could feel no pulse. She bent over him but there was no hint of him breathing. His legs were bent backwards and his arms were weighed down with sand. She tilted back his head, covering his mouth with her own. She tried breathing in hard and watching for movement. There was no response.

'Come on, come on.' She pumped his chest. Hands trying to pull her away but she kept going, pumping to the rhythm of 'Keeping Alive'. Micki's eyes were open, staring, registering nothing. Onlookers were taking photos on their mobiles. Nobody offered to help. Then she was pushed out of the way and someone else took over. Someone who knew what he was doing. Luca. Kate watched his frantic rhythmical movements and knew it was hopeless.

\*

Demonstrations in Ladram Heights were becoming so common place that nobody at the police station took them very seriously. Jacqui looked up with surprise as her uniform colleagues limped into the locker room looking and smelling like they'd returned from a nuclear attack. She often took refuge in the locker room to write up her notes: it was the best place to avoid interruptions from her sarcastic boss. The new case she was working on was complicated and she needed some thinking time. The victim's family were alleging their three month old baby had been injured by burglars. Jacqui wasn't convinced. They said the baby had been left outside in her pram while her father watched the football match on television. After Exeter City had won, he'd 'popped down' the road to celebrate with his mate and his wife had returned from shopping to find the house ransacked and the baby with a broken arm, exhausted from screaming. There were no forensic traces of anyone other than the parents near the baby and only their fingerprints and DNA on the pram. They were both being cagey about their movements when interviewed.

Loud voices in the corridor invaded her quiet space which was filing up with uniform lads looking blood smeared and dirty. One of them nodded his gratitude as she moved aside to let him sit down. From his riot gear he must have come straight in from the demonstration and looked exhausted.

'That bad?'

'It's all getting out of hand. My sergeant sent us back to get cleaned up and send out more back up. An old woman's got mugged up there. One of those migrant workers apparently, and she's ended up critical in hospital. The mass mobsters of Ladram Heights are having a field day. You can forget your paperwork; all hands are needed on deck.'

She didn't respond immediately. Last time she'd got geared up and trundled out to a so called riot they had all dispersed except for a couple of drunken teenager girls squabbling over a boyfriend.

The uniform guy she'd given up her seat for smelt of petrol and was bleeding all over the locker room floor. She reached up into her locker for her first aid kit and tried to stop the bleeding from the gash on his hand with some thick dressing.

'What's the matter with your leg?'

He looked pleased with her interest and she realised how young he was. 'Bottle bomb. I didn't lower my shield in time. The dam flames went right up my leg. Hurts like hell.'

His bravado didn't fool her; from the way he was swaying he could collapse at any moment. She gave him her best smile, 'You need some medical attention.'

'You offering?'

Jacqui shook her head. Was he flirting with her? She was nearly old enough to be his mother. Still, she couldn't help smiling as she knelt down in front of him to look at his injury. Then wished she hadn't. The fabric from his trouser leg had melted into the flesh.

She was grateful when the police surgeon arrived and moved her out of the way.

'Hospital for you,' he told the young officer, 'there's an ambulance on its way.' Then to Jacqui, 'I think you're needed out on the streets.'

By the time she got outside to the car park all the police vans had left, so she had to drive to Salterton Avenue in her own car. When she arrived the riot was far from over. Besides the usual chants of 'Immo's out' and the stamping feet, women and children were screaming and running out of the way of bricks and metal missiles. The demonstration had turned into a riot.

She looked around trying to decide what to do. Most of the other cops had gone ahead of her in police vehicles, one of which had been turned on its side and set alight in the middle of the road. She was separated from her colleagues by a barricade of burning cars but could see that beyond it they had formed a defensive line to try and stop the progress of the mob. It seemed to be working and as she secured her protective vest the message came over her radio that reinforcements were needed at an incident at the building site. There was no way she was going to get there by car.

She started making her way through the crowd when someone grabbed her arm.

'You're a police officer aren't you? You've got to stop them. They're going to kill him and it wasn't his fault.'

Before Jacqui could ask what she meant, two burly demonstrators pushed between the two of them. The woman started shoving back, determined to keep Jacqui's attention. 'You've got to stop them.'

She saw the demonstrator raise his baseball bat and bring it down hard into the woman's face. Jacqui had to choose between chasing the youth or helping the woman who had stumbled over and was now in danger of being trampled by the crowd. But before she bent down to help the woman, she did manage to capture the assailant and a good view of the dragon tattoos on his neck on her helmet camera - then call an ambulance.

The woman was getting weaker and closing her eyes. Jacqui was relieved to hear the siren of an approaching ambulance as the injured woman's hands felt very cold. She was telling her she would soon be at the hospital when the ambulance drove straight past them. It had a police escort and she jumped up to stop one of the cars. The officer slowed down to tell her the ambulance was needed for someone who'd fallen from some scaffolding but there was another ambulance right behind. He'd driven off before she could argue.

# 38

Kate stared after the ambulance. Luca had got in with his son and the ambulance had driven them away, its siren blaring. She didn't notice Jacqui at first, and when she did, all she could say was, 'It's far too late,' but Jacqui seemed to understand how she was feeling without the need to explain and took her to a rundown pub smelling of cigarettes where she bought her a brandy – then took her back to Elaine's.

When they arrived at Hawke Towers Kate wanted Jacqui to stay, but Elaine dismissed her like she was a supermarket delivery person and led Kate into the drawing room. All she could do was stare ahead of her, it was as if she was functioning in someone else's body. It felt completely different from when Dad died. She hadn't believed that he'd gone at first. When she woke in the mornings, she expected to see him until her rational self took over and she remembered what death meant - but with Micki it was all too real. A young life cut short. She would never see his cheeky grin again or hear him call her Dr K. When she'd first heard that her father hadn't made it she was paralysed with grief - now she felt a deep and resigned sort of sadness and couldn't stop reliving the last few moments before she'd found Micki's body - the smell of burning, the sound of the vengeful crowd, the thrust of elbows in her side, fists in her face and the look of hate on the faces of everyone around her as they looked on at Micki's body like foxhunters at a kill.

The sound of a door opening brought her back to the present. She hadn't noticed Elaine leaving the room but now she was coming in with a tray of tea.

'Nothing can hurt you while you're with me,' Elaine said, putting down the tray and taking Kate into her arms.

It felt good to be held and Kate gave in to her grief as tears flowed out of her. When Elaine released her, Kate looked towards the door and saw Ian Ross standing looking at her.

He handed her a cup. 'I was with Elaine at the police station when we heard you were caught up in the riot. Do you want to talk about it?'

Kate shook her head. The last thing she wanted to do was relive the experience.

He nodded, then turned on the television news. An old woman's face filled the screen before the camera switched to the studio where Ian Ross was on camera. She looked up at his face which was full of a smug admiration.

Elaine picked up the remote. 'I'm not sure Kate wants to see this.'

But Kate was interested in Ross's reaction and said, 'Leave it.'

On screen, Ian Ross was saying, 'Mrs Renton had no connection with the demonstrators. She was just in the wrong place at the wrong time. She was struck a number of times then forced to the ground where she was kicked. It was a vicious and cowardly attack. Her shopping bag was found near to where she fell and her purse was missing, believed stolen. She sustained a number of serious injuries and is recovering in hospital ...'

The reporter interrupted him. 'Were other people injured in the riot?'

'My officers were fully engaged dealing with the rioters. The protest had become violent - residents were caught up in it, cars overturned and the emergency services firebombed. Several police officers were hurt and some members of the public were also injured and are being treated in hospital. The only fatality was the young man believed to have been Mrs Renton's attacker. It seems his callous attack of a defenceless old lady in front of so many demonstrators seems to have sparked a reaction of community anger.'

'What!' Kate shrieked. 'But that wasn't Micki!'

The televised Ross went on, 'We are still trying to find out what happened and would ask anyone who saw the attack on Mrs Renton or the incident at the building site to contact Ladram Heights police on 0140 ...'

She leapt to her feet to confront the real Ian Ross, spilling the tea. 'How dare you accuse Micki of attacking the old lady? Community anger! He didn't do it. It was just an excuse to hound an innocent boy to his death. Mrs Renton was attacked by the gang that tried to rape Danuta – then they blamed Micki. It's them you should be investigating – not Micki.'

A view of the Ladram Heights estate filled the screen, the strapline underneath reading 'Mugger dies after chase by demonstrators'. The

170

camera focused back on the reporter with his coat collar turned up against the rain. The crowd were giving him a difficult time and it was hard to hear him over the noise of their shouting. The camera panned round showing some kids mooning in the background. 'As you can see, feelings are running high here. Local residents are horrified by what happened.'

Then, turning to the youth standing beside him, 'This man witnessed the attack on the woman.' He offered him his microphone. 'Tell us what you saw.'

The camera zoomed in on the ring leader of the gang who had accused Micki. There was no mistaking the purple hair - he was the same hooligan she'd caught on her phone video attempting to rape the waitress in the cafe.

'Yeah, it was frightening. That immigrant barged into the old girl and knocked her to the ground, started kicking her all over, then took her bag. We tried to stop him but he was too quick for us.'

The reporter said, 'It's been suggested that the protesters gave chase and threw burning banners at him, causing him to fall.'

'Nah. They just had him cornered and were waiting for the police. He must have slipped. It's sad but he got what he deserved.'

'Well, thank you very much ...'

Kate grabbed Ian Ross's arm. 'That's completely wrong. It didn't happen like that. I was there. That yob was one of the gang that attacked Mrs Renton. He tried to rape a waitress in the cafe – you've got it on video. Why the hell haven't you arrested him?'

Ian Ross snatched his arm away as Elaine tried to guide her back to the sofa but not before Kate caught the look of surprise on his face. She shook off Elaine's hand and searched for her iPhone. 'Here, I'll show you.' But however many times she scrolled through the video clips on her phone she couldn't find it.

Elaine placed her hand back on Kate's arm, 'You've had a terrible shock and you need to rest for now. I've got some pills upstairs that'll help you sleep.'

Kate studied Elaine's face and thought she looked unusually flustered. Right now, Kate had as much as she could take of Elaine's Good Samaritan act. The woman was right, she did feel shaky. But not so much that she wasn't fit to start looking for somewhere else to live, first thing in the morning.

# 39

It felt strange returning to the office. So much seemed to have happened since Kate was last there. She paused outside the meeting room to collect her thoughts; they were a long way from anything on Jake's agenda for the team briefing. She was still furious with Ian Ross for blaming Micki for Mrs Renton's mugging and doing nothing to find his or her dad's killers. Then there was Jake. She wasn't looking forward to seeing him again. They hadn't met since Elaine's party but she'd spotted his Porsche outside Hawke Towers last thing at night and first thing in the morning enough to know there was something going on between him and Elaine. She felt guilty about neglecting the anti-migrant research. After Micki's death the research was even more important and she wanted to get back to work on it, as a kind of memorial to Micki. And she was feeling suffocated by Elaine and her exaggerated concern about Kate's welfare, waking her with her breakfast and insisting Kate took her bloody pills.

She heard the news coverage as soon as she entered the room. All the team where crowding round the television screen. Ginny moved aside to make room for her to squeeze in next to her. 'Have you heard what happened in Ladram Heights last night?'

Kate nodded. Denise, noticing her arrival, said, 'Apparently, the boy who died was one of the Kidpower youngsters, so he was probably a bit of a rogue.'

The TV coverage changed to show a photograph of Micki in a smart school uniform with his collar fastened and his striped tie in a perfect knot. He looked younger than Kate remembered. Instead of the eager schoolboy on the screen, Kate saw his distorted body lying in the sand. She shut her eyes but the image was still there.

When she opened them again, Denise was holding the TV control and had turned off the television.

Ginny broke the silence. 'You knew him, didn't you - the boy who died? Wasn't he the boy you rescued from those bullies?'

Kate nodded.

'That's so awful. He looks such a nice young lad. They're saying he was driven to his death by mob violence.' She looked closer at Kate. 'Are you sure you're all right? You don't look it.'

She swallowed hard before replying. 'That's right. Micki Hamereski. He was bullied a lot at school for being foreign. He was a smashing kid - I was there when he died.'

She was aware that the whole team were still looking at her, expecting more explanation.

'Sorry, I've had a shock. It was awful – sorry, I can't…'

'Well, take it easy today,' Denise interrupted, then raised her voice to include the others. 'OK, let's get on with our briefing.'

The other team members were already sitting down at the conference table. As usual, Ginny had arranged glasses and a water jug ready for their meeting and replaced the box of chocolate biscuits with a bowl of fruit. Documents for the team briefing were laid out in front of each chair. All Kate wanted was to get the meeting over with and felt irritated when a well-built young black guy burst into the office.

'Sorry I'm late, folks. The traffic through Ladram Heights is deadly. Some sort of protest going on, police cars and banners everywhere. I think it's to do with that poor kid who died yesterday. Emotions are high; the atmosphere in Ladram Heights is toxic. We can use it to our advantage? Isn't this just what we need to find out what's really happening?'

He stopped as he noticed Kate. Denise took the opportunity to explain, 'Kate Trevelyan, this is Leon Thomas, our new research assistant.'

'Wow! Dr Kate Trevelyan!' He grabbed her hand, pumping her arm for longer than necessary. 'I wondered when I'd meet you, you're the reason I've joined CCR. I've read all your research papers. I think your work's brilliant.' There was a time when Kate would have been flattered; now she just stood and stared back at him. It didn't seem to put Leon off. 'Jake said when you're better we can work together on the anti-migrant research.'

Everyone looked uncomfortable. Even Denise looked embarrassed. 'Well, you haven't discussed it with me, Leon, and this boy's death isn't going to help. Residents are reluctant to report anything to the police as it is, they're afraid of reprisals. All this is going to do is make them even more afraid to talk about the demonstrators.'

174

Leon wasn't going to be put off. 'I don't mean go in with clipboards and recorders. We'd need to be more subtle - the sort of research that Kate's done so successfully.'

Denise dismissed the idea immediately.

Leon looked expectantly at Kate for support but Denise hadn't finished. 'You're right, Kate has had some success in using undercover methods with sex workers or community activists. But it can be risky and it's not something Jake approves of.'

Leon wouldn't let the subject drop. 'What Jake wants is for us to get some results to send to the Home Office. I understand we are doing so badly, we're in danger of losing the contract.' He was so fired up he squeezed Denise's arms, 'It's a golden opportunity – a young migrant killed by demonstrators. We need to find out what's behind it.'

Kate didn't like the idea of treating Micki like a research specimen, she also knew how risky covert research could be and didn't want to encourage him. 'Your idea might work, Leon, but it takes months to set up and get approval from the ethics committee. And Denise is right, Jake doesn't like it. So however unsuccessful it seems we have to stick to the original research brief.'

Leon couldn't hide his disappointment. 'Well, it's still something I'd like to try.'

Before she could respond Jake strode into the office.

'I don't know about that – but you're asking the right questions, Leon.' He'd obviously been listening to their conversation. 'Denise is right, people will be more afraid but that means they will open up more, not less. That boy's death could provide a real breakthrough opportunity. At the moment we're in danger of missing it. We need to get out on the streets, talk to the demonstrators; get inside the homes. Kate, go and find the boy's parents, if he had any, and take Leon with you.'

How could she ever have thought Jake attractive, Kate thought. He was a stuck-up, egotistical prig who thought making money out of contracts was more important than people's feelings.

'The boy was called Micki and he has a loving father who will be absolutely distraught. There's no way I'm going in to trample on his emotions. Get real.'

Jake gave the familiar deep sigh that Kate was starting to hate and glared back at her. 'You've changed, Kate. You were always the first to grab an opportunity. Since when have you cared about other people's emotions if it served your purpose? We need to exploit this boy's death and if you can't handle it you'd better go back to the London office and crunch statistics.'

She was about to tell Jake he was being grossly unfair when Ginny leant across to him and said quietly, 'Kate knew the boy who died. He was helping with her research, and of course we can't go bursting in on his bereaved parents.'

It wasn't in Ginny's nature to contradict people and it took some guts to interrupt Jake. Kate was touched by her loyalty, she could usually take Jake's insults and give back as good as she got but seeing how upset Ginny was, she said nothing, just mouthed her thanks.

Jake was tapping his watch. 'We need to move on and reschedule the interview programme. Kate, you can finish your interviews with members of the local council. Denise get the police perspective on these demonstrations - how seriously are they taking them? How many arrests have they made and do they know what's behind it - and why Ladram Heights?' Then, turning to Leon said, 'You can have a go at finding some demonstrators to talk to, but do it by the book, no undercover stuff, OK?

'And Kate, you're upset, I guess that's understandable, but we can't let our feelings get in the way of making progress.'

Kate ignored his smile; it didn't work on her any more.

The silence was broken by a polite cough. 'I hope I'm not interrupting anything, but I wanted to see how Kate was.'

Elaine Pierce was standing in the doorway, looking cool in a stunning purple silk dress. Elaine glided over to Jake who rushed to offer her a chair.

She pushed it away with a smile. 'I'm not stopping. After Kate's dreadful experience I thought she might like to come out for lunch. Take her mind off the whole ghastly ordeal.'

Kate stared back, wondering how Elaine knew she'd be at the office, but Jake looked flustered. 'That's a very generous of you, Mrs Pierce. I'm sure we can manage without her for a couple of hours.'

He was rewarded with a brilliant smile. 'Thank you, I knew you were an understanding boss.' As she guided Kate towards the door she added, 'There's no need to be so formal, Professor Williamson - it's Elaine.

Remember?' With a confidence that confirmed what Kate had suspected about their relationship - but didn't care.

# 40

Elaine wanted to take her to Combe House Hotel but Kate wasn't hungry and knew she wouldn't be able to do justice to the expensive food served there. Instead she insisted that they walked to the Esplanade and settled for a sandwich in Duke's pub. Kate didn't touch the sandwich but the wine spritzer suited her fine. She was relieved to be out of the office and away from Jake. Her feelings towards him were in turmoil. She'd been furious with him for his crass remarks about Micki and had no desire to continue with their occasional sexy nights, but she still didn't like the thought of him and Elaine being together.

The barman placed their drinks in front of them. Elaine said, 'I couldn't help overhearing your discussion with Professor Williamson. He seemed rather insensitive. Has he no idea what you have just gone through? Witnessing a violent death and mob hostility so soon after the death of your father. You needed rescuing.'

'No,' Kate said, sipping her spritzer, 'my emotions may be a bit shaken, but rescuing - no way.' Her emotions were all over the place, but Elaine was the last person she'd turn to for sympathy. She thought back to the first time they'd met. The way Elaine had smooched up to her dad, all smiles and understanding. After taking another gulp of her drink she said, 'Jake's always been good to me and he's really helped build my career. He's one of the best researchers I know, and he's effective and ruthless when it comes to competing for contracts and funding. But sensitivity isn't one of his strengths, as I'm sure you've found out.'

Elaine smiled.

'So how do I feel now?' Kate continued, 'I'm not so sure. I still admire him. But you're right, I was upset by his callous remarks about Micki. All he cares about is exploiting the situation to benefit our research.'

'Have you thought that, professionally, he might be right?'

Kate gripped the stem of her wineglass so hard it was in danger of snapping. 'At university you're taught to be objective, to regard your research population as subjects with behaviour to investigate. But objectivity is an ideal; it's impossible to reach. Researchers are shaped by their values and social experiences as much as their subjects. We can't escape what's going on inside our heads. Or at least, I can't. Micki wasn't a research subject. He was a sweet, caring boy trying to get his head round becoming an adolescent – and trying to understand why so many people hated him. Jake seems to find it easy to turn him into a statistic.'

'Maybe he finds it as hard as you do. He's just been doing it for longer and knows what works?'

'I don't think so.' Kate took another sip of her drink, swirling it round her mouth and enjoying its sharpness against her tongue. She hadn't wanted to lunch with Elaine but the more she talked, the better she felt.

Elaine asked if she wanted another drink. Kate was starting to feel the effects of the first one on an empty stomach and hesitated. Elaine said reassuringly, 'It's only a spritzer, and I won't let you have more than two.'

'I'd better not. I'm driving up to London to see Nan.' But when Elaine ordered two large glasses of spritzer and pushed one towards her, she didn't protest. As Elaine withdrew her hand, Kate noticed the scar tissue at the back of her wrist. She reached across to Elaine's arm, 'Suicide attempt?'

Elaine snatched her arm away, 'Oh that, bad times in a toxic place. I was young – it's a reminder to never to go back there again.'

She was studying Kate intently. 'How are you really doing? You've had a lousy time. The deaths of two people you were close to must be very hard to deal with.'

'I'm probably not coping as well as I think.' Kate sighed, 'The hollowness I felt every morning when I woke and remembered Dad was dead was starting to ease off. I really liked Micki. He must have been terrified - I know I was scared.' Thinking about him made the image of Micki's broken body appear in her line of vision. Kate blinked hard, 'He tried to ring me before he was chased by the mob but I was driving and didn't have a signal. I should have been there for him. Now I've failed them both.' Kate found she was blinking back tears.

Elaine passed her a handkerchief. 'You haven't failed anyone. It just feels like it at the moment. You're a loving, caring daughter and friend. What about your grandmother, would talking to her help?'

She'd been so caught up in what was happening to Micki she'd almost forgotten about Nan. 'Yes, I'm sure she can. Last time I visited, the doctor said she was making a remarkable recovery. They're arranging for her to convalesce in Westfield Nursing Home in Sidmouth. I'll be able to see her every day soon.' As she said the words she felt that things would start to feel better once Nan was close by.

Elaine raised her glass and said, 'Well, let's drink to your Nan's recovery.'

*

Jake arrives almost as soon as I call him and sweeps down to kiss my cheek, then sits down on the chair Kate has just vacated placing his beer on the table. The movement is accompanied by a waft of aftershave. He wasn't wearing any at the office this morning – I'm pleased he's made the effort to impress me.

'You wanted to see me? I hope it's important, I've got a busy afternoon.'

Kate is right; he's not in a very good mood.

The remains of the scowl remain on his lips but his grey eyes stare back at me. I lean forward and slip the straps of my dress further off my shoulders. His eyes flicker down to my cleavage and linger on my erect nipples that I know are obvious beneath the thin silk of my dress. I wait to see what he has to say. Will it be personal or business?

He leans back in his chair and looks back towards the entrance, 'I saw Kate as she was leaving. She looks awful. Her father's death has affected her badly.'

I'm glad he thinks so. 'Yes, she's not holding up very well, I'm afraid.'

'You're worried about Kate too?'

'I think she's having a breakdown. It's not surprising. First the death of her father and then that boy she was getting close to.'

He takes another sip of beer before replying, 'She's probably not at her best at the moment but she's one of our top criminologists. The one who sees beyond the obvious and spots the connections the rest of us miss. She'll come round.'

He seems a lot more sympathetic than Kate gives him credit for. Does Professor Williamson have feelings for her or is she just another commodity like his research subjects? It's time to find out. 'I've been reading up on her work. Her track record is impressive. But it's sometimes controversial; she takes risks and sometimes people around her get hurt. I wouldn't want that to happen in Ladram Heights.'

He glances coolly back at me. 'It won't.'

Maybe I need a different approach? This isn't the whole hearted agreement I was expecting from Jake. He goes on the defensive when his professional judgement is being challenged. Somehow I don't think sex appeal is going to work – time to try coercion.

'I hope you're right.' I say.

'Dr Trevelyan may be an eminent criminologist, although there wasn't much evidence of it at the Business Forum she attended at Pierce Enterprises, but she seems to have lost her way, interfering in things outside her jurisdiction. The police investigation into her father's death for example, insisting there's been foul play when there clearly hasn't. I am worried about her state of mind and how that might affect the research, which as you know I sponsor as well as the Government. Her headaches and blackouts are getting worse, she has panic attacks that make her incapable of making decisions – then there's her delusions, she sees dead people and animals where there are none. I think she's becoming a liability.'

'You think I should take her off the work?'

'I think Kate needs to be referred to a psychiatrist.'

He jerks back as if I'd hit him. 'That bad?'

This is better. 'It's not bad at all. She just needs the right treatment. I can recognise what she's going through. I know a bit about psychiatric treatment.'

He's thinking over the significance of what I've just told him before he replies, 'Kate's very headstrong. She won't take any notice of anything that I suggest.'

He's just confirmed my assessment of him - weak.

'Let me make it easier for you. You are the CEO of CCR and the person ultimately responsible for this research work in Ladram Heights - and I am a woman with a great deal of influence and friends in high places. As the Chairwoman of the Devon Business Forum, I have received lot of complaints about Kate's work. New businesses about to move to the new business park here are threatening to pull out. She's already upset too many people. If she continues to work on this research I will withdraw my support for your work. You might find that the current small germ on CCR's reputation turns into an organisational epidemic – one that kills your whole organisation. If you don't take action soon to dismiss Dr Trevelyan, it won't only be *her* career that goes down the toilet.'

# 41

Nan was looking forward to transferring to Devon, she told Kate. The nurses had recommended Westfield Nursing Home and she'd booked a place for a week's time. Kate was relieved to see the colour had returned to Nan's face and she was full of conversation, wanting to tell her all the gossip about the nurses' private lives and other patients' medical conditions. Much more like the Nan she remembered. Kate didn't want to dampen her good mood or hamper her grandmother's recovery, so she decided to postpone a conversation about her father's and Micki's deaths until Nan had moved to Sidmouth.

On the drive back to Devon, Kate had the car roof down and sang along to her favourite Queen songs. They'd been Dad's favourites too. Knowing that Nan would be nearby soon had given her strength and a new-found determination to get her life back under her control. She was starting to find Elaine's constant surveillance stifling and had decided it was time to move out of Elaine's place as soon as possible, find whoever had set fire to Brathcol and bring the gang responsible for Micki's death to justice. So she drove on, past the turning to Hawke Towers, to Ladram Heights Police Station, where she was pleased to find that Jacqui Sunday could see her straight away.

'You got my messages then?' Jacqui asked as she arrived in the interview room with two coffees.

'No, I've been driving back from London,' Kate replied as she scrambled through her bag for her mobile, 'and I've had my phone turned off.'

Jacqui shrugged. 'That's OK. You're here now so I can tell you in person. We're opening the investigation into your father's death again. So I'm back as your FLO - that's if you'll have me.'

Jacqui held up both hands to show Kate her crossed fingers. However angry Kate had been after her visit to the Coroner's office it felt good to be on speaking terms with the policewoman again. 'The investigation into Dad's death is live again?'

'Yes.' Jacqui looked rueful. 'But I'd understand if you haven't got much faith in us. I know you were upset when I couldn't produce the Fire Inspector's Report or tell Vera Thomas much about the fire.'

'Doesn't matter,' Kate interrupted. 'Why the change of heart?'

'Well, partly because we messed up. But mostly because Vera Thomas rang to say the tox report was back and showed your father had a suspiciously large amount of Restoril in his system.'

'What!' Kate knew her father was supposed to be taking it for his anxieties about the troubles at Ladram Heights Community School, Vera Thomas had told her as much, but she went cold at the thought that he might have been so distressed that he'd overdosed and she'd never even noticed he was worried about anything.

'That's not all,' Jacqui was keen to tell her. 'Our analyst got the forensic team to check your father's shed again and they found evidence of a cat being butchered there, just like you said. I'm sorry I doubted you.'

Kate was still trying to make sense of everything Jacqui was telling her. 'So there is forensic evidence to prove the fire was started deliberately?'

'They found traces of ethyl acetate. It's an accelerant used in the pharmaceutical industry. It also takes the caffeine out of coffee. We're not sure what that means yet but we are checking to see if it's used locally.'

Kate was thinking of Derek Droney's suspicion that Kidpower was somehow behind the fire. 'So not the accelerant of choice by your everyday arsonist?'

'No, not easy to come by, apparently.'

'And all that stuff Vera Thomas was on about involving my dad's state of mind? Is that still relevant?'

Jacqui looked embarrassed. 'Well, your dad was being given a bad time by some of the kids' parents. But I think Vera overdid the significance of it. She thinks so too now.'

Jacqui paused, then said, 'I tried to get hold of you at Elaine Pierce's place. You're still staying there?'

'Yes, but I'm hoping to move.'

Jacqui grinned. 'Too posh for you?'

Kate smiled back. 'She keeps trying to mother me. I just want to have some space and time alone.'

As they drank their coffees Jacqui asked Kate what she was going to do about finding somewhere to stay.

'Well, Nan's coming to Devon next week. They've found her a place in a nursing home in Sidmouth. Maybe I could hole up there?'

Jacqui laughed. 'You think an old folks' place would keep you out of trouble?'

Kate shrugged. She hadn't given any thought to where to stay and as it was the May Bank Holiday weekend everywhere would be booked up.

'I think I can help you out,' Jacqui said, grabbing her car keys. 'My brother is the manager of the Belmont Hotel. Let's go and see if he's on duty.'

Jacqui drove her to Hawke Towers to collect her things. Kate was relieved when Elaine's housekeeper told her Mrs Pierce was in London for the day. Jacqui's brother was behind the reception desk when they got back to Sidmouth and managed to find Kate a room. It was waiting for refurbishment and looked out on to dustbins but she didn't care. She told him she'd be back to check in soon for an early night, then accompanied Jacqui back to her car.

But as they approached the car park someone called out, 'Kate!' It was the journalist, Derek Droney, leaning across his E-Type Jaguar smoking. His face was alight with excitement until he saw Jacqui. He studiedly ignored her as he muttered urgently, 'You've got to come with me, Kate. You're going to want to hear this.'

'Is this man being a nuisance?' Jacqui asked Kate stepping between Kate and Derek.

Kate looked hard at Derek before replying, 'Not really. I think he's harmless.'

'I should bloody well hope so,' he said looking hurt.

Jacqui smiled and said, 'Mr Droney and I go back a bit. He kept trying to spin me fabricated stories about the intrigue and mayhem in Ladram Heights when I first arrived here.'

'A journalist has to have something to write about and quotes are always needed. Especially from a detective sergeant from the Met.'

Jacqui ignored the comment and turned to Kate, 'If you're sure you'll come to no harm, I'll leave you to it. A bit of excitement is probably just what you need. Forget the early night.'

Derek opened the passenger door of his Jaguar. Kate cleared all the empty plastic boxes of convenience food away from the car seat and sat down, 'Where exactly are we going?'

'We're following DS Sunday back to Ladram Heights Police Station.'

*

Derek found them a couple of seats at the back of the briefing room which was already full of journalists. He'd refused to tell her any more during the short and bumpy drive from Sidmouth in his ancient E-Type. Derek seemed to know everyone and was busy catching up with other journalists. Kate scanned the room. There were a couple of TV cameras and she recognised Simon Hall, the West Country's crime correspondent. She was trying to look over the heads of the chattering journalists for a better view when Derek poked her in the ribs.

'The fun's about to start,' he shouted in her ear. 'I know your father was interested in the lad that died and I think his death has got something to do with Kidpower.'

'You mean the gang that did the mugging were from Kidpower?'

He winked back at her. 'You'll see.'

The talking subsided as Chief Superintendent Ross strode out from a side door, accompanied by a frizzy-haired grey-suited woman carrying a number of files. They took their places on the platform at the front of the room.

Ian Ross smiled and acknowledged a couple of the journalists on the front seats; the woman with him whispered something in his ear and he nodded and adjusted his microphone.

'Welcome, ladies and gentlemen. This morning's conference concerns an incident that occurred in Ladram Heights two days ago. We're seeking your readers' help in establishing what exactly happened.'

A couple of flashbulbs went off around Kate as she strained to get a better view. A few journalists had already started to shout out questions.

Ian Ross's confident voice rang out above their heads. 'I'm glad you are so interested but please hold your questions while I outline what we know so far. At around nineteen hundred hours last Wednesday, a number of people assembled in the centre of Ladram Heights for a peaceful protest about the employment of migrant workers. The demonstration was hijacked by unscrupulous trouble makers. While my officers were occupied dealing with the riot, an eighty-three-year old lady called Gladys Renton was knocked to the ground and her handbag stolen. The crowd chased the assumed assailant, Micki Hamereski, who ran off into the new development site at the edge of Ladram Heights. He climbed up scaffolding to escape the crowd but lost his footing and fell. He was declared dead on arrival at the Royal Devon and Exeter Hospital.'

A flurry of hands went up all round Kate but she could hardly see them for the anger burning inside her. 'That's so wrong,' she shouted, despite Derek's instructions to her to sit quietly and listen.

Ian Ross's statement had prompted a number of questions so that apart from Derek no one took any notice of her. 'Kate, I told you to listen. Remember that or you'll get us both thrown out.'

'But it's not true! Micki didn't assault Mrs Renton. It was a gang of teenagers. They started the hue and cry after Micki. They were part of the crowd that drove him to his death. I tried to stop them but no one took any notice.'

She started to feel dizzy. The hubbub of the shouting journalists had become, to Kate, the roar of the mob that night. She was back inside the riot, trying to find Micki. All around she could smell rubber and wooden pallets burning. She started to rise from her chair, desperate to get outside and was held up by Derek. 'You're sure about that?' he was asking. 'Micki didn't do the mugging?'

Kate nodded, trying to make sense of what was happening to her. Derek raised his hand and waved a rolled-up copy of the Ladram Heights Gazette violently enough to make the journalists around him move smartly out of the way, 'Over here, Chief Superintendent.'

Ian Ross picked him out. 'Oh yes! Mr Droney, our local Ladram Heights correspondent. We're honoured by your presence.' The comment caused a ripple of laughter at Derek's expense.

Derek seemed unperturbed. 'You say this boy Micki was the one that assaulted and robbed the old lady, but I have a witness who was there and says Micki Hamereski was innocent. That in fact he was the subject of mob violence incited by the real muggers. And despite the many police in attendance, they did nothing whatsoever to stop it.'

Derek had got into his stride now and Kate kept her head down, hoping that Ian Ross wouldn't notice her sitting next to him. 'It seems that not only have the police screwed up again, but they are blackening the name of an innocent young boy who came over to this country for a better life.'

The response to this from the other journalists was so loud Kate couldn't hear Ian Ross's reply. There were shouts of 'Disgraceful!' and 'Shame!' Ian Ross turned and spoke urgently to the lady with the frizzy hair who was struggling to pack up her files.

At last the uproar subsided and Ian Ross made himself heard. 'If Mr Droney is right, this witness should come forward and talk to us immediately.'

'They may be too scared,' interjected a stylish woman next to one of the TV crews. 'What were the police doing to allow a demonstration of this sort in the first place? Sounds like you could have prevented this boy's death if you'd had acted properly.'

Ian Ross was starting to look strained and started to pack up the papers in front of him. Journalists were pushing forward with their microphones as he stood up to leave.

'Thank you, ladies and gentlemen. That will be all for now. I would just like to repeat if any witnesses can give us more details of what happened in connection with the mugging of Gladys Renton and the death of Micki Hamereski, we would like to hear from them.' Then he was gone, leaving the door swinging behind him.

Kate forced herself to stand and push her way through the throng of journalists out of the conference room. How could Ian Ross denounce Micki so publically as if there was no room for doubt? He obviously didn't believe what she'd told him at Elaine's, now she had to convince him Micki was innocent.

The way to his office was blocked by a security door. She reached it just as a young police officer in uniform arrived, carrying a tray of tea. Kate smiled, she might have a splitting headache but she could still recognise an opportunity, and held out her hands for the tray.

'Here, let me take that for you. Is it for Chief Superintendent Ross?'

The young officer looked awkward and slopped some of the tea before passing the tray to Kate, while he keyed in the security code then held the door open for them both to go through.

'It's so nice to meet someone with manners,' she said, then headed down the corridor to Ian Ross's office.

A bulldoggish personal assistant was sitting in the outer office and dismissed Kate's request to see her boss.

'Leave the tea here,' she instructed. 'Chief Superintendent Ross is far too busy for unexpected visitors.'

'Tell him it's the witness who caused the fuss downstairs in the press conference and if he doesn't come straight out I'm going back down to give some interviews.'

The woman looked flustered, uncertain what to do next. Ian Ross, who had obviously heard their exchange, came out of his office, looking surprised when he saw who had been speaking. 'Kate, what a pleasure. Please come in.'

She followed him inside where he gestured for her to sit down. 'You've looked better, are you OK?'.

'I'm fine,' she snapped back, selecting the chair the furthest away from him.

'What can I do for you?'

'It's more what I can do for the Ladram Heights police to stop them tarnishing the reputation of a dead thirteen-year-old, before the tabloids get hold of the details of your incompetence.'

'Oh that? You made your views quite plain last night.'

She didn't think he was taking her seriously yet. 'For the last two days your officers have been issuing statements accusing Micki Hamereski of assaulting and robbing Mrs Renton, and implying that he got what he deserved. He was an innocent victim who actually went to help her. You should be looking for the gang members who carried out the assault and then blamed Micki. They encouraged the crowd to chase him. Although they didn't take much encouraging, seeing as he's a foreigner.'

'So you're the witness Derek Droney was talking about?' The boyish smile had gone but at least she had his attention now.

'Yes, I saw it happen. I was looking for Micki because his father thought he might be hurt by the demonstrators. Turns out I was right.'

'I didn't take you seriously Kate because you were in shock and when you tried to show me a video that you'd taken on your phone of the gang members who had mugged Mrs Renton, you couldn't find it. Are you

189

sure you're thinking straight?' His tone was no longer friendly. 'This Micki was one of your father's protégés, wasn't he?'

Kate felt the room spinning around her. The stabbing pain in her head was getting worse. She groped inside her handbag for her migraine tablets and was relieved to find the new full pack that Elaine had collected for her from the chemist. Now she had to get out of Ian Ross's office so he didn't see her take one.

# 42

I'm parked outside the Royal Free reluctantly; anything to do with hospitals gives me the creeps. When Ross rang last night to tell me how Kate strode into his office demanding justice for Micki Hamereski or she's going to the national press, I couldn't leave it any longer. Just as well I've destroyed the video of that stupid idiot Connor's attempt to rape the waitress. His obsession with appearing on the media is becoming a liability; always searching for new TV moments to post on YouTube. I did consider giving Ross Kate's video and letting him arrest the little shit. But it's too big a risk. At first I thought he'd stolen my camera, the one I keep for my special sex parties, to put them on You-Tube. But when I looked at the security cameras I saw the boy had taken it. Surely not for his own gratification, someone else must be behind it. And just in case it was Lyndon, I'm feeding morsels of information about him to Ross.

As for Kate Trevelyan, she's too stubborn for her own good, insisting it was time for her to move out. The little bitch had already booked a room at the Belmont. That's very foolish; she doesn't seem to recognise how ill she is. She could hardly see straight last night but she insisted on packing. Just as well I collected her migraine tablets for her before she left. She's going to get a lot sicker.

So here I am in the hospital reception to visit a patient. Before I go to see her I ring to check that the she is awake and ready for visitors. They tell me Mrs Trevelyan is in a private room on the second floor. This place is as bad as I expected, with its entrance hall lined with wheelchairs and zimmer frames and smelling of disinfectant and old people's ailments. But the private rooms are well away from the communal areas. That's so much more convenient. An old dear in a faded dressing gown shuffles past and I move on quickly following the signs for women's orthopaedics. I don't want to be remembered. I look into the communal lounge where residents are watching Pointless. There's a faint aroma of boiled cabbage and mothballs in the room. I continue up to the second floor, stopping occasionally to make way for patients with walking frames or porters pushing trolleys. Then finally, I'm outside her room where a woman in a blue nurse's uniform is coming out of the door carrying a bedpan covered in a white cloth. So the patient inside is still bedridden.

Let's hope the old lady isn't so gaga she's forgotten me. She's lolled over to the side with an oxygen tube half in her mouth. She seems to be asleep. I have time to check her chart at the end of the bed. She's on plenty of medication but I can't see any lying around. The nurses must dish it out.

I've bought her favourite flowers. When she opens her eyes I'll give them to her before I tell her why I'm here. Let's see if she remembers the last occasion we met - how her insistence on having those highly polished floors caused me to fall and fracture my wrist. How that might never have happened if she hadn't made me carry her huge vases of hydrangeas and treated me like her skivvy. That was years ago, but the wrist still keeps me awake at night. It's never healed properly.

She moans and rolls on to her side. She's going to need a little encouragement to wake up so I throw the flowers across her bed, scattering their blue petals and leaving splash marks on the hospital green bedcover. She groans and opens her bleary eyes.

When she sees me she jerks away, dislodging the catheter from her scrawny arm. Blood trickles out from the hole it leaves behind as she tries to reach across for the red panic button.

'Don't worry, Nan,' I say, 'we are quite alone.'

# 43

Maurice Denman, influential chairman of the Centre for Criminal Research, was waiting for Kate in Jake's office accompanied by a smartly-dressed young woman of Indian origin she didn't recognise. Jake sat in the far corner, refusing to look at her. There were copies of the Ladram Heights Gazette spread out on his desk. Kate got on well with Maurice Denman. She liked his no-nonsense way of handling things. If the Ladram Heights research needed a boost, she had every confidence he would provide it.

Maurice gestured towards the Indian woman, 'Kate, this is Dr Santos.'

The woman held out a cold hand and Kate shook it reluctantly, then looked back at Maurice. 'I'm sorry I wasn't here when you arrived.' She'd slept in longer than intended and put it down to the comfort of the bed at the Belmont Hotel and the absence of Elaine bringing her an early morning cup of tea.

It was Maurice who replied, 'I understand you've been having a bad time and I'm very sorry about your father's death. I hear you are taking it badly. That's why I've asked Dr Santos to see if she can offer any help.'

This wasn't what she expected at all. 'I'm not in need of a doctor,' she snapped back.

'Kate,' Maurice cautioned, 'none of us know how grief will affect us.' He took hold of her arm. She shook his hand away. 'Your work has suffered. You've ignored Jake's advice to take some time off to grieve.'

'That's what I keep telling her,' Jake interrupted.

Maurice glared at him. 'So why did you do nothing about it when the complaints started coming in?' Jake turned and stared out of the window obviously still annoyed with her.

Maurice was looking uncomfortable. 'You are one of our top criminologists, Kate, but your usual standard of research has deteriorated alarmingly. You've missed appointments, left your colleagues to cover for you and behaved in a manner that brings discredit to our company.' He pointed to her photograph on the front of the newspaper. 'But giving confidential information about one of our backers to the press is unforgivable, especially when it's not true.' Kate stood transfixed, trying to take in what Maurice was saying and snatched up the newspaper. The headline read '*Business magnate responsible for local riots.*' She quickly scanned the article to find it quoted a Dr Kate Trevelyan who said the research being carried out by The Centre for Criminal Research showed beyond doubt that Pierce Enterprises' recruitment of migrant labour was the cause of the recent riots, fatalities and injuries in Ladram Heights.

She slammed the paper down on the desk. 'This isn't me. I never said that. I'd never say anything was beyond doubt.'

Maurice interrupted her, 'I've already had the Minister on the phone threatening to close all our contracts. When our competition hears about it we may never get another Government contract again. You know that's what keeps us in business.'

'I said it wasn't me.'

'Look, why don't you and Dr Santos go somewhere you can talk in private? Jake and I are going to re-allocate your work. He's been worried about you.'

Now she could see Jake for what he was - her most enthusiastic supporter when she was a success, but now she was in trouble he couldn't ditch her quickly enough. She strode over to the window where he was standing and said, 'I am perfectly fine. There's no need for you to re-allocate anything.' She did think a lot of the content of article was true but she'd never tell that to a journalist. How could anyone, especially Jake, believe she'd disclosed confidential information to the media?

Maurice's usually benign face looked strained. 'That was an instruction. For the sake of everyone else in the office I'm telling you to take some time off. Go back to the Belmont Hotel where I believe you're staying and take Dr Santos with you. I'll come round later and we'll decide what to do about this.'

This time she didn't resist as Dr Santos took her arm and guided her out of the office, past the other members of her team and out to the street below. Too many things were happening to her that she didn't understand but she'd never betray a confidence. She knew it would ruin her career.

*

They walked to the Belmont Hotel in silence. Kate could sense Dr Santos wanted to talk but she ignored her. The shock of the last hour had

194

cleared her head and her doubts about her competence were disappearing fast. Someone had leaked that information about Pierce Enterprises to the press and it wasn't her. She would ring Derek Droney as soon as she could to find out what was going on.

Inside her bedroom she was stunned to see her wardrobe was open and empty; her clothes and personal possessions were missing. The calm exterior she'd been trying to put on for Dr Santos was disappearing fast.

'Is something wrong, Kate?' The psychiatrist was standing in the open doorway watching Kate's frantic search for her possessions.

'My clothes have gone. Someone's been in my room.' She looked behind the bed and she saw her overnight bag was bulging; further examination showed it was all packed and ready to go.

'I asked the maid to pack your things. Mr Denman has booked you in to my clinic while you recover from your anxiety problems.'

Just as she started pulling everything out of her overnight bag and putting it back in the cupboard, Maurice Denman entered the room. She swung round to face him, a crumpled pair of pyjama bottoms in her hand.

'Kate, you need to calm down. First the fire destroying your home and killing your father, then being swept along by a mob to witness that poor boy's death. It's not surprising you're suffering from stress. It's nothing to be ashamed off.' He tried to guide her to an armchair in the corner of the bedroom, whilst Dr Santos started to repack her bag.

Kate brushed past him and snatched her bag back. 'I'm as calm as anyone who found that someone had been rifling through their possessions.'

Dr Santos turned round with one of Kate's silk shirts still in her hand. 'I think we should get you to my clinic as quickly as possible.' She handed the garment back to Kate. 'Of course, if you'd prefer to pack yourself ...'

They were interrupted by a knock at the door and Jacqui Sunday walked in and flashed her identity card. She pushed past Dr Santos and went over to Maurice Denman. 'Ginny told me what's been happening. I think you're in danger of over-reacting. True, Kate has been under a lot of pressure but she's used to it, if what I've heard about her is correct. I think she seems to be coping.'

Maurice gave her the sort of look he reserved for waitresses who brought him the wrong sort of tea. 'You're an expert in mental health, are you?'

'I've worked with a lot of bereaved people who've managed fine without any medical intervention. I'd say this is more about punishing Kate for what's happened to your company's recent failures. You want to turn her into a scapegoat.'

Maurice screwed up his face. 'Her recent behaviour is all the justification I need. But you're right, CCR isn't doing so well at the moment and I won't let Kate Trevelyan ruin it completely.'

But Jacqui wasn't finished. 'I may not be an expert in mental health but I know about the law. You can't take Kate to a psychiatric clinic against her will unless you get her sectioned.'

Maurice turned his back on Jacqui but looked ruffled. 'It's your choice, Kate. Either you go to the clinic with Dr Santos and get the treatment which I think you need - and I'm willing to pay for - or I will terminate your contract at CCR.'

All the highs of working for the Centre flashed through her mind. The excitement of finding something new and significant, trips abroad, recognition at conferences, the media accolades, the admiration of colleagues like Leon. The friendships she'd made with people like Ginny and being close to Jake. She'd worked so hard to build up her career and now it was crumbling at her feet. Then she thought of her dad, looking forward to her visits that she failed to make. And Micki, who she could have helped more.

She squared up to Maurice. 'In that case it's easy. I'm just starting to recognise what's important in my life and it's not CCR.' She started tipping everything out of her overnight bag and mouthed a silent 'thank you' to Jacqui, who was holding the door open for Maurice and Dr Santos's departure.

As the bedroom door slammed behind them Jacqui said, 'Good for you,'

Kate grinned back. 'I may be homeless and jobless but it's a lovely day out there. How about going down to the beach to get an ice cream? I think we have a lot to catch up on.'

# 44

Jacqui couldn't remember the last time she'd been sunbathing, but lying on Sidmouth's warm sand, the tang of seaweed in her nose, listening to the lapping of the waves, she promised herself she'd do it more often. After all, what was the point of moving to the beautiful Devon coast and leaving all your friends and family behind in London if you never got to see the sea. Kate Trevelyan was making the most of the waves, jumping over the spray oblivious to how wet her skirt was getting. It was good to see her carefree and prancing around - such a contrast to the intense and angry Dr Trevelyan she'd met at the hospital after her father had died.

It felt good to be her Family Liaison Officer again. Jacqui was glad she'd been assertive and refused to comply with Chief Superintendent Ross's instruction to dismiss Kate as a trouble-making neurotic. She should have known when Kate rang to tell her about finding the dead cat and could hardly get her words out that she wasn't making it up. Then Jacqui'd followed it up and got the forensic team to re-examine Mr Trevelyan's shed. What a result - even Chief Inspector Ross had complimented her detective skills and she was assembling a growing dossier of evidence to prove that Trevelyan fire was arson and Kate's father's death was murder. She still hadn't worked out who had done it or why, although after her visit to Bill Brewster, the force analyst, she thought the Ladram Height gangs were the most likely suspects. And now Kate was no longer burdened with her urgent drive to find whoever was behind her dad's death. She seemed content to leave it to Jacqui.

Kate's mobile ringing interrupting her thoughts. Jacqui picked it up and headed for the water's edge so that Kate could answer it.

\*

'Dr Trevelyan?' Kate didn't recognise the voice. 'It's Nurse Bryant from the Royal Free Hospital. It's about your grandmother. I'm sorry to tell you Mrs Trevelyan's had a stroke.'

Kate's new found feeling of happiness vanished. She grabbed her bag and started running to her car. 'I'll be there straight away.' Please God, she prayed, keep her alive. Don't let Nan die too.

As she reached her car the familiar aura of a migraine was starting up. She rummaged through her bag for her car keys and felt relief when not only did she find those but also her migraine medication. She stopped off at a roadside cafe to buy a bottle of water to wash down a double dose of tablets. She just hoped her vision was good enough to get her to London.

By the time she arrived at the hospital she could hardly see through the flashing dancing lights before her eyes and pulled over to the edge of the car park to be sick in the flower bed. She wasn't unduly worried; she knew the progression of her migraines. Once the pills kicked in the headache would go, she would regain full vision and soon be feeling fine.

Nurse Bryant was waiting for her by the entrance. She must have seen how white she was and asked if she wanted a glass of water.

'No, I just want to see my grandmother.'

'Follow me then.'

The corridor was very hot. It took all Kate's concentration to keep up with the nurse. As they passed the TV lounge the noise was deafening and Nurse Bryant asked if she'd mind waiting while she sorted it out. Kate just wanted to get to Nan. She felt dizzy and had to lean against the wall of the corridor to stay upright.

The music had turned into shouting. 'Kill the immo. Kill him. Kill him. Kill him.'

The sounds were ringing round her head. She couldn't see the ward entrance any more. People were crowding round her; she was being jostled and pushed and couldn't keep her balance. Acrid smoke filled her lungs so she couldn't breathe. The crowd were mainly men, shouting and jeering, their faces distorted with hate. However hard she dug her heels in to resist, she couldn't stop them dragging her with them. She knew she needed to get to the front of the crowd but she couldn't make her legs move. Then she was on the ground and angry feet were trampling over her. She recognised the thick sole and dark stained leather of builder's boots. Luca was standing above her, but she couldn't get her breath because his boots were pressing down, crushing her chest. She tried to tell him it wasn't her fault. The crowd had stopped jeering and in the gap through their legs she could see Micki lying in a pool of blood. His arms and legs were misshapen and there was just a black space were his face should have been.

*

When Kate opened her eyes, bright lights hurt her head. Strong arms were lifting her up and the dazzling lights were replaced by the medicinal green of a cotton tunic which smelled of sterilizing solution.

'Thank goodness you're back with us. You gave us a fright. Just sit there until you feel better.'

But as she recognised Nurse Bryant, she was already remembering. Nan had had a stroke and needed her. What was she doing sitting on the floor propped up by two nurses?

She started to get up and slipped back down again. The nurses helped her on to her feet. 'I've come to see my grandmother. Where is she?' The words felt like they were sticking in her mouth but they seemed to understand.

'Mrs Trevelyan's condition has stabilised. She's awake now,' Nurse Bryant told her. 'We are more concerned about you. Have you hurt yourself?'

'Is Nan better? Can she speak?' Kate didn't know much about strokes but she had expected to find her grandmother unconscious.

'She's doing really well now. But it's hard to make out what she's saying. Doctor's just examining her. Then you can go in as soon as you feel better.'

Kate stood up straight and saw that a cluster of patients in dressing gowns had gathered round and were watching her with interest. Kate felt stupid and desperate to see Nan. 'She's not dead?'

'Heavens no,' Nurse Bryant said. 'The stroke has left some side effects but nothing she can't recover from. We're more concerned about you. Sit down for a bit until the doctor's finished. You're as white as a bed sheet. You don't want to alarm your grandmother. She's still quite poorly.'

As soon as Kate saw the doctor coming out of Nan's room, she was up on her feet to ask him how Nan was.

'Mrs Trevelyan is making a good recovery but her mobility and speech are limited at the moment. You mustn't be too upset by her appearance. There's no reason to think she won't make a complete recovery.'

199

With Nurse Bryant keeping a steadying hand on her back, Kate went in to see her grandmother. Nan looked much worse than the last time she'd seen her. The left side of her face had slipped, leaving her mouth hanging open. There were tubes attached to both arms and her eyes were closed. Suddenly Kate experienced a sharp pain in her chest and she felt wobbly. She had to force her legs to carry her the last few yards to her bedside.

'Hallo, Nan.'

No response. She swallowed hard to drive back her tears and tried again. This time Nan opened her eyes but didn't seem to recognise her. Nurse Bryant came round behind her with a chair.

'She's a bit confused at the moment, but sit down and hold her hand. She'll know you're there.'

So Kate sat and held Nan's hand. It felt cold and brittle and nothing like the warm touch she associated with her grandmother. It was hot in the room and Kate felt like her whole body had gone through a giant wringer but at least her headache and all the visionary distortion seemed to have disappeared with her fall. She shuddered, remembering the images of Micki lying on the ground. The images had been so real.

Nan opened her eyes a couple of times but didn't seem to know she was there. After an hour Nurse Bryant came back again to check Nan's vital signs and administer an injection and told her visiting time was over and to come back tomorrow.

'You look all in, love. I don't think you should drive. There's a direct phone link to some taxi companies out in the entrance. Treat yourself to one and a train back to Devon and I'll ring our parking people and explain why you're leaving your car.'

Kate would usually have dismissed the idea as ridiculous but didn't have the energy to disagree. She kissed Nan goodbye and promised to be back to see her in the morning. Finding her way back to the main entrance seemed more hazardous than she remembered, with lots of trolleys and wheelchairs to avoid, but eventually she made it and managed to secure a taxi and catch the next train to Exeter.

*

The taxi from the station to Sidmouth was uncomfortably hot but her stomach felt like it was filled with ice. She'd never experienced such extreme symptoms before with her migraines and the tablets weren't helping. She felt very alone and couldn't shake off the image of Luca staring down at her in hatred. She felt an urgent need to see him again, to explain, to tell him how hard she'd tried to save Micki. That she would never forgive herself for failing him.

'I've changed my mind about going straight to the Belmont Hotel. There's someone I want to visit first,' she told the taxi driver. Someone who would be feeling more alone and far worse than she was. She gave him directions to Luca's house.

Salterton Avenue was no longer full of demonstrators but burnt-out cars remained on both sides of the road as a legacy of the riot.

The taxi driver looked uneasy when she asked him to wait outside. A large van was parked in the kerb and men were loading rucksacks and boxes into it. She hoped it didn't mean that Luca was returning to Poland.

A tanned young man with floppy blond hair asked, 'What do you want?' He didn't sound friendly.

'I'd like to see Luca, please.'

'You the police?'

'No. A friend.'

The expression on the young man's face hardened. He looked back at her with pure hatred in his eyes.

'He has no friends here. Especially white trash like you.' Each word was spoken like a weapon and Kate reeled back as if he'd hit her. 'You're one of them. One of those English bitches that drove Micki to his death.'

He pushed her back down the path and Kate felt her dizzyness returning as the shouts of the angry crowd were starting up again inside her head.

The driver was revving up his engine and she stumbled back into the taxi.

'They are a bad lot up here,' he said as he slammed the door shut behind her. She could just make out the driver's words before she blacked out.

# 45

It was getting late by the time the taxi arrived at the Belmont, although Kate wouldn't have known except for the driver shaking her hard to wake her up. Her head hurt like hell and she had difficulty finding her purse to pay him. In the end she'd thrust the purse at him and told him to take whatever was owed. He returned her purse and insisted on getting someone from the hotel reception to escort her to her bedroom. She guessed she must have looked as bad as she felt because the receptionist kept fussing around, wanting to call a doctor.

In the solitude of her room she drew the curtains, poured a gin and tonic from the fridge and swilled down three more migraine tablets. The tablets must have worked because when she next woke the room was dark. Her headache had gone but she still felt groggy. She lay on the bed with closed eyes trying to get back to sleep but memories of the last few days kept stealing back, together with an overwhelming sense of guilt. Everyone she cared about was dead or dying, and the career she loved was over. What was there to live for?

She couldn't stop these negative thoughts. She needed to know why Dad and Micki died and if she could have done anything to prevent their deaths. She felt if she could work this out, maybe Nan would pull through.

Thinking she'd go mad if she stayed in her room a minute longer, she made her way downstairs and out of the hotel. It wasn't as late as she thought. With no plan of action she followed a group of men down to the beach where the sea lapped against the rocky walkway. The men took off their jackets and sat on the rocks laughing and passing round cans of beer. As Kate walked past them she thought one looked familiar but in her present muddle-headed state she didn't bother to look back. She expected the images of riots, broken bodies or dead cats to come back. Living seemed pointless, so she carried on walking into the sea.

For some reason she thought of Virginia Woolf and how she filled her pockets with stones to make sure she drowned. There were plenty of stones below her feet but she couldn't reach them. She gave in to the buoyancy of the sea and let her body drift. It felt safe and protected. Then suddenly strong arms took hold of her and pulled her roughly back towards the shore. As the moonlight lit up his face she recognised Ian Ross.

His friends gathered round them and someone draped a jacket round her shaking shoulders. He guided her towards a beach hut, unlocked the door and hunted for some towels. She stood in the entrance staring at him as he closed the door. Then he started to remove her wet clothes.

He held her to his wet body for warmth and she was aware of a tingling sensation spreading through her body. He pressed his thighs hard against her and his touch seemed to burn through her skin. They stood wrapped together for what seemed a long time. Then he kissed her hard on her mouth. He tasted of beer and seawater. She didn't want to return the kiss but the impulses of her body had taken over. Their hands were all over each other. She couldn't wait to get his clothes off. He kissed her breasts and sucked her nipples but she just wanted him inside her and pushed him back against the wall, forcing his hips down towards hers, guiding him in. He picked her up and she was riding him like a wild animal. She heard someone screaming and realised it was her. She was oblivious of what he wanted from her. She just needed to get through it.

Then it was over.

Thrusting him away, she sank to the ground. She was wet and sticky from damp salt and semen and the sand from the floor stuck to her body. The musky smell of him was strong on her fingers as she tried to wipe away the tears that seemed to be pouring down her face. He tried to touch her. She recoiled, slapping his hand away.

He threw on his wet clothes and left her huddled in a corner until daylight crept under the door. No amount of sea water could wash away her loathing of what she'd just done.

# 46

The red cliffs of the Jurassic coastline looked amazing from Kate's sun lounger as she took in the view from Elaine Pierce's yacht. They were sailing towards Lulworth Cove and the outline of Dundle Door rock looked like a dinosaur sipping the shimmering sea. It was a glorious day; baking hot but with enough wind and sea swell to power the yacht and provide some respite from the heat. She'd always loved sailing and had cruised this coast many times with her father. She'd loved their fishing trips together even though he'd tease her for refusing to remove the hooks from any unlucky fish that she caught. She didn't think much about him these days. In fact, she hardly felt any emotion at all. Occasionally she tried to think about why he was killed, then more memories from her childhood came back. They weren't especially happy ones, apart from the fishing trips.

Kate didn't think much about anything now. Elaine took care of everything and Kate was happy to exist in the sealed bubble she thought was caused by the extra-strong migraine tablets Elaine had obtained from her doctor. If Elaine wanted to organise her life for her, it was fine by her.

The tranquillity of the moment was shattered by the sound of the table scraping against the polished wooden deck and a familiar male voice saying. 'Sorry to interrupt your sunbathing, but lunch is ready.'

Kate sat up abruptly and had to scramble to retrieve the top of her bikini and tie it back in place before swinging round to face Ian Ross. His suntan stood out against his white trunks and his bare arms glistened with sweat as he carried a tray loaded with tempting-looking savouries of smoked salmon on brioche, mini cheese flans and sushi, which he set down on to the table next to her. Kate looked round and noticed Elaine watching them.

Ian Ross was the last person she wanted to meet. She hadn't seen him since the night in the beach hut, and she'd no idea he would be joining them on the cruise. But she wasn't going to let his presence spoil her day. He divided the savoury delicacies onto three plates, then poured some wine from a cooler into a tall stemmed glass and handed one to Elaine and one to Kate, which she knocked back in a couple of gulps. He passed her a plate of food which she waved away. The memory of their last meeting was seared on her brain.

Elaine took a long sip of her drink and said, 'Are you sure you won't have something to eat, Kate? I can recommend anything Ian gets his hands on. He seems to know what all the ladies like.'

'Well, maybe I will.' Kate said, snatching both the plate he was holding out to her and the wine bottle from him and pouring herself another drink.

Kate rearranged the savouries on her plate and tried to work out if Ross had told Elaine about dragging her from the sea and their sex together.

Elaine threw an ice cube at him. He grinned and took some more food across to her and then pulled up a sunbed besides Kate. 'How is your grandmother getting on? Elaine said she was in the Westfield Nursing Home recovering from a stroke.'

After the tense atmosphere between them, it was a relief to have a conversation. 'Hard to say, I haven't seen her for some time. But I think she's a long way off recovering fully.'

Ian Ross looked genuinely concerned. 'I'm so sorry. She hasn't recovered any speech or mobility yet.'

Elaine answered for her, 'Kate's been so ill recently she hasn't been able to visit so I've been going instead.'

'Do they know what caused the stroke?' he asked Kate, offering her more food. 'Was it anything to do with your father's death?'

'It's hard to say.' She stared intently at Elaine's sombre face. 'Dad's death didn't seem to affect her recovery from the hip operation. The doctor at the hospital thought it had been brought on by a shock of some kind.'

'Maybe she fell?' Elaine suggested.

But Kate wasn't going to miss the chance to get back at Ross. 'She was very worried about the fire, though, and it didn't help to be told there were no suspicious circumstances when there obviously were. Or for her dead son to be accused of starting the fire himself.'

He had the grace to look embarrassed. 'Yes, I'm sorry you were both misled. We're making better progress with our investigation now.'

'Any suspects yet?' Elaine asked, as she topped up her sun lotion.

'Or any links to Kidpower?' Kate found herself asking. She glanced at both Elaine and Ian Ross to check their reactions.

'I hope you're not still jumping to conclusions again like you did with Connor O'Brian. You know he's dead I suppose. Looks like he was taking part in some kind of sexual ritual in a brothel in Exeter that went wrong.'

'Children, that's enough,' Elaine chided, her cobalt toenails shimmered as she stretched her tanned legs out along her sunbed. 'That's enough shop talk. Poor Ian will think he's back at the police station.'

Kate shuddered and fell silent thinking that Micki would never get his justice now. Then she stood up and poured out two more glasses of wine, handing one to Elaine. She was pleased to see Ross's look of annoyance.

After downing a large gulp of Chablis and moving next to where Elaine was lying, she said, 'It must be amazing to own a yacht like this. Does Pierce Enterprises have a nautical arm?'

'Not yet. It's got nearly everything else,' Ian Ross replied.

'Really? What sort of everything?'

'He's joking,' Elaine put in, 'but we're not doing badly. We do nearly everything now from development of sites like Ladram Heights to producing fair trade decaffeinated tea and coffee.'

Kate looked hard at the elegant woman lying next to her. Something Elaine had said sparked a half formed memory. She thought it was important but couldn't remember why. As a cloud moved over the sun and the wind quickened, Ross squeezed between them and told Elaine they needed to get moving again if they were to reach their Exmouth mooring before low tide.

They were soon underway. With the sun directly overhead, together with the wine and all the food she'd consumed, Kate felt sleepy. She dragged her sunbed closer to the guard rail so that the spray caught her face. She wanted to stay there forever looking out at the sea; it was hypnotic. Then she felt the warmth of a hand pressing down on her back.

'You're looking a bit red, Kate,' Elaine said. 'Lie back and I'll put some sun cream on.' Kate didn't have much choice but obey. 'You're not still thinking what happened to Micki was your fault because he was probably out there looking for you.'

The pressure from Elaine's hands was getting harder, pushing her back down into the sunbed with more force than was necessary, making her wince. She was about to protest when Elaine bent down and whispered in her ear. 'And you mustn't think that not going to see your grandmother was why she had her stroke, or that putting your work and your social life before your father had anything to do with his mental state that caused the fire at Brathcol.' Kate sat bolt upright. It was as if Elaine was reading her thoughts.

'Good,' Elaine said, moving back to stretch out on her sunbed. 'I'm glad because you know what Philip Larkin said about parents fucking you up. I think that's true.'

Kate didn't know what Elaine was talking about. She recognised the famous line from Philip Larkin's poem but neither Dad nor Nan had ever fucked her up, as Elaine put it.

'Don't look so alarmed. They say we never really know our parents and sometimes it takes a major tragedy like a fire and a death before we realise it.' The sky was clouding over and a swift breeze ripped through the pages of the magazines lying on the decking.

Kate said, 'I think I'll go back down and get changed.'

Elaine smiled. 'Look, there's the Cobb at Lyme Regis. We'll be back at our moorings and then Hawke Towers before you know it.'

# 47

Kate was in the kitchen at Hawke Towers making some coffee when the security buzzer went off. She didn't usually check the monitor and opened the gates to visitors, but the security room with the screens was next to the kitchen so she went in to see who was calling. Jacqui was waiting by the gates, holding out her identity badge. It seemed ages since she'd seen her, so Kate went to let her in.

Elaine arrived at the front door at the same time that Kate did and pushed her to one side whilst she opened the door to their visitor.

Jacqui flashed her identity card again. 'DS Sunday, ma'am. I've come to see Dr Trevelyan.'

Elaine stepped in front of Kate as if to shield her. 'Dr Trevelyan is still recovering. You'll have to come back later?'

Jacqui pushed her way inside. 'Sorry, Ms Pierce. I need Dr Trevelyan to come with me to the police station to help with our enquiries into possible fraud at The Centre for Criminal Research.' Elaine looked about to protest, 'Don't worry, I'll make sure she gets back safely.'

In the car, she turned to Kate. 'Let's get you away from here and go for a drink. I've been wondering how you were.'

Kate was confused by Jacqui's appearance and surprised that Elaine had let her go outside Hawke Tower. That hadn't been permitted since she'd arrived back two weeks ago. 'Aren't I being arrested?'

'Oh, that. I just said it in case Ms Pierce wouldn't let you come out.'

'I'm surprised she did. She almost had me convinced I was an invalid. I was getting flashbacks of the riot and my migraines were becoming more extreme - I've really deteriorated since I went back to live there. I think it was the pills she gave me, so I've stopped taking them.'

'Good for you.' Jacqui said, slowing the car. 'I think we've got a lot to talk about - can you face the Clock Tower Café?'

Kate soon found herself back at Micki's favourite cafe where the waiting staff, including Danuta, crowded round her; even Derek Droney was there.

Over an excellent cappuccino Jacqui explained why they had all been worried about her. 'Even Jake rang me to ask if you were OK. My brother at the Belmont told me how an elegant woman in a Ferrari kept calling round to see you. He was worried because you'd been spending all day in your room and looked awful. He felt better when the elegant woman said she was taking you home to look after, but no-one knew where you'd gone.'

'I couldn't understand it.' Derek cut in. 'You'd been fine at the press call about Micki. When Jacqui came round to The Gazette to ask if I'd seen you I couldn't believe you'd gone missing. Fortunately, I was able to use my superior detective skills,' he said grinning at Jacqui, 'Well, some of the extensive network of useful men I've met since I joined Fathers4Justice.' He put his hand up to stem Jacqui's question. 'Don't ask. Anyhow, turns out one of them reads electricity meters.'

'So I sent him off with a photograph of you and a list of likely places to try and find you.' Jacqui added.

'Yeh, he saw you in the garden at Elaine Pierce's pile.'

Kate looked from one to the other of them, touched by their eagerness to find her. 'Great to see you've become such good friends. Who'd have thought it?'

'Yeh,' Derek said, 'And who'd have thought that confident sassy young woman who I met outside that burning wreck of her father's would become an invalid who needed looking after in less than three weeks.'

Kate was trying to take in what they were telling her. She'd felt vague and exhausted when she was at Hawke Towers and was always forgetting things, even the rawness of her grief had been subdued by Elaine's medication.

'The flashbacks were getting worse, along with the headaches. I kept blacking out - so I took the pills. They didn't help but it was easier to do as Elaine said. So I did. But however vague I felt the memory of Micki's death was always with me, and it made me angry. It was about the only emotion I was capable of feeling. Elaine couldn't see it. But it was enough to make me strong enough to start hiding the pills she gave me.'

She reached out to put one arm around each of them and pulled them close. 'Thank you for rescuing me.'

They sat in silence drinking their coffee. Memories of the time since her father's death were coming back to Kate. She pulled away from them panicking and said, 'What about Nan. I haven't seen her. She's moved to the nursing home at Sidmouth but Elaine wouldn't let me see her. She went instead.'

'Your grandmother is fine,' Jacqui reassured her. 'I called round at the Westfield Nursing Home to try and find where you were. She's a still a bit confused and wondered why you'd deserted her, but she's improving no end.'

That was all Kate needed to hear. She got up to leave.

'Hey, not so fast,' Derek said. 'If you need a lift I'll take you round to see her.'

'Better if I go,' Jacqui said, finishing her coffee. 'Afterwards I'll show you your new room at the Belmont.'

\*

Nan gave Kate a lopsided smile. The plastic tubes and oxygen feed had been removed. Her mouth drooped at the corner but otherwise she looked like the Nan Kate loved and thought she'd lost. She sat next to her, holding her frail hand and chastising herself for leaving her for so long.

'You look so much better.'

She waited for Nan to reply and thought she said she was better. But it was hard to tell.

'I'll talk, you just listen,' she said as Nan gave her a half smile.

She told Nan she was sorry that she hadn't been to see her but she'd been ill. She talked about her childhood in Devon and the summers she'd spent with Nan in Bermuda, knowing that memories could help stroke patients recover. Nan pressed her hand occasionally to show she was remembering too.

A care assistant came over to Kate. 'We were told you'd been ill and couldn't visit. Your grandmother was worried, but it's great you're better. You've made her day now.'

It was only three hours since she'd left Elaine's and already Kate was starting to feel more normal. Thoughts were crowding in on her, but she welcomed them. So much better than the empty zombie-like state she'd existed in before. She felt alive again but she didn't want to tire the old lady. As she bent over to kiss her goodbye, Nan mumbled something and

Kate looked up at the care worker to see if she could help her understand what her grandmother was trying to say.

'Is it the letter? The one from the school? You wanted to show it to Kate?'

Kate was impressed with the way she made sense of Nan's faltering speech and saw from the way her grandmother relaxed back into her pillows that the care assistant was right.

The nurse took an envelope from the locker drawer. 'I know she wants you to see this. A woman from the community school brought it in.'

Kate took the letter out of the envelope and skimmed through its content. It was an invitation to a memorial service for her father at the Ladram Heights Community School - and it was happening later that afternoon.

She looked at her grandmother. 'Nan, would you like me to go?'

Nan moved her head and said something about Kate's father that she couldn't understand.

The care assistant helped out again. 'I think she wants you to say something, a eulogy for your father.'

Kate reached for Nan's hand. 'Of course I will. I'll come back tomorrow and tell you all about it.'

Jacqui was waiting for her outside the ward. She dropped her off at the school after Kate had handed over the migraine pills Elaine had given her, to have them analysed.

Clusters of school children and teachers were already making their way into the school hall when Kate arrived. She followed them inside, looking around and thinking of all the days her father must have spent in here.

A small woman in rimless glasses came over and held out her hand. 'You must be Kate Trevelyan, Terence's daughter. I'm so glad you could make it.'

Kate confirmed who she was and was introduced to some of the other members of staff. She felt very awkward as they mostly looked embarrassed to meet her or avoided looking at her.

Ms Blundell glanced at her watch and indicated that Kate should go ahead of her to the front of the hall. 'I can tell you're Terence's daughter. You're just like the photo he kept in his office. He was very proud of you, my dear.' Then after checking that all the staff and students had arrived told her, 'His students will be so glad you came.'

Kate doubted that. From what she'd heard, some of them had made her father's life hell and the staff, including Ms Blundell, hadn't supported him either.

As they reached the stage Miss Blundell indicated where she should sit and handed her the order of ceremony. Kate tried to concentrate on thinking about what she was going to say but it was hard in front of a few hundred of her dad's students. Some of the student audience were starting to shuffle and she gazed out across the sea of heads, wondering if Micki's persecutors were sitting out there somewhere in front of her.

Miss Blundell stood up to explain the reason for the assembly and invited some teachers and students to come up on to the stage and say what they remembered about her father. Kate listened, hoping to learn more about her father's time at the community school, but their descriptions were insipid and could have been about anyone. It seemed he did his job as Head Teacher well, was liked by most of his students, but very little of what was said was personal or sounded like her father. As she'd expected, no mention was made of the pressure he'd been under, or any of the recent police raids or allegations of bullying. The students sitting in front of Kate were passing round sweets and chattering between bursts of giggling.

The whole event was turning out to be so disrespectful to Dad's memory. Kate was thinking it couldn't get much worse when Miss Blundell stood up and introduced her.

'We are privileged to have Mr Trevelyan's daughter, Dr Kate Trevelyan, with us. I'd like to end our memorial service by asking her to share some of her favourite memories of her father.'

Kate stood up and looked around. 'Thank you for giving me this opportunity to talk about my father. I loved him a lot. What else is there to say? Would he be delighted to see how you all remember him? I don't think so. Listening to you just now, I don't think you knew my father at all. He was a man who cared deeply for people, especially his students. He hated racism and bullying. No-one's mentioned that or how he tried to stop the hostility between students from different backgrounds that went on here on a daily basis. Or that some of you leaked spiteful allegations to the press about his alleged mismanagement.' She was feeling stronger now, boosted by the words she found she was saying.' I think Dad would have liked me say something about another recent death. Micki Hamereski was a student at this school. In the four months he was here, you made his life hell. With your constant teasing and bullying you found every opportunity to let him know how much foreigners are resented at Ladram Heights Community School. Terence Trevelyan was trying to stop this despicable behaviour, but it seems his efforts weren't supported by everyone, especially the staff.'

She stopped to let her words sink in.

'So I hope those of you responsible feel very guilty. If you really want to do something in Dad's memory - put a stop to this kind of persecution. I don't believe Micki was the only one to suffer. So do something now to help the living. It's too late for my father and Micki Hamereski.'

A couple of people started to clap but her words were mostly greeted with silence. Kate marched down the steps off the stage and made straight for the exit door without turning back. Behind her she heard a burst of chattering. She hoped she'd done justice to Dad and Micki's memory. She was starting to feel a lot better.

The thunder claps breaking through the humid late May weather seemed appropriate for her mood. Sharp pellets of hail bounced off her face as she ran down the drive to Jacqui's car.

'Wait!' Someone called out. Kate didn't recognise the voice and ran on. She was only a few metres from Jacqui when they called again. 'Dr K, don't go.'

For a moment she thought Micki was calling her and felt her heart racing. She swung round to see a small figure with purple and red striped hair plastered to her face. It was Girl. Kate ran towards her and held the girl as she burst into sobs.

When she got her breath back Girl said, 'What you said about Micki was true. It needed saying.'

Kate gave her a packet of soggy tissues. 'Thank you, but you might be the only person who thought so.'

Girl sniffed. 'I miss Micki a lot, he was fun, you know. I tried to be his friend.'

Kate struggled to think of some words of comfort. 'I know your friendship was important to him.'

Girl blew her nose and threw the packet of tissues on the floor. 'You're wrong. I was a cow. I let him down.' She started sobbing uncontrollably. Kate stood and waited, holding her close. Eventually Girl said, 'It was all my fault.'

'No, how could it be?' Kate protested.

'It was my fault he died. I didn't know what Connor was going to do. But I shouldn't have helped him.'

Confused, Kate asked, 'What shouldn't you have done?'

'Lead him on. Connor made me. He said ring Micki and get him to come to the shops. He said he'd beat me if I didn't.'

'Micki was set up?'

'Yeah, I think Connor was jealous 'cause I liked Micki. He was clever.'

'Come on,' Kate said, shivering from the rain, 'get in the car.'

But Girl pulled away. 'I got to go. I can't tell you any more - but it was her.' She wiped a sleeve across her face, gulped and went on, 'It was her, not him. Her that wanted Micki dead. Not Connor. He just did what she told him.' With that she took off across the car park.

'Wait,' Kate shouted after her, 'you'll get soaked. Get back in the car and we'll go to the police.' But Girl was running through the rain, already half way across the playing field, leaving Kate to make sense of what she'd just been told. She'd been certain that Connor was the cause of most of the trouble in Ladram Heights and that Lyndon Crud was almost certainly behind Connor. But Girl had been emphatic that Connor was controlled by a woman - and now he was dead.

# 48

Jacqui was still worried about Kate's safety. She dropped her off at The Belmont Hotel after the memorial service and sat in her car examining the packet of tablets Kate had given her. The label said *'Maxalt - to be taken at the start of a migraine attack. Do not exceed the dose of two a day.'* Jacqui googled Maxalt and found they were a genuine, if very strong, remedy for migraine but if taken too often had lots of side effects, including dizziness, chest pains, exhaustion and confusion – they could also make the original migraine symptoms much worse. So it would be hard to prove that Elaine Pierce had intended any harm by giving them to Kate.

She picked up her phone intending to ring Kate's doctor to find out why he'd changed the prescription but progress was halted by an incoming call from Derek Droney. He shared her concern about Kate and wanted to meet up to discuss it. Although, this time it had to be in a pub.

They settled for the Otter Inn and found a table in the far corner of the garden overlooking the river Otter. Jacqui went to get two beers and left Derek reading the information she'd found about ethyl acetate, the accelerant that was found in Terence Trevelyan's burnt out house.

'Looks like arson then?' Derek said after he'd downed most of his pint.

'It's looking that way. Apparently, it is hard to get hold of, which implies the fire was planned, but it's also been used in a number of similar house fires around Otterford'

'Any idea where it comes from?'

'Not yet.'

'Well, I have.' Derek's gold front tooth glinted in the evening sunshine. 'According to your notes it's used in the pharmaceutical industry and in the making of decaffeinated coffee. Now there's hundreds of pharmaceutical plants all over the UK, but not many coffee processing factories.'

Jacqui was following his logic, surprised that he was so methodological for a middle-aged local hack. 'Go on.' Derek picked up his empty glass and held it upside down indicating he was thirsty. Jacqui sighed, 'OK I'll get you a refill when you've told me what you're getting at.'

'The only factory that processes decaffeinated coffee round here is in Ladram Heights Business Park and it's a subsidiary of Pierce Enterprises.'

He held up his glass and Jacqui reluctantly went to get him a refill and a bottle of water for herself. There was no way she was matching Derek's capacity for alcohol, she didn't trust him that much.

Back at their table, Derek gulped down some more beer. 'So Terence Trevelyan was killed and his daughter held captive by the woman who had access to the accelerant that killed him.'

'That's a bit of a big leap.' Jacqui said. 'But it could be someone working for Elaine Pierce who killed her father, possibly under instructions.'

Derek tapped the side of his nose, 'I might be able to help you there. I've been investigating Kidpower and I think that young and recently dead tearaway Connor O'Brian may have something to do with it. I have a source who's been tipping me off about his illegal activities.'

'A source?'

'OK, a whistleblower, someone who knows what's going on both at Kidpower and with Pierce Enterprises. The point is, I've followed Connor to Heathrow where he regularly collected young migrant girls, then took them to private houses.'

'You mean people trafficking?' Jacqui said, her interest increasing.

'Just so. The girls are always taken to somewhere well out of Devon, but I wouldn't be surprised if some of Pierce Enterprises bulky builders don't get involved. Anyhow, if you want evidence, my whistleblower can provide it. But you can't have it until I've published my exposure.'

'That's a big scoop for The Ladram Heights Gazette.'

'I'm not planning to sell it to The Gazette.' Derek grinned back at her. 'Then there's another thing. I saw Connor outside Terence Trevelyan's house around the time of the fire.'

'We can hardly arrest someone who's dead.'

'Yeah, but if you do your job right it might lead you to who sent him to the airport and who's behind the trafficking.'

As Jacqui stood up to leave before Derek Droney persuaded her to buy him another drink he said, 'What about Kate?'

'I'm going to ask my cousin at The Belmont to look out for her, but there's not much more we can do. Maybe the best way to help her is to get whoever sent Connor to kill her father.' Jacqui hoped that would be enough.

*

When Kate arrived back at the Belmont she was exhausted and ready for an early night. The memorial service at the school had been upsetting and was reviving memories from her childhood of time spent with her father. And she still didn't know what to make of Girl's suggestion that a woman was behind Micki's killing. But when she collected her room key, the receptionist told her she had a visitor waiting in the lounge. She hoped it wasn't Jake or any of the research team. Since she'd been unceremoniously marched out of the CCR office she didn't think she could face them. But when she saw it was Luca waiting, her legs nearly gave way.

Kate was delighted to see him but was momentarily dumb. She wanted to commiserate, to tell him how grieved she was about Micki, but words didn't seem sufficient or perhaps necessary.

He saved her the trouble of speaking by moving towards her. 'I hope you don't mind me coming to find you.' Then paused as if he expected her to say she did.

In answer she hugged him to her and felt him slowly respond.

When she released him he said, 'I saw you the day you came to the house and Daz was so rude to you. I'm so sorry. I tried to catch you but by the time I got downstairs you'd gone.' She pulled at her earlobe with embarrassment as she remembered how she must have looked. 'I tried to find you at Mrs Pierce's house but she wouldn't talk to me, her maid said you'd left. Then tonight I went to the police station and saw DS Sunday and she told me you are staying here.'

He was fidgeting with the rolled-up newspaper in his hands and some of the pages fell onto the floor. They both bent to retrieve them and their heads nearly collided. He smelt of Imperial Leather soap. He was wearing a suit instead of the usual jeans which made him look older.

'I've come to ask a favour.'

Whatever it was, she knew she'd agree. 'Of course, anything.'

He smiled briefly. 'You don't know what it is yet.'

'I'll risk it, just ask me.'

'I've got to sort out Micki's things.' His shoulders sagged at the mention of his son's name and Kate's heart went out to him. 'There isn't much but I've been . . .'

She interrupted him in her eagerness to accept. 'Of course I'll help.'

'I've been putting it off. I need to do it soon, before I leave for Krakow.'

Her elation that was escalating by the sight of him was swept away by his last words. Of course he was going home. Why would he want to stay in a place that treated outsiders so despicably?

'When do you fly off?'

He gave her an apologetic look. 'Tomorrow.'

Biting back her bitter disappointment, she said, 'We'd better get started then.'

*

Micki's possessions lay in a corner of the bedroom. Luca had piled the mattresses and bedding that usually covered the floor into a heap in the middle of the room. Kate found returning to the hostel was bad enough. Now, looking at the few things which Micki had owned, she felt tears well up, but knew she mustn't cry for Luca's sake. But she couldn't help the swell of happiness sweeping over her at being in his company again. It was good to feel emotional again. Whatever Elaine had been giving her had made her into a zombie and now she was coming back to life.

She knelt down close to Luca and together they started sorting through Micki's things. Micki's clothes on top of the pile were in need of washing. She would have offered to wash them for him but there wasn't time. She'd no idea if they would be a comfort to Luca or his mother and daughter back in Krakow and didn't like to ask. All her father's things had been destroyed in the fire, and although she wished she could have salvaged something other than a few paintings, she was grateful not to have to deal with the disposal of his unwanted items like Luca had to do now.

Micki's collections of magazines and school books were underneath the clothes. She put them to one side, intending to throw away the magazines and return the books to Ladram Heights Community School after Luca had gone.

'What about this?' she said holding up a bunch of paper held together by an elastic band. At the front was a cover with 'Sara's Diary' written on it.

'I've never seen it before; perhaps it's a school project.' Then seeing her start to leaf through it Luca said, 'Would you like to keep it?'

Kate put it in her bag to read later. Luca stood up to stretch, then leant against the wall watching her. She could tell he was finding the task hard to bear and suggested he got some drinks as a distraction.

'Of course, I'm forgetting my manners. What would you like tea, coffee or a cold beer?'

She chose the beer and carried on looking through the diminishing pile of possessions. There were matchboxes filled with assorted things, foreign coins, dried up insects and rocks with ammonites. In one of them she found a strand of red and green tinged hair. Underneath all the matchboxes was a red Nikon camera wrapped in one of Micki's socks. Touching the lock of Girl's hair felt like an invasion of Micki's privacy, but she took it to give to Girl. It might make her feel better. Then disposing of the sock, she placed the camera to one side to give to Luca. It might have photos of Micki that he'd want to keep.

'I've found this.' Kate told Luca as he came back with two beers. She held up a turquoise silk scarf and a birthday card still in their packaging.

'Misha's birthday,' was all he said. Kate knew Misha was Micki's little sister. She rewrapped the scarf carefully in some tissue paper.

After they'd finished packing Micki's things, Luca said the least he could do was take her out for a meal before he flew and he hoped she would come to see him in Krakow.

# 49

Kate felt very alone after seeing Luca off at Exeter airport. She'd really enjoyed his company over the last twenty four hours but hadn't realised how much she'd miss him, especially as she was unlikely to ever see him again. They'd sat up talking until three in the morning when Luca kissed her and she hugged him close hoping he would stay. But after giving her a longing look, when she hoped he'd change his mind, he'd stood up and left, telling her he'd see her in the morning for their last morning together.

To take her mind off Luca's imminent departure after he'd gone she'd spent most of the night reading through Sara's diary. Sara seemed a fascinating character who obviously had a serious mental problem. But after reading through the progressively more incomprehensible entries, Kate still had no idea what the diary was doing among Micki's things. She hoped Girl could provide an answer.

So after leaving the airport Kate found she was driving Luca's hire car back to Ladram Heights to find Girl. Her quick visit to the community school turned out to be a waste of time. The reception staff said they were unable to help her without Girl's name. As she was leaving the building some of the kids hanging around in the entrance confirmed that Girl hadn't been seen at school since Micki died. Kate still had access to all the CCR search databases if only she knew Girl's proper name. She walked up the street following a stream of students and bought a packet of cigarettes, which she quickly exchanged for information. Girl was called Mathilda Murray. Back in her car, she soon tracked down Girl's address. After waiting outside her house for three quarters of an hour her patience paid off; Girl came swaggering down the street, earphones in position and singing out loud.

*

It felt right to bring Girl to the Clock Tower Café. Over toffee apple gateau and an extra large milkshake the young teenager started to relax. She told Kate about living with her dippy mother and her brothers from different dads, and how she wanted to be an artist but knew the best she could expect out of life was shop work, if she was lucky.

Kate had been waiting for the right time in the conversation to mention Micki. She'd brought Sara's diary with her as well as Micki's box with his memento of Girl's hair. After she'd told her about sorting out Micki's possessions, she gave her the box with the lock of her hair. Girl looked so sad.

'You mustn't feel bad about what happened to him.' Kate told her, 'It wasn't your fault. Connor made you do it, and from what you told me someone else was pulling his strings.'

Girl stirred the frothy bits left at the bottom of the glass with her straw and didn't answer. Eventually she whispered, 'I miss Connor. He might have been bad to me but I miss him.' Tears ran down her face. She went across to the wood carving that lined the walls of the cafe and ran her fingers along the dolphin's back. 'It was Micki's favourite. You can feel the love that went into making these,' she said.

Kate handed Girl a tissue and tried to change the subject. 'Ladram Heights wasn't built when I was growing up. What do you think of it?'

Girl gave Kate a scornful look as if she'd asked if she took her tea with strychnine. 'I hate it. Everyone's out to get you. We lived in some right dives in Plymouth but everyone was scruffy together and we helped each other out. Not like here, you have to look out for yourself.'

Girl's face was flushed and she was slapping her hand on the table to reinforce what she was saying. 'You wanted to know. OK, that's why I went with Connor. All right, he beat me up and he's as bad as the rest of them when it comes to hating foreigners, but he looked after me. It doesn't matter if you come from Plymouth slums or a posh pad in Poland. You're an outsider – and you get blamed for whatever goes wrong in other people's lives.'

She sniffed, drawing a grubby hand under her nose. 'I never meant for Micki to get hurt. I was angry with his dad for throwing me out. Parents are all the same.' She gave Kate a hostile look as if she was included in this grouping. 'Then there was the diary. He really cared about that and I nearly destroyed it.'

Kate sighed inwardly with relief - at last she had an opportunity to say something encouraging. She reached across to hold Girl's hand. 'You didn't destroy it. I found it in Micki's things. From the tape stuck all over it I think he repaired it. But who was Sara and why was the diary so important to him?'

'Sara's - the mad woman in the hospital.'

'Which hospital?'

Girl's scowl was back and Kate realised she was on shaky ground. She had to stop interrogating her like a policewoman. It would be better to just to let her talk. So she pushed Girl's plate with the half-finished cake towards her, 'It looks good,' and was rewarded with a brief smile.

Girl devoured the rest of the cake in silence. When she'd finished she said, 'The old hospital that's falling down, up beyond Ladram Heights, near the caravan site.'

Kate remembered an old mental hospital near Ladram Bay, she thought it had been knocked down years ago. But Girl seemed to have found her voice so she didn't interrupt.

'Micki broke in and found a diary written by this Sara. He wanted to find out all about her. First of all we thought the doctors were forcing bad treatments on her and she was real unhappy. Then she started to do bad things herself: real bad, like she made people kill themselves – and she killed her baby while it was still inside her. He kept trying to tell you. To ask you to help him understand the big words but he didn't get the chance with you being right pally with his dad.'

Kate blushed. She hadn't realise her attraction to Luca was so obvious. But Girl carried on regardless. 'Micki wanted to find out if Sara was still alive – he thought she sounded lonely like him. And then he found her.' Her eyes filled with tears. Kate squeezed her hand. Girl snatched it away to blow her nose then carried on, 'He broke into her house, Lyndon made him. He sent him in to get her camera said he needed the photos. She had a bedroom with walls covered in animals and insects. Weird he said it was. It had doors in the wall that lead into other rooms. Micki found the camera in a room he thought she used for sex, and he took some photographs with it. He knew she was the Sara from the diary from the stuff she had on the walls.'

Kate was stunned. From her reading of Sara's diary she sounded a dangerous psychopath and the room Girl had just described sounded like Elaine Pierce's bedroom. Was it possible that Elaine was Sara – and if she was, and had found out Micki had taken her camera, was she responsible for getting him killed?

'You want to know about Sara?' Girl said. 'Come on I'll show you.'

*

Kate wished she'd been wearing flatter shoes as she followed Girl through the undergrowth to see Pastures Hospital for herself. She stopped by the half-broken sign. Shouldn't they have called it a psychiatric hospital? Then she remembered it had closed down in the late eighties, so they probably weren't infected with political correctness that far back.

She was just slim enough to squeeze through the gap in the fence and the broken window after Girl, but wished she'd bought a torch when she landed in the dark and rather creepy corridor. Girl seemed quite at home in the musty space and they soon reached what she said Micki had called his office. At least that room had more light and what Girl had called Micki's 'crime wall' was clearly visible. He'd put a lot of effort into his work and two complete walls were covered in photographs, drawings and writing. Large letters spelling out 'Finding Sara' stood out in the centre of the display. She started reading Micki's notes about Sara, surprised by how neat his handwriting was and felt deeply sad as she imagined his look of concentration as he carefully recorded all he'd found out.

There was loads to read and sketches of the hospital including something that looked like a torture machine.

'Surely they didn't use this in the 1980's?'

Girl turned round and gave her an imperious look, 'Micki did very though research at the library. He had loads of books. If he thought that was used to treat mad people, he was right.'

Kate considered what she'd read in Sara's diary. Perhaps she had to put up with this sort of thing. Kate knew enough about ECT to know it was widely practised in the 1980's and was a frightening and uncomfortable treatment. Sara had sounded terrified at first, then her diary had got a bit sinister with lots of talk of blood. If Elaine really was Sara she must have had a horrible experience here. She wasn't very old and losing a baby must have been very distressing. Kate remembered asking Elaine about the scar on her wrist. Maybe this was the bad times that she was referring to and Pastures Hospital was the toxic place.

Before she could read everything in front of her, Girl called her over to the far wall. 'This stuff's new. I haven't seen it before.'

She joined Girl, who was pointing to a sheet of paper covered with of a group of photographs. They were monochrome images with curled-up edges but had been photographed with a modern camera.

'Micki must have taken these and put them up on the wall when he was here by himself.'

Kate studied the old photographs. She looked closer and saw the building in the background of most of the photographs looked familiar. It was Brathcol and the young man in the photographs with long hair could have been her father.

Kate felt cold all over as she tried to work out the connections. 'Where did this come from?'

'Dunno. But Micki didn't have a camera of his own, so he must have used the red one he stole from the rich ladies house.'

So the camera she'd found with Micki's things and given to Luca was Elaine's camera, and Micki had used it to take photographs of what he'd found in her secret room because he thought she was Sara - and wanted them to complete his crime wall.

'That's you, isn't it, Dr K?' Girl was looking hard at the photographs and pointing to a grainy image of a child on one of the images.

Kate screwed up her eyes and peered closer. It was really too dark, and the reproduced photograph too small, but the more she looked the more she recognised the taffeta dress and fluffy angora bolero. Nan had it made especially for her fifth birthday party. She'd loved that dress with its flounces and stitched in petticoat.

'This is definitely you,' Girl shouted, grabbing her hand and placing it next to an article torn from a magazine. There was no doubt about this one, the article was written three weeks ago. The picture accompanying it was of her wearing her favourite emerald dress as she collected the 'The Young Criminologist of the Year' award at The Stakis St Ermine Hotel.

'What an earth was Micki doing with this?'

Girl didn't answer, just tugged at her arm, pulling her away. 'I don't like it here, I'm off,' she shouted as she ran out of the room.

The room was closing in on Kate and she knew she had to leave as well. It was all starting to make horrible sense: Girl's reference to the rich woman at the top of the hill who controlled Connor, Elaine's eagerness for Kate to stay at Hawke Towers so she could make her ill.

She still had no idea why - but Micki must have believed it had something to do with Sara.

# 50

The sensual aroma of frangipani fills the bathroom and for once I've got time to enjoy my bath after a long lingering massage. Outside the open door I can hear the hotel staff removing the massage table and getting breakfast ready. I've left the door open on purpose. These days I don't care if my special hotel service is provided by men or women. It's still a thrill being watched by those paid to care for my needs. But those voices are definitely masculine and my towel rail appears to be empty.

'Hey, out there - can you be darlings and bring me my robe and some towels?'

The voices stop abruptly. I can hear footsteps and then a cough. I don't need to look to know someone is standing in the doorway. So I stand up and let the last of the bath foam slide down my body. A young man in uniform walks hesitantly towards me holding out a robe as I step out of the bath, enjoying his look of admiration.

'Thank you, you can go, now,' I tell him, reinforcing the dismissal with a toss of my head.

He turns abruptly and I follow him out into the lounge. The other waiter is still arranging my breakfast. He's older and better looking and I feel a stab of disappointment as he hardly glances at my half-naked body.

The younger man holds out a chair. At least he can't take his eyes off me. He points to his name badge. 'I hope everything is to your satisfaction. If not I will personally come to attend to it.'

I let my robe slide off my shoulders and smile up at him as he pours me a glass of champagne. Looking into his brown eyes I think he's not that bad and tell him, 'Maybe later?' But right now I have to get ready.

They leave me alone to eat. It's my favourite breakfast of fresh figs and pancakes stacked with maple syrup and cardamom cream. My mobile rings and I reject the call when I see it's Ian Ross. I walk over to the window and looked out at the triangular sign of New Scotland Yard and the sixties concrete-and-glass edifice opposite my hotel room, not caring if the police officers looking out of the window across the road are looking back at me. It turns out Ian is in London as well but I don't want him around today. Today is all mine.

I move across to the mantelpiece and pick up the gold embossed card.

*To commemorate your services to industry we are pleased to inform you that you have been shortlisted for the prestigious 'Business Woman of the Year' award. The successful candidate will be announced at a special luncheon to be held at the Stakis St Ermine Hotel, London.*

I replace the card, knowing I will win.

*

As Kate looked around the splendid ballroom of the St Ermine Hotel she was reminded of her own award ceremony just over a month ago. Diners were starting to arrive for the celebratory luncheon and hotel staff were busy finishing off the table decorations and hanging five huge blown up photographs of each of the shortlisted candidates. She shuddered as she walked past the larger-than-life image of Elaine Pierce. If calculated confidence was the main criteria for success, Elaine would win hands down.

She was still finding it hard to accept all the awful things that woman had done and how she'd deceived her so badly. Something she would be haunted by for some time. Right now there were things to organise if she was going to deliver a revenge ritual of her own.

The sound of a piercing whistle cut through the clatter of tables being set for luncheon and caused the other diners to turn towards the part of the room reserved for the press. Typical of Derek Droney. Never one for understatement, he was standing waving wildly as well as whistling to catch her attention. She strode across to prevent him drawing any further attention to them.

He ambled over and hugged her. 'You certainly look the part. Ever thought about taking up journalism?'

She wasn't sure if he meant this as a compliment. She'd tried to dress like the female newsreaders did on TV, and had splashed out on a red shift dress and some long gold earrings. But she couldn't stop smiling as she took the press identity pass he was handing over, and put it round her neck. Her heart rate was accelerating as she smoothed down her dress and thought about what she had to do. It was the same adrenalin rush she got before she addressed a conference - but this time it would be Elaine and not her who was going to be in the spotlight.

Kate grinned back at Derek. 'Everything go as planned?'

He looked hurt. 'As if I'd forget. Look, I'm going to enjoy this as much as you are. I've tipped off a few colleagues,' he gave a grand sweep of his hand towards the rest of the press area, 'but I'll make sure I get the scoop on all the Devon stuff.'

Her hand shook with excitement as she handed over the DVD. 'Where did you say they were setting up the audio visuals?'

'Behind us in that small room.' Kate looked where he meant as he started walking towards it. He called over his shoulder, 'Don't you want to come with me?'

'No need, I'm better staying here.' She watched him go into the small technicians' room that he'd had pointed out to her. That was where all the technology for the ceremony was controlled, including the visuals showing the highlights from each shortlisted candidate's work. Kate smiled as Derek appeared again in the doorway giving her big thumbs up sign. He was incorrigible but such a useful person to know. He'd persuaded the techies in the control room that he was making a documentary about their work and they had readily agreed for him to join them. As for the DVD, it had been touch and go to get it ready in time. Kate had filmed the background shots herself, Pierce Enterprises marketing division had provided material about the businesses, Jacqui acquired a copy of the video of Connor and his gang that Ian Ross had recovered from her phone and Derek had adding some shots from his own investigation into Kidpower. The finishing touches had been provided by the images on the red camera that Micki had taken from Elaine's bedroom. Luca had posted it back to her but Derek had insisted he examine it first. She suspected it may contain some shots of Jake and Elaine together that he didn't want her to see.

She found a seat at the very back of the press corps where she had a direct view of the tables where the shortlisted nominees were seated. Elaine Pierce was the last to arrive, accompanied by two young men who looked like they'd been hired from an escort agency. She looked amazing in a dramatic leopard-skin off-the-shoulder dress.

The lights dimmed, signalling the ceremony was about to start. Kate swallowed, crossed her fingers and tossed some salt from the salt cellar on the table in front of her over her right shoulder. The diners' murmuring ceased as the MC, a comedienne who Kate hadn't heard of, stood up with a microphone in her hand. She welcomed everyone to the award ceremony and cracked a couple of jokes. Hardly anyone responded; the sense of expectation was building up.

Across at her table near the front of the room, Elaine was laughing with the man sitting next to her.

The audience gave the comedienne a flutter of applause as she handed the microphone over to a stern-looking older woman.

'Now for the moment I know you have all been waiting for - our announcement of this year's Business Woman of the Year. There are some truly exceptional contenders. But before we find out who it is, let's take a look at some of their remarkable achievements.'

The woman sat down to more applause as the lights dimmed and the video about the first shortlisted candidate played across the huge screens covering the walls. Kate realised she was holding her breath. The first video was about a woman from Scotland who had developed her now multi-million dollar orthopaedic appliances business from her front room while caring for her disabled son. Kate thought back to her own moment of glory. Her award of 'Young Criminologist of the Year' really was a surprise and Jake must have nominated her for it. It seemed such a long time ago since she'd felt successful and had hopes of a permanent relationship with him, and yet it was just over a month ago. To stop thinking about what might have been, she tried to focus on Elaine's reaction. She was sure she would have her acceptance speech ready and be enjoying the anticipation.

Three more accounts of business success were displayed around the room. Then the final video started to play and the spotlight picked out a beaming Elaine confidently sipping her wine. The shots of her various companies were accompanied by a voice-over describing how she'd developed Pierce Enterprise from scratch. She was shown visiting some of her factories, chatting to workers packing meals then looking elegant in a hard hat striding around a building site. The voice-over explained that Pierce Enterprise was renowned for its exemplary personnel practices and employed five times more people with disabilities than any other British company. Then the video stuttered slightly and the voice-over changed from a plummy woman's voice to a male commentator. Kate held her breath and dug her fingernails into her palms.

'Some of Elaine's most impressive results have come from her investments and support of local charities.'

The picture changed to show the logos of a number of charities for young people, including Kidpower. Before the audience could focus on them, the screens were filled with images of young girls in scanty clothes. Their faces were blocked out except for their red lipsticked mouths. The camera lingered on the marks and bruises on their adolescent bodies. The images speeded up to resemble an American gangster film as men threatened the girls with knives and coshes and made them stand shivering as they were hosed down in a rubbish-filled back yard while Alsatian dogs strained at their leads. Then the scene changed to Heathrow airport, where Connor and some other men with shaved heads and multiple tattoos were meeting some young scared-looking girls at Arrivals. The voice continued, 'Elaine takes a very personal interest in her charities. She has set up youth projects all around the country to recruit violent gang members whose sole purpose is to support her corrupt businesses and the destruction of her rival companies.'

The multi-screen images changed to shots of the Kidpower intake room where Connor and other gang members were forcing young girls to take cocaine. It switched to show the same men jumping out of white vans and throwing firebombs at shops in Ladram Heights. Connor was easy to recognise despite his dark stained skin and black curly wig. He featured again on the video from Kate's phone as he struggled with her over the waitress, Danuta's, half undressed and spread-eagled body and Kate pulled off his balaclava. The Connor sectioned ended with clips from his recent news broadcasts blaming migrant workers for the riots in Ladram Heights.

People were starting to react, especially the journalists sitting around Kate. Someone turned on the lights but not before the voice-over praised Elaine for taking time out from her busy schedule to give her very personal support to some of the neediest young people in her projects. The visuals showed close-up shots of Elaine Pierce in glittering party gear partying with Connor and friends, joining in their consumption of drugs washed down with copious amounts of alcohol. Derek had assembled the last part of the DVD for her. It featured some of the film from Elaine's red camera, shot in the hidden room she kept for her sex

230

games. She was clearly visible sitting naked astride a man who was handcuffed to an iron bedstead.

Kate knew that plain clothes police officers were waiting to move in to arrest Elaine for her father's murder. She felt elated; the same euphoria that she had experienced at her own award ceremony. Smiling to herself, she looked across to see Elaine's reaction. The spotlight shining on Elaine's table only revealed an empty chair.

*

As pandemonium broke out all round her, Derek spirited her away from the hotel ballroom to take her to celebrate at a restaurant across the road. Kate tucked into her tapas and champagne, enjoying the accompanying Flamenco music but her overall emotion was disappointment. Nearly everything had gone as planned; her research into the failures and bankruptcies of Pierce Enterprise's rival companies, which hadn't featured much on the video but was of great interest to the police, together with Jacqui's contribution and Derek's dossier of incriminating evidence had produced a masterpiece, worthy of an award in its own right. More importantly for Kate, Elaine's moment of glory, that would have been so important to her, had been crushed, she'd been disgraced - but the final part of the plan hadn't worked out. The plain clothes detectives mingling with guests at the ceremony had failed to make an arrest. No one seemed to know where Elaine had gone.

Derek was topping up her glass. 'Here's to sweet revenge,' and when she didn't immediately respond said, 'Look, we pulled it off. The police will get her soon and there's no way she'll know it was you.'

Kate doubted that but knocked back the champagne and held out her glass for more. 'You're right. Even if she escapes the police her reputation's ruined and her multimillion dollar enterprise discredited. Everything she cares about has been destroyed.'

Derek scratched his nose. 'You bet. Connor's dead and the other yob that torched your dad's house is banged up. She'll go down for a long time when they catch her; it's a sure-fire certainty.'

She was doubtful but couldn't help grinning back, his enthusiasm was infectious, 'And how can you be so sure?'

'Their gangmaster told me. He's the one who told me where to find Connor meeting those girls for trafficking and supplied the film of Elaine partying and sharing her cocaine. He told me a lot about Pierce Enterprises corrupt and illegal dealings.'

'You mean Lyndon Crud?' Kate exclaimed, visualising the dark glasses and stout physique of the man who had caused Micki and her father so much misery.

'Yep, my best whistleblower.'

'You mean he's not going to be arrested?'

'No, he'll give evidence against them all. He's probably in protective custody as we speak.'

The thought didn't make Kate feel any better.

# 51

Back at the Belmont Hotel, a posse of press were waiting for Kate. She hadn't given much thought to her future but was staying in Devon until Nan fully recovered. She was looking forward to a quiet afternoon with her grandmother in the nursing home, not this rowdy reception better suited to a celebrity. Derek seemed to know them all and ushered her through the crowd of waiting journalists. He promised them Kate would be out to talk to them after she'd freshened up.

'I thought you said no one would know I was responsible for the video.'

'They don't know. They're here to interview the victim's daughter now that the shocking truth about her father's death has been revealed.'

She had to search his face twice to check if he was joking, 'You don't mean it? I've got to talk to the press?'

He grinned back at her. 'Of course not. But it would give you the chance to clear up any doubt about your dad's reputation. You can tell them all about the good he was trying to do - and slag off Lyndon Crud and Kidpower all you want.'

'OK. Tell them I'll be back later for that press call. Are you really going to interview me about Elaine?' She could never tell if he meant what he said.

'What do you think?' Then, spotting the hotel manager, waiting anxiously in the foyer said to him, 'I'm sure the Belmont will make a back room available for some refreshments. The TV chaps will want to take some shots of this splendid building as a backdrop. Just think of all the free advertising.'

Kate made a dash for the lift. As the lift doors closed behind her someone squeezed in through the diminishing gap. Glancing across at the overweight middle-aged man in a Hugo Boss suit and gold cufflinks she told herself not to be so paranoid since Elaine's disappearance. She had to stop seeing danger everywhere. The lift stopped at the third floor and they waited for the doors to open.

He followed her out and called after her, 'Dr Trevelyan?'

She pushed past him as quickly as she could, her room key ready in her hand to stab in his eye if he tried an attack. She could hear the tap of his shoes as he followed her down the corridor.

'Hey, wait. I didn't mean to alarm you. I wanted to thank you - but not in public.'

His Texan drawl sounded friendly enough and now she was more curious than scared. She stopped outside her door and turned round to face him, but the key was still ready in her hand if needed. 'You think that following me to my bedroom is friendly?'

'Shucks, I guess I just didn't think. Can we go somewhere else to talk then?'

She remembered the journalists milling around the hotel entrance. 'How about the bar? And this time we'll take the stairs.'

Downstairs in the bar, he ordered her a gin and tonic and a Becks for himself, then handed her a glossy brochure with his photograph on the front cover. Underneath Kate read that her new companion was called Franklin J Hurst and was the CEO of FJH Services, a large US security company.

She raised her eyebrows. 'What has this got to do with me?'

'You'll notice in the company's yearbook that two years ago we were one of the United States top companies. Then Elaine Pierce decided she didn't like our success, we were outselling Pierce Enterprise. So she decided to remove the competition and arranged for FJH marketing to be corrupted: got her goons to use malware to zap all our customer databases, changed their orders and overloaded our online registration process so that it ground to a halt.'

Kate had heard about malware invasions but computer fraud wasn't her speciality. 'Was your company ruined?'

'Not entirely, and I've still got plenty of successful alternatives. Now we'll be able to take back our share of the market, thanks to you. What really hurt me about Elaine Pierce was when she got personal. She burnt down my racing stables. I loved those horses more than I do my wife. All those beautiful intelligent animals burnt to death. Still makes me cry.'

'You mean, she found out what would hurt you the most and destroyed it?' Judging from the copy of the hand-written notes Kate had found on Micki's crime wall that would be her style of operating.

'Yep, she came to stay with us when she was setting up her security arm. Came out riding with me. She knew those horses were what I got up for in the mornings, they kept me sane. Well my horses and my family.'

'She didn't harm your family, did she?', she said with alarm.

He shook his head. 'No, I've been married too long.' Kate thought he was lucky, Elaine Pierce must have thought he cared more for his horses than his wife. 'My wife didn't believe the stories in the press about my other women and I've got enough security around to keep the kids safe. But you achieved what my team of investigators couldn't do. You secured enough evidence against Elaine Pierce to destroy Pierce Enterprises.'

She wondered about Elaine Pierce's other victims. How many other businesses had been destroyed, relationships broken, youngsters drawn into crime, people injured or killed? From reading Sara's diary she knew Elaine had a history of mental illness and had driven her psychiatrist to take her own life. She was an evil woman and the ripples of her mania had spread across the world, but Kate wasn't sure she should be taking the credit for stopping her.

Franklin J Hurst was still talking. 'I've checked you out. Your academic work is well regarded by the University of Chicago; I gather you did some work for them. That's my home town, you know.'

Kate lightened up. 'I spent some time with Dr Sampson, evaluating their programme on neighbourhood policing. My time there was awesome. The paper I wrote about it gave my career a huge boost. I think it was why the CCR employed me.'

'And now they've sacked you.'

She sucked the lemon slice from her gin and tonic, wondering where the conversation was going.

'So I'd like to offer you a job, lady. Come and work for me.'

'Doing what exactly?'

'Research. Come to Chicago and head the research side of my charitable foundation. I fund lots of neighbourhood projects and it would be great to work collaboratively with some British universities. With your connections and my money, think of what could be achieved.'

Kate was starting to take him seriously. It was an exciting proposition but did she want to move to Chicago? A month ago she was all set to go there and leave her father and Jake behind for the opportunity of working with some of the world's leading criminologists. But now the thought of leaving Nan alone again made her shudder.

'I know you have connections here in Devon. So the appointment would be on a part-time consultative basis, but it would pay so well you wouldn't need to do any other work – unless you wanted to.'

Was there anything he didn't know about her? Still, his offer could be just what she needed. After what happened to Micki and all the hostility against migrant workers in Ladram Heights she'd been reading up on community conflicts and the best methods of preventing them. If she worked for Franklin she could relaunch her career and still have time to develop some of her ideas back in Devon. His proposal was well worth considering.

'My grandmother's recovering from a stroke and I've my father's funeral to organise…'

'Of course. I don't expect you to decide here and now. I know your grandmother's from Bermuda.'

'You do?' She was starting to feel uneasy with all he knew about her.

'I've done my research too - and if your grandmother wants to return to Bermuda I'm setting up a new branch of my research company in Hamilton and you'd be perfect to head that up. There are some great opportunities for you with FJH Securities - so think about it.'

# 52

It had been a chaotic but exciting twenty-four hours and Kate was more than ready for a long soak in a hot bath and an early night. She'd gone down to be interviewed by the journalists gathering round the hotel and hoped she'd vindicated her father's reputation, explaining how Elaine Pierce was behind so much of the hostility that her dad was trying to stop. The bath water was getting cold but Kate didn't notice. She was excited about Franklin J Hurst's offer. Part time hours sounded ideal, especially if the pay was better than her full-time income at CCR had been. She could spend more time with Nan and have time to visit Luca in Krakow. It was such a brilliant opportunity to get her career back on track. She felt a bit smug thinking of Jake finding out that she would be working in the USA after all and earning a hell of a lot more than he would have paid her.

She plunged back under the water to give her hair a quick wash and when she re-emerged the hotel fire alarm was ringing. She had shampoo in her eyes as she stepped out of the bath, groping for a towel. Someone handed it to her.

Elaine was standing in the doorway.

She was alone with the mad woman who had killed her father and probably just set fire to the hotel. The wail of the alarm stopped suddenly. The only sound in the room was the soft humming of the fridge.

'Must have been a false alarm,' Elaine said. Kate wrapped the towel tightly round her body and held her gaze. Elaine looked like a coiled snake about to strike. It was the first time Kate had been face to face with her since finding out that Elaine had employed Connor to kill her father. She knew she should feel afraid or angry but found she just felt curious.

Elaine moved towards her and, despite thinking she wasn't afraid, Kate flinched - but Elaine only pulled out the bath plug. 'I was impressed with your work at the award ceremony yesterday. I misjudged you, Kate. I didn't think you had the intelligence to work it all out or the style to carry it off. Well done.'

Kate was younger and fitter than the older woman. If she could get past her she could get away. She started edging towards the door.

But Elaine read her thoughts and moved back to lean on the closed door. 'I came back because you'll want to know why I killed your father. If you don't find out it will eat away at you.'

Elaine was right; she did need to know. Kate squared up to Elaine. 'After reading your teenage diary I think it must have been for some sort of twisted revenge, although I can't imagine what he did to deserve it.'

Elaine's green eyes narrowed with hate. 'Can't you? Not as clever as I thought, then.' And when Kate refused to give her the satisfaction of a reply went on, 'He married me. Believe me that would have been motive enough. Sentenced to a life of boredom. Of course that was thirty years ago. Then we met up again, at a Business in Education conference where I was the guest speaker. He hadn't changed of course. He still wanted to do all he could to please me. The stupid fool even thought we could get back together.'

Kate knew her moment to escape was passing and Elaine was deliberately trying to goad her into a reaction. She didn't believe this madwoman. Dad had never mentioned a first marriage.

'You mean you killed him because he divorced you?'

Elaine's face was a mask of confident gloating. 'Oh no. I divorced him. Your Nan will tell you all about it if she ever recovers. Seems I got it wrong, I thought a big shock and major stroke would finish her off. Such a tough old bird. But she hasn't changed - she's still an interfering old crone. I gather she never told you the truth about me.'

Kate went cold. 'You caused her stroke?'

'I didn't need to. I just told her I'd tell you the truth about your mother.'

A shiver went through her. 'What about my mother?'

Elaine moved closer and ran her finger along Kate's cheek. 'You still can't recognise me. And we're so alike!'

It was too horrible to think about. Her mother was dead. If Elaine was inferring she was her mother to unsettle her she was succeeding. Kate felt hot and the room was starting to swim in front of her eyes. If she was going to escape it had to be now.

She tried to shove Elaine away from the bathroom door. The other woman's strength surprised her. Kate found she was being pushed back against the wall. Elaine's hand was crushing her throat with such force that she could hardly breathe.

She brought her face up close to Kate's and spat, 'I expected better of you. For all your fancy education and degrees you're remarkably slow. You made it so easy for me - destroying everything you cared about - your career, your pathetic relationship with your boss, your friendship with that meddling boy, Micki.'

Elaine's nails were slicing deeper into her skin. 'Let's not forget your precious family. Your father was always so weak. Your grandmother had more balls. The old bat never liked me. She tried to get me put away for good in that dreadful hospital. I couldn't wait to get away from you all - especially from you. Always screaming, never content, such a little misery.'

Kate closed her eyes as more saliva hit her face. She tried not to look at Elaine's distorted face, eyes so full of hate. But Elaine's response was to smash her head back against the wall. 'Look at me when I'm talking to you! It's you I blame for ruining my life. I never wanted a baby, they made out I was a bad mother - but I didn't want to be one in the first place, I was having too much fun. Then I was sent away to be punished. Locked up in that horrible place. Your father was so weak, always giving in to his mother's wishes. He left me there to rot - but make no mistake; I only killed Terence to get back at you.'

Elaine's words were like weapons releasing her anger, and from somewhere deep inside Kate found the strength to fight back. She felt Elaine's nails scratch through the bare skin of her arm as she wrenched it free. But she had broken her grip and caught her off balance and before Elaine could recover, Kate was through the bedroom door and dashing down the corridor.

Elaine screamed after her as she ran. 'Who do you think you get your long legs and pretty face from? Ever wondered why you could turn Ross on so easily? You look a lot like me.'

She didn't stop running - she had to get away from this monster who'd taken so much delight in destroying her and her family.

Hotel guests were making their way back to their rooms after the fire alarm had stopped. Kate pushed between them, clutching her towel. It couldn't be true. The woman was deranged. Playing some sort of mind game. There was no way on earth Elaine Pierce could be her mother.

She stopped running when she reached reception. Looking around, she saw she wasn't the only scantily-clad guest, except unlike her they'd been fleeing from the alarm that Elaine had obviously set off. She was standing in the entrance to the hotel lounge getting her breath back when someone grabbed her arm and she screamed.

'Hey babe, it's only me.' She spun round, relieved to see Derek. He took off his jacket and draped it round her shoulders. 'Did the fire alarm catch you out?'

'Elaine Pierce set it off to clear the hotel. To have me all to herself. She had me cornered in my hotel room.'

Her words wiped his grin away. 'Christ, are you OK? Is she still up there?'

'I doubt it.' Then, as she saw him take out his phone, 'I think it's too late for the police. She'll be long gone.'

In the end they settled for ringing Jacqui and waited for her in the bar. Kate sat drinking the triple brandy that Derek had insisted in buying and going over everything Elaine had told her. How her hatred had built up and been sustained over all these years and had resulted in the deaths of her father and Micki.

As soon as Jacqui arrived, she wanted to take Kate to hospital to get the cuts on her neck and arms attended too, and then take her statement. Kate couldn't stop shivering and Jacqui said it was the shock kicking in. She didn't want to return to her hotel room alone, although she suspected Elaine would be well gone. But there was no way she was setting off for the hospital in a towel. Jacqui went upstairs with her and opened the door of her bedroom. They checked round but there was no sign of Elaine - except for a note she'd left on the bed.

*Your grandmother knows the truth. Ask her - if you dare*!

*

Jacqui had rung her police colleagues and sent them ahead to check on Kate's grandmother. Although she thought it unlikely Elaine would risk returning to the nursing home, Kate wasn't so sure. She'd persuaded Jacqui that her injuries were superficial and agreed to let her swab them down and apply a temporary dressing. Watching Jacqui at work with her first aid kit brought back memories of Luca dressing Micki's wounds. She wondered how he was getting on. He hadn't been in touch since he left for Krakow. Maybe she'd never hear from him again.

All the way to the nursing home Elaine's words echoed round her head.

*Who do you think you get your pretty face from?*
*I blame you for ruining my life.*
*Don't think I haven't been watching you.*

Now she was trying to remember anything from her early childhood that might refute Elaine's claims. She'd always believed her mother had died giving birth to her and that was why her father had been rather remote when she was a child. When she asked about her mother both Dad and Nan discouraged her from talking about her. There were no photographs in the house; Nan said it caused her father too much pain. Kate had always believed a loving father and grandmother were all she ever needed, and secretly made the most of being the child of a dead mother. It gave her a kind of status at school. But at home, no one ever talked about it.

Kate had already worked out that Elaine was Sara and, from the treatments Micki had described, her detainment at Pastures Hospital was probably for some kind of psychosis. The diary was written in 1987 when Kate was only a few months old, so why did Elaine blame her for her illness? She said she'd killed Dad to get even. But what had she done as a baby that was so bad that Elaine hated her?

When they arrived at the nursing home she dashed out of the car leaving Jacqui to park. The care assistant called out to her as she sped down the corridor and stopped her rushing in to see Nan.

'The police are here ahead of you. What an earth's happening? We've moved your grandmother to a different room.'

She didn't want to waste any more time. 'Please, I need to see her.'

'Your Nan is fine. She's slept through all the excitement, even when we moved her bed.' The care assistant hesitated and looked intently at Kate. 'The police said a woman might try to see Mrs Trevelyan and do her some harm.'

Jacqui's arrival saved Kate from further explanation. 'Which room is Nan in now?'

'Upstairs in room thirty five, but she's still very frail. You won't upset her, will you? She tires very quickly ...'

Kate dashed up the stairs then stopped. Rushing in to demand to know the truth about her mother was just what Elaine wanted. The note she'd left was intended to make her go crashing in, making Nan's condition worse. When she reached her grandmother's room she needn't have worried, the police officer standing outside room thirty five refused to let her in, until Jacqui arrived.

Nan was sitting up in bed looking much brighter. She still had a drip attached to her arm and an oxygen tube to help her breathe but the colour had returned to her face. When she smiled at Kate she looked a lot like her old self, except for her drooping mouth. She tried to speak as Kate approached.

As she sat down beside the bed Nan was trying to speak, strange sounds Kate couldn't understand. She reached out to hold Kate's hands.

Kate said, 'Let's just sit here together. There'll be plenty of time for chatting when you're better.' Feeling the bones through the thin skin reminded her how vulnerable Nan was already, thanks to Elaine. Plying her with questions which she couldn't answer would just make things worse. She wasn't going to do what Elaine had expected. Whatever had happened when she was a child, it was the people they'd all become that mattered. Nan would tell her the truth one day.

She sat holding Nan's hand until the daylight started to fade and Nan had fallen asleep. Kate eased her hand away and bent over to kiss her grandmother goodbye. Resting her face against the person who meant so much to her, she knew she'd done the right thing.

But as she picked up her bag to leave she muttered, 'I don't care if Elaine is my mother.' She hadn't realised she'd said the words out loud or that as she left Nan had opened her eyes.

*

One Year Later

Kate was standing outside the brand new Micki Hamereski Centre for Community Mediation in what used to be the garden of her old family home. The early summer sunshine emphasised the new growth in the old hedgerow surrounding Brathcol and a soft breeze rippled through the pink and red rhododendrons. Even Nan seemed to have more energy than usual and her enthusiasm to be shown around the Centre was contagious. Kate was flushed with pride as she looked at the purpose-built glass and metal edifice. The opening ceremony was going to be a great celebration in Micki's honour but she knew her father would have wanted this too.

Kate hadn't been back to Brathcol since she started working for Franklin. The memories of life with Dad and the brief time she'd spent with Micki were too painful. She'd overseen the planning and construction of the new Centre from a distance. Her work had taken her round the world, interspersed with management meetings and fund raising back in Chicago. She'd fitted in a few weeks helping Nan settle back in Bermuda. The pace of life since she'd worked in Ladram Heights had been hectic, but she preferred being busy, to keep memories at bay as much as possible.

It had been a whirlwind week preparing for the grand opening and she still felt a little jetlagged after her long flight from Bermuda to accompany Nan back to Devon. Her grandmother wanted to know all about the mediation centre and Sophie Wippelston, newly graduated and appointed as the centre manager, couldn't wait to tell her all about it.

Now, as Kate pushed the wheelchair around the grounds trying not to think of what had been here before, Nan reached out her hand indicating she wanted to speak. 'Your father would have been so proud of you making this happen. You've turned a tragedy into something that will help so many people.'

Kate stopped the wheelchair, blinking back the tears she was trying to keep under control. 'I hope so.'

Everything was going smoothly in her life and it was a joy to see old friends again. Jacqui had been promoted to Inspector and had returned to London to work for The Met. Derek had left Devon too after securing a job with the Manchester Guardian. Kate was touched that they'd both returned to Devon for the opening ceremony. Ginny and Denise were here too - but no Jake, of course. Sophie had invited some of the other sex workers from London who were attracting some curious looks, and Kate was delighted to see them again. Nan's recovery had been erratic after her stroke, but she had gained back most of her speech and a lot of her mobility. Enough for her to visit Brathcol occasionally and keep Kate well informed of the progress of the building work during recovery in Devon.

Life was good. So why, she wondered, did she have this empty feeling and the long nights when she lay awake thinking about her childhood? There was so much she wanted to know, especially about Elaine. This desire was an obsession that she hated herself for. In the weeks after their last meeting in the Belmont, Kate had checked out family records, databases and newspaper cuttings to find out more about her. Apart from the commercial information about Pierce Enterprises, there was very little to find. She'd obtained a copy of her birth certificate which confirmed her mother's middle name was Sara and she was the same age as Elaine.

She studied her grandmother's face to check she didn't look too tired and noticed how her face had recovered and how much more upright she was holding her head. Her speech was nearly back to normal too. Maybe this was the moment to ask her what she'd been putting off.

She squatted down in front of Nan to make sure she could hear what she was saying. 'You never told me what brought on your stroke. Do you think you can tell me now?'

Nan's eyes clouded over and she looked away. Kate didn't want to ruin their day of celebration but not knowing was eating away at her. So she carried on, 'Was it Elaine Pierce?'

Nan gasped and put her hand over her mouth. Kate could barely make out her words. 'She's someone I hoped I'd never hear of again.'

Kate felt she wasn't approaching this very well. 'I'm sorry ... please forget it.'

'No Kate, it's me that should be sorry. It's time I told you the truth about your mother.' Nan reached out for her hand and looked her straight in the face. 'You found out she was Elaine, didn't you? When you came to see me at the hospital after my stroke you thought she might be your mother - and you were right. But neither of us has been able to talk about it since.'

'You heard me? I thought you were asleep.'

'I can't remember much but I knew my stroke had something to do with your mother. After she came to see me ...'

The sense of Elaine's presence was so strong that Kate could smell her perfume. The side of Nan's face had dropped and her mouth looked slack. Kate started to panic, fearful that her stupid questions might trigger off another stroke. But Nan's eyes shone as bright as ever as she continued, 'Elaine came to see me and threatened to tell you she was your mother. After all those years of protecting you from her I couldn't let her do it ... then she said some dreadful things about Terence and I tried to hit her. The next thing I knew I was on the floor and Elaine had gone. I couldn't hold on, everything went black - that was when I had the stroke.'

Kate squeezed her hand gently to reassure her. Nan's voice had dropped to a whisper. 'I thought you'd found out already. I was so worried when I realised that you were staying with her and you thought she was looking after you. You seemed to admire her so much. I was terrified she was going to tell you the truth but I couldn't tell you. I couldn't even write it down.'

Kate hugged Nan close and felt her damp cheeks against her face as their tears mingled. She whispered, 'It's all right. Elaine was evil and I was deceived into telling her so much about you and Dad and Micki.'

'I should have told you the truth about your mother instead of pretending she was dead. When she escaped from Pastures Hospital it was all in the papers. The police thought she'd been killed and I kept praying she had, but your father always thought she'd come back. She deceived him too - and then she killed him.'

Kate thought of the nightmares she'd been having and realised she had already known the truth. 'She tried to kill me when I was a baby, didn't she? Was that why she was in the mental hospital?'

'She was ill, Kate. She still is but Terence never believed it. She sent him letters asking him to get her out and when I went to see her she threatened to try and harm you again. I told Dr Sands and she intercepted the letters to stop your father finding out.' Nan's voice faded again and Kate had to strain to catch her words. 'I never thought she'd come back.'

'She told me she killed Dad to get even with me.'

'It wasn't you, Kate. She's ill. It's such a shame the police never caught her, but they will.'

Kate didn't want to ask her next question but she had to know. 'When did she start being mentally ill?'

'The doctors said her psychosis was brought on by her pregnancy but it started before then. She always had mood swings: one minute she was all calmness and charm, the next full of angry outbursts. She had hallucinations, spent hours living in a world of her own where you couldn't reach her.' Nan tightened her grip on Kate's hand. 'You mustn't think it was because of you. You didn't cause anything. She was ill before you were born. Terence never saw it because he loved her so

245

much. If she told you anything different she was playing with your mind.'

Nan's description of Elaine had echoes of how she'd been feeling since her father was killed. Her mood swings and hallucinations - her flashbacks were less frequent but still alarmingly vivid. Anything could trigger them. One minute she'd be sitting on a train, or queuing in a crowded shop - then she'd be back in Ladram Heights hearing the demonstrators and seeing Micki lying distorted and bleeding. If Elaine had a mental illness... was it hereditary?

Suddenly the older woman sat upright and pointed behind her. 'That man has been staring at us for the last five minutes.'

Kate spun round and all her negative thoughts were swept away. Luca had come to the ceremony after all. She ran towards him and was engulfed in a big bear hug.

She hadn't seen him for months - just one visit to Krakow where he was working in the hospital as a consultant. Neither his mother nor daughter wanted her there. She reminded them of what happened to Micki, so she hadn't stayed long.

As she broke away to look into his strong face and responsive eyes she wondered if it was time to put aside her own career plans and concentrate more on the people she cared about.

As if on cue, Sophie rushed up to them. 'Hi there, gorgeous,' she said to Luca, treating him to one of her best flirtatious smiles. Then turning to Kate, 'You're not looking so bad yourself.'

They all exchanged hugs. It was impossible to stay serious for long with Sophie around. She circled round them, her arms stretched out towards the new centre. 'What do you think then? Does it live up to your expectations, Kate?' From the confident look on her face, Sophie already knew the answer.

'This place is amazing. I hadn't realised you'd achieved so much while I was in the States.'

She noticed Luca was impressed with Sophie too and introduced them. 'Sophie is the person responsible for getting this place finished and ready to open.'

'And the proud owner of a sparkling new first class honours degree in criminology,' Sophie piped up. 'My main achievement recently though is hooking a merchant banker with loads of spare cash. He comes complete with a rent-free apartment.' She winked at Kate. 'You see, I've learnt something from you. Your research was not in vain - it's much safer than working on the streets.'

*

It had been a brilliant day. It was the first time Nan and Luca had met and she had completely fallen for his charm. After the opening ceremony he'd insisted on taking them both out for dinner. Kate relaxed as she saw Nan respond to his compliments. In the ladies' toilets she wanted to know all about him and by the end of the meal she had fixed up a date for Luca and Kate to stay with her in Bermuda.

Kate was enjoying Luca's company too. It felt good to reawaken the attraction between them. They saw Nan safely to her hotel room at the Belmont and then Luca suggested a walk along the sea front. They stopped to look up at the Clock Tower Café and remember Micki. Luca pulled her towards him. She could taste the sea salt on his lips as he kissed away her tears.

They made love on the beach in the moonlight. For Kate it was a kind of exorcism of the sex she'd had there with Ian Ross and this time she didn't want it to stop.

Back in Luca's hotel room she kicked off her shoes as he poured out some wine. Kate felt a draft and notice the curtains blowing into the room through the open window.

'Didn't we close all the windows before we went out?' she asked Luca.

He responded by kissing her nose. 'There are more important things to think about than windows.'

Still glowing from their lovemaking, she sat on the end of the bed and watched him undo his tie and start to remove his shirt. She pulled him towards her, enjoying the feel of his skin against her own and lay back, nearly squashing a bunch of oriental poppies lying on the bed, their blood redness in stark contrast to the white broderie anglaise quilt.

Smiling, she picked them up, holding them to her face. 'Oh Luca, what a lovely thought...' but her smile froze as she read the card attached to the stems. Written there in black spidery letters was 'From your loving mother.'

*

They've dimmed the lights in the cabin and, apart from a few fellow travellers still watching inflight movies, everyone is sleeping. Or trying to. I signal to the stewardess to bring me another glass of wine. I lie back in my seat and swap my sunglasses for the Virgin Atlantic eye protectors, although I don't need to sleep. Instead I think back on a very successful day. I hadn't been back to England for a year, but when I heard about the Micki Hamereski Centre opening today it was too good an occasion to miss.

They all looked so well, my daughter and her grandmother. But then they should. Kate's earning far more than any CCR criminologist could hope for and Terence's mother looks well on the way to recovery. It seems my daughter has inherited my resilience. She won't let an unpleasant discovery about her background prevent her from enjoying life. She's even found a sexy new man. Although I'm not sure that relationship is going to last - too much history. And I'm glad to see she's turned down the offer of police protection. That's my girl - carefree and brave. I think a lot about being a mother these days. Sometimes I wonder if I missed out, not being around. They say having children and watching them progress through life is one of its greatest experiences. I wouldn't go that far of course. But I intend to stick around to see how she's doing.

# Author's Note

The New Town of Ladram Heights doesn't exist. Pastures Mental Health Hospital is also an imaginary place. Otterford, home of the Trevelyan family is based on the picturesque village of Otterton. All other places in East Devon mentioned in this book are real, beautiful and well worth visiting. More information about the settings in this book can be found on my website: cjbrownecrimewriter.com

Love and thanks for believing in me to Martin, Dan, Julie, Tess and Chris

CJB